Dessau

ICEBREAKER

LIAN TANNER

FEIWEL AND FRIENDS
NEW YORK

A FEIWEL AND FRIENDS BOOK
An Imprint of Macmillan

Feiwel and Friends books may be purchased for business or promotional use.
For information on bu᾽ purchases, please contact the Macmillan Corporate
and Premium Sales Department at (800) 221-7945 x5442 or by e-mail at
specialmarkets@macmillan.com.

Originally published as *Ice Breaker* in 2013 in Australia by Allen & Unwin.

First published in the United States by Feiwel and Friends.

Library of Congress Cataloging-in-Publication Data Available

ISBN: 978-1-250-05216-2 (hardcover) / 978-1-250-08017-2 (ebook)

Book design by Anna Booth
Feiwel and Friends logo designed by Filomena Tuosto

First U.S. Edition: 2015

10 9 8 7 6 5 4 3 2 1

mackids.com

For Margaret Connolly, with love and thanks

MAIN CHARACTERS

PETREL — an orphan and an outcast; known to the crew as Nothing Girl

MISTER SMOKE — a rat, and a law unto himself

MISSUS SLINK — another rat, and one with a talent for stitching wounds

ORCA, *First Officer* — a woman with little patience for fools (Braid)

CRAB, *Second Officer* — a man who values tidiness above all things (Braid)

DOLPH, *Orca's daughter* — a girl as sharp and proud as her mam (Braid)

KRILL, *Head Cook* — a huge man whose gruffness is all on the surface (Duff)

SQUID, *Krill's daughter* — a young woman with quick wits and a kind heart (Duff)

ALBIE, *Chief Engineer* — a cunning, vicious-tempered man, and Petrel's uncle (Grease)

SKUA, *Albie's son* — a bully, but not as dangerous as his da (Grease)

THE SLEEPING CAPTAIN who may or may not exist

A NAMELESS BOY found on an iceberg and brought onto the ship

OTHERS

THE MAW a monstrous fish that follows the *Oyster*

BROTHER THRAWN leader of the fanatical Anti-Machinists known as the Devouts

THE THREE TRIBES

THE OFFICERS They navigate and steer the ship. They live on the upper decks of the *Oyster*, which are called Braid.

THE COOKS They feed the crew and keep the stores. They live on the middle decks, or Dufftown.

THE ENGINEERS They keep the ancient engines running, and anything else mechanical. They live on the lower decks, which are known as Grease Alley.

PROLOGUE

THE CHILD'S FACE WAS BEATEN SILVER. His mind held the knowledge of ten thousand libraries. His fingers were so cunningly made that they could mend the broken bones in a kitten's paw, setting each one in place with care and precision.

So far, every moment of his short life had been spent hiding from the Anti-Machinists.

For all his cleverness, the child could never understand why his enemies hated him so much. "They have not even spoken to me," he said to Professor Serran Coe. "They do not know me."

"Ah, but they *think* they know you," said Coe with an angry laugh. "They think they know all about you. According to them, you are an abomination, even worse than the automobiles and trains that they delight in smashing. They say you are too clever to be trusted. That you wish to set yourself up as a false god."

"That is not true," said the mechanical child.

"No, of course it isn't," said the man who had made him.

"The whole thing would be laughable, if only their aims were not so deadly. Last week they burned seven libraries and besieged a university. Their ideas are spreading, and not just in this country. A battle is being fought all across the world, between knowledge and ignorance . . . and ignorance is winning. I fear we are heading into a new Dark Age—"

A knock interrupted him, and a young woman peered anxiously around the door. "The Antis have found us again, Professor. They are twenty minutes away, a hundred or so of them, shouting their stupid slogans and brandishing their axes. We must leave, immediately. The carriages are waiting."

Serran Coe did not move. Instead, he sat and stared at the mechanical child, as if trying to fix those fine silver features in his mind.

"Professor?" said the young woman.

"Yes, yes, I heard you." Coe stood up and stuffed various papers into the pockets of his coat. "I will take him to the ship," he said over his shoulder.

The young woman's face lost its color. "Must you?"

"We cannot put it off any longer. You and the others had best go to the university and begin packing up the laboratory. I will meet you there as soon as I can. Be careful. The mobs will be watching for us."

The young woman bit her lip. "I wish they would chop each other to pieces," she said fiercely. Then she rushed forward, kissed the mechanical child on his forehead and hurried out of the room with tears in her eyes.

"The ship?" said the mechanical child, staring after her. "I do not know of any ship."

"It is my finest creation, after you," said Professor Coe, taking a long metal box from a cupboard and placing it carefully on the table. "There has never been another ship like it. It could cruise for a hundred years at the farthest end of the earth if necessary, and never come to port."

He grimaced. "Perhaps such a long voyage will not be needed. Perhaps this Anti-Machinist nonsense will fizzle out by summer's end. But somehow I doubt it. Come here, my dear."

The mechanical child stood trustingly while a panel in his shoulder was unscrewed. "Will I like the ship?" he asked.

"You will like it—very much." Professor Coe swallowed, peering down at the screwdriver in his hand as if it were an assassin's knife. "Forgive me," he mumbled. Then, before he could change his mind, he dipped his fingers into the child's body and removed two intricately wired devices.

The light in the child's eyes died immediately and he fell against Coe in a jumble of limbs. The professor cradled him, then laid him carefully in the box, straightening his arms and legs and stroking his silver face.

"I have hired the most trustworthy crew I could find," whispered Serran Coe, "but I dare not give you the run of the ship, in case there are Anti-Machinist spies among them. Sleep well, my dear. You are my joy, and the hope of the world."

It was only when he had kissed the child's cheek and closed the lid of the box that he took a second box from the cupboard.

This one was considerably smaller, and when Serran Coe opened it, a reluctant smile flickered across his face.

"You will be his guardians," he said. "And when the world is safe again, your sacrifice will wake him."

Before he left the house, the professor paused in the hallway to wrap his cloak around the boxes. Then he threw open the front door, looked both ways for signs of the approaching mob and ran down the steps to the waiting carriage.

PROFESSOR COE WAS RIGHT—THE ANTI-MACHINISTS DID NOT fizzle out by summer's end. Instead, their grip on the world gradually tightened. They infiltrated armies. They toppled governments. They killed anyone who disagreed with them.

In this way, a hundred years passed.

AND ANOTHER HUNDRED YEARS . . .

AND ANOTHER. At the farthest end of the earth, the ship kept its course. But on board, much had changed . . .

CHAPTER I

NOTHING GIRL

PETREL WAS ASLEEP WHEN THEY CAME AFTER HER. She'd made a nest of rags in the narrow space around the shaft of the wind turbines, and for once she was warm and almost happy. The familiar sound of the icebreaker's engines rumbled through her dreams like a lullaby, and she smiled, and snuggled down deeper into the rags.

The Officer bratlings might've caught her there if they'd had more sense. But they were so sure of themselves—so certain that *this* time they had her trapped—that they didn't even try to be quiet. Petrel woke to the sound of eager voices coming at her from two directions, and the smell of hot tar.

"This way! This way!"

"We've got her!"

There were ten of them, mostly girls, with Dolph grinning in anticipation at the front. Petrel saw them out of the corner of her eye as she sprang from her nest and leaped for the iron ladder above her head.

Dolph screamed, "There she goes! Quick, grab her!"

But by then Petrel was halfway through the rusty hatch that led to the next deck, and running for her life.

As she tore desperately along the passageways she could hear the bratlings a little way behind her, laughing and shrieking, "Rat hunt! Rat hunt! Catch the rat!"

"I found her paws," cried one of girls. "Look, I've got her nasty little paws."

Which was when Petrel realized she had left her gloves behind.

Furious with herself, she snarled over her shoulder as if she really *were* one of the ship's rats. Then she ducked into a cabin, scrambled under a hammock full of wailing babies, dived through a rusty hole in the bulkhead and threw herself beneath the first berth she came to, with no idea whether it was occupied or not.

The footsteps pounded past. As soon as they were gone, faded into the distance along with the ugly clank of the tar bucket, Petrel scrambled out from under the berth. An old man peered up at her from his pillow. She made a clumsy curtsy to him and crawled back the way she had come.

The babies had quieted now, soothed by their mothers, a trio of women with Officer stripes tattooed on their muscular arms. As Petrel tiptoed past, hunching her shoulders and making her eyes blank and stupid, the Officer women whispered to each other.

"She's a strange one."

"Not Officer nor Cook nor Engineer. Imagine not having a tribe!"

"Well, you remember what her parents did."

"Disgraceful . . ."

Petrel goggled witlessly at them.

"What are you doing in Braid, Nothing Girl?" one of the women asked loudly.

Petrel didn't answer. Silence was one of the few weapons she had against the crew that had rejected her. Silence, stubbornness and the knowledge that she was not who they thought she was.

"It's no use talking to her," said a second woman. "She's as thick as winter ice. You might as well chat to a toothyfish." She made a shooing gesture. "Go away, Nothing Girl. We don't want you here."

Petrel crept down the passageway and through the hatch, hoping that her pursuers might have dropped her gloves in the excitement of the chase. But there was no sign of them, no sign of anything except for the dollops of tar all over her nest.

She sighed. "Can't stay here now," she muttered in her hoarse voice. "Dolph'll be watching for me, sure as blizzards. Better keep away from Braid for a while; find somewhere safer to sleep . . ."

The trouble was, nowhere was *really* safe, not for Petrel.

During the *Oyster*'s long voyage, the ship had accumulated centuries of rust, and a hull as battered as an iceberg. But that wasn't the worst of it. Roughly two hundred years ago, a midwinter disagreement between crew members had flared up into three months of violent warfare. Nearly half the crew died in that war, and precious books and papers were burned, among them the ship's log, with all its history and instructions.

In the bitter aftermath, with everyone blaming everyone else, the *Oyster* had been divided into three territories, each of them jealously guarded. The bottommost part of the ship, with its engines and batteries, was called Grease Alley—that was where the Engineer tribe lived and worked. The middle decks, which included the kitchens and storerooms, was Dufftown. That was Cook territory. And the upper decks, Braid, belonged to the Officers.

Petrel, who had no tribe, was the only one who could move freely between the three groups. But that freedom came with a high price. None of the tribes turned her away at the border, it was true. But none of them welcomed her, either, or fed her, or protected her against cruelty.

As she stood there, thinking, she thought she heard the clank of a bucket. *Dolph*, she thought, and she rose on tiptoe, as alert as a gull. The clanking sound came again, and Petrel ran.

Braid, where the Officers lived, was a maze of cabins. Most of them were floored with iron, but in others the original deck had rusted away long ago, and been replaced with driftwood or netting, or bones scavenged from ancient whaling stations.

There were folk everywhere on the Braid decks—bratlings hopping from one whale rib to another in a game of chasings, babies tied to their hammocks with seal gut, grown men and women rubbing their eyes as they woke, and calling greetings to their neighbors.

Petrel shuffled between them, eyes lowered. Most folk ignored her; they were too busy with their own lives to bother themselves over a witless girl.

Which suits me, thought Petrel. *Safety lies in being ignored.*

She trotted along the passages until she came to one of the Commons ladderways, where fighting between the ship's three tribes was forbidden. Her nerves were still jangling, and she had a sudden overwhelming desire for sunlight and salty air.

She glanced around to make sure the Braid border guards weren't watching, then fumbled behind the ladderway for her ancient and very ragged sealskin jacket.

"You're getting old, you are," she muttered to the jacket as she wriggled into it.

As if in answer, there was a dull tearing sound and several gray scraps fluttered to the deck.

Still, the jacket was better than nothing. Petrel fastened the strings, then scurried up the ladderway to the hatch that led to the *Oyster*'s foredeck.

There must have been a time, centuries ago, when the hatch had been weather tight. But now the damp and the cold seeped through it like sea fog. Petrel drew the tattered hood of her jacket over her head, then she turned the clamp, pushed the hatch open and stepped out onto the deck.

The cold air hit her like a bucket of water.

"Oof!" she yelped, then jammed her lips shut and scuttled away from the hatch in case someone had heard her.

The sea was dotted with icebergs. The morning sky was yellow. Petrel ran for'ard across the snowy deck as quickly as she dared to where an ancient crane loomed, and the wind fiddles sang their endless song.

There was a sheltered area there, beneath the body of the

crane, and she tucked herself into it, out of the wind. Spring was on its way to the frozen south, and the song of the wind fiddles was luring penguins, seals, whales and every other speck of life back to their summer haunts.

But the air was still cold.

"Ice cold," mumbled Petrel. "Bone cold!" And she stuck her hands into her armpits and wondered whether Dolph would think to look for her out here.

Probably not. The fishing shift would start soon, and men and women from the *Oyster*'s three warring tribes would have to work together to feed the ship. Like the Commons ladderways, the open decks were neutral territory where knives, poison and pipe wrenches were forbidden. Even hot tar would be seen as a weapon on the foredeck.

Which meant that the only *real* danger for Petrel—apart from the cold—was that someone might creep up behind her and push her overboard.

"Trouble is," she muttered, "if I stay out here for much longer my nose'll fall off. I'll have to take my chances inside."

With a grumble, she stepped out into the wind. On the horizon, something flashed white . . . and was gone. Petrel squinted after it.

"Must've been a berg. Though I've never before seen one so neat and square."

The next moment she had completely forgotten that odd glimpse. Because the ship was sailing past another berg, and this one had an ice cave near its summit.

Petrel never tired of watching ice caves. Some of them were

so blue and so beautiful that they made her heart ache. She leaned on the rail, stamping her feet for warmth. The berg came closer.

That's when she saw him. A boy, laid out on the ice like a dead fish, with a scattering of snow almost covering his face. A boy, where there should have been nothing but the memory of winter.

A frozen boy.

CHAPTER 2

THE FROZEN BOY

PETREL WAS SO STUNNED AT THE SIGHT THAT HER WITS almost deserted her.

"A—a—a *stranger!*" she whispered.

She had to dredge the word up from the depths of her memory. She'd never had need of it before. In all the hundreds of years that the *Oyster* had been trudging around the southern ice cap, there had been no strangers. Not a single one.

There were stories, of course. There were always stories, especially in the long winter dark when there was nothing much else to do but mend clothes and fishing lines, plot against the other tribes, and listen to the blizzards thrashing about the ancient iron hull.

But no one took those stories seriously. So what if there were other folk in the world? They were of no interest to the *Oyster* and its crew. The ship was what mattered. The ship was a world in itself, it was life and shelter, birth and death, love and hatred and protection against the elements. It was all any of them had ever known or wanted.

Until now . . .

Petrel pinched herself. The *Oyster* was already more than halfway past the berg, and if she didn't act quickly it would retreat into the distance and she would never find out who this—this *stranger* was, and where he had come from.

She dived through the hatch, pulling it shut behind her and taking a stub of iron from her pocket. There was a pipe running along the base of the bulkhead. Petrel banged a message on it in Engineer code.

TO CHIEF ENGINEER ALBIE. STRANGER ON BERG. STARBOARD BOW. ORCA SAYS DON'T STOP.

She didn't sign it; no one would take any notice of a message signed *Petrel*. She just sent it on its way with an anonymous *tap tap tap*, so that it could have come from anyone. The echoes rattled through the pipe, all the way down to the engine rooms. Petrel pictured her uncle, the Chief Engineer, cocking his head to listen. She imagined his lips curving in a humorless smile.

The lack of other messages in the pipes told her that she was the only one who had seen the boy. The Officers on the bridge *should* have seen him, but maybe they had been looking the other way, or had mistaken him for a seal. Whatever the reason, it meant that First Officer Orca, who was Dolph's mam, could not possibly have said, "Don't stop."

But it was the best way that Petrel knew of making the Chief Engineer do exactly the opposite.

She went back out to the foredeck and waited, shivering, until she heard a change in the constant grumble of the engines. It was only a minute or two, but it seemed like forever. The boy on the berg, slowly retreating into the distance, didn't move.

"Maybe he's dead," whispered Petrel.

But she would not let herself believe it. She wanted to know who this stranger was, and how he had come to be on a berg in the *Oyster*'s path. She wanted it more than anything—except perhaps a good feed and a warm safe bed.

As soon as the ship stopped, Petrel slipped back inside the hatch and tucked herself into a corner where no one would notice her. The pipes were rattling again—this time in general ship code. Furious messages raced between the bridge and the engine room, and Petrel automatically translated them.

TO CHIEF ENGINEER ALBIE. WHY HAVE WE STOPPED? SIGNED, ORCA.

TO FIRST OFFICER ORCA. NUMBER TWO ENGINE OVERHEATING. SAFETY ISSUE. SIGNED, ALBIE.

TO CHIEF ENGINEER ALBIE. RUBBISH. GET UNDER WAY IMMEDIATELY. SIGNED, ORCA.

TO FIRST OFFICER ORCA. CAN'T. SIGNED, ALBIE.

Petrel could hear a score of feet pounding up the Commons ladderway. She felt the blast of cold air as the hatch was dragged open, and heard the footsteps race towards the only seaworthy lifeboat. Then the hatch slammed shut again, and she was left chewing her nails, with no way of knowing what was happening outside.

She closed her eyes and tried to picture it. The berg would be well past the *Oyster*'s stern by now. Perhaps the Engineers would decide it was too late. Perhaps they would think the boy dead, and not worth rescuing.

"Or maybe the Maw's out there waiting," she whispered, "and they won't dare set the lifeboat into the water, stranger or no stranger."

Petrel shivered and pulled her ragged coat tighter. The monstrous fish known as the Maw had been following the icebreaker for as long as anyone could remember. Sometimes it wasn't seen for weeks, or even months. But as soon as someone died, and occasionally even *before* they died, it roared up from beneath the waters with its massive jaws agape, waiting for the corpse to be thrown overboard.

The Maw frightened Petrel more than anything in the world. More than Orca. More even than Uncle Albie. According to Dolph—the information shouted across the afterdeck two years ago—shipfolk had argued long and hard over Petrel when she was a baby. Many of them had wanted to throw her to the Maw, along with her parents.

"A traitor, your da was," Dolph had shouted, "and your mam was mad. Shipfolk killed 'em and chucked 'em overboard, and good riddance. Pity you didn't go with 'em. Reckon the Maw thinks so too. Reckon it feels cheated. Reckon it's down there waiting, and one day it's going to get you!"

And having delivered that terrible opinion, Dolph had linked arms with her friends and strolled away laughing.

Today however the Maw must have been elsewhere. Petrel sat bolt upright as the pipes rattled out a new message.

TO CHIEF ENGINEER ALBIE. LIFEBOAT FOUR LAUNCHED WITHOUT PERMISSION. EXPLAIN. SIGNED, ORCA.

TO FIRST OFFICER ORCA. NOPE. SIGNED, ALBIE.

The next thirty minutes passed so slowly that Petrel felt as if the world had come to a standstill. There were no more messages in the pipes, but Orca's anger seemed to filter through every part of the ship, so that even the gurgle of the ballast system and the crack of ice against the hull took on a furious note.

The Braid border guards were doubled, then tripled. As Petrel watched, a dozen of them positioned themselves on the Commons ladderway, arms folded, so that no one could pass.

They're going to fight, thought Petrel, pressing farther back into her corner. *Except they can't, not on the Commons. It's not allowed!*

At last something thumped against the hatch. Petrel heard voices, then the hatch flew open and one of the Engineers hurried through it, with ice in his beard and the boy over his shoulder. His fellows were right behind him.

When they saw the Officers blocking the ladderway, the Engineers quickly closed ranks around the first man, so that he and his burden were hidden. Then they moved forward in a solid block, men and women together. The scars on their cheeks, that marked them as belonging to Grease Alley, twitched with unconcealed hostility.

"Out of our way, Braid!" snapped one of the women.

The Officers stood their ground. "What's that you've got?" demanded a man with a square face. "What've you brought onto the ship?"

The woman narrowed her eyes. "None of your business. Let us pass."

"You can pass whenever you want, Grease," sneered the square-faced man. "No one's stopping you."

Except they were—everyone could see that, including Petrel.

If this had happened at any other time of year, it would probably have ended with nothing more than a bruise or two and a promise of revenge. The rules against fighting on the Commons were strict and seldom broken.

But the winter just gone had been a long, hungry one, and folk were strung as tight as a stay line. As Petrel watched, the Engineers growled deep in their throats. The Officers flexed their tattoos and grinned nastily. Hands slid into pockets and came out holding pipe wrenches and knives . . .

Petrel held her breath. But before the first blow could be struck, a voice came bawling up the ladderway, full of iron and authority. "No fighting on the Commons! Let 'em pass or I'll chuck the lot of yez overboard."

It was Chief Engineer Albie.

Every single person in Braid hated the Chief Engineer, but they respected him too, in a reluctant sort of way. He was ferocious and clever, and only a fool would turn their back on him. More importantly, he knew the *Oyster*'s ancient engines better than anyone; knew how to bully them through yet another winter; knew how to patch the unpatchable and mend the unmendable. Sometimes it seemed to Petrel that her uncle *was* the ship's engines, and that without him they would give up the struggle and die.

The Officers blocking the Commons swore, and for a second or two their knives wove ugly patterns in the air. But then they moved aside, and the Engineers clattered down the ladderway, jeering at their enemies as they passed.

Petrel tucked her jacket back into its hiding place and crept after them, low and silent and stupid-faced. Five decks down, she was close enough to hear them call softly, "It's a bratling, Chief. A boy."

Another deck. Then Albie called up to them, "Is he alive?"

"Too cold to tell," said one of the rescuers.

"Well then," said Albie, his voice closer now, "we'll warm him up and see what happens. Who is he, d'you reckon? Where'd he come from?"

"No idea. Dropped out of the sky maybe."

And with that, the rescuers stepped off the Commons and hurried towards the Engineer sick bay.

They'll put the boy under close guard, thought Petrel. *They won't let anyone through, much less me. But I'll get to see him somehow. I will!*

In the meantime, she had better tell Mister Smoke and Missus Slink what was happening.

She hurried down another ladder—this one steeper than those above it—and past the ancient batteries that were fed by the wind turbines. She edged past the digester, which took all the ship's waste and turned it into fuel for the engines, and followed a narrow passage to the propeller shaft. A walkway ran alongside the shaft, and at the far end of the walkway, tucked into the bulkhead like an afterthought, was a cramped, disused workshop.

Just as Petrel was mostly forgotten, so were certain parts of the *Oyster*, and this was one of them. The lights along the walkway were broken, and the workshop itself was only dimly lit. But Petrel did not need light to find her way around. She squatted down and clapped her hands to attract the attention of the ship's rats.

There were two sorts of rats on the *Oyster*. The black rats ran across folk's toes as they slept; they chewed the charts; they haunted the Officers' mess and the galleys. Head Cook Krill set traps for them, and sometimes in the long winter dark they turned up in stews.

Petrel liked the black rats for their quickness and their cunning. But it was the gray rats she loved.

"Mister Smoke," she hissed. "Missus Slink. Are you there?"

There was no response, but Petrel suspected that at least one of the two grays was somewhere nearby.

"Listen," whispered Petrel. "There's a stranger on the ship."

There was a moment of utter stillness. Then the darkness in the corner of the workshop seemed to bristle. "A *stranger*?" cried a small rough voice.

"Is that you, Mister Smoke?" whispered Petrel. "Aye, a

stranger, dropped out of the sky. *I* spotted him and told Albie, and he sent a boat—"

She stopped, as the pipes above her head began to clang out a message in general ship code.

STRANGER ON BOARD! STRANGER ON BOARD! STRANGER ON BOARD!

Petrel imagined Dolph and her friends staring at the pipes openmouthed. She grinned. "That'll put the wind up 'em," she whispered.

But as the clanging of the pipes died away, the grin slid from her face. Because Mister Smoke had limped out of the corner and was standing in front of her, his ragged whiskers twitching with agitation.

"What 'ave you done, shipmate?" muttered the rat, and in all the years Petrel had known him, she had never heard him so horrified. "*What 'ave you brought upon us?*"

CHAPTER 3

A STRANGER ON THE SHIP

The boy was alone, trapped in a nightmare of ice and snow. He had never been so cold. It slid into his bones like a knife, and he thrashed from side to side.

"Help me!" he cried, but the words turned to frost on his tongue and fell silent to the ground. His mind tumbled from one useless question to another. Where was the ship? Where was the demon? Where was his dream of winning a Name and becoming part of the Circle of Devouts . . .

He woke then, for a second or two. Just long enough to know that he was not cold after all, but warm, and that the ice was nowhere to be seen. He sighed with relief.

But then he became aware of a relentless *thump thump thump* close by. He had never heard the sound before, but he knew immediately what it meant.

Machines. The plan had worked. He was on the ship.

He rolled his head to one side, to make sure he was alone. A sly smile touched his lips.

"Send a boy," he whispered. "They will never suspect a boy."
Then he closed his eyes and fell back into unconsciousness.

By the end of the day, the *Oyster* was awash with
rumors. No one knew where the stranger had come from, but
everyone had an opinion. Braid folk said that he must have
stepped out of the mouth of a whale, right into the path of the
ship. Grease Alley believed that he had fallen from the sky, and
in Dufftown they claimed that he was made from seaweed and
old bones, like winter soup.

Overnight, the rumors grew even wilder. And so, as soon
as the next morning's fishing shift was underway, the rest of the
crew donned their outdoor clothes (which had been handed
down over the centuries and patched and mended until there
was not a scrap of the original material left) and headed up to
the neutral territory of the foredeck.

None of them saw Petrel. She was hiding in Lifeboat Three,
just above their heads, with her ragged hood drawn around her
ears and the breath issuing in clouds from her mouth. Beside
her crouched the large gray rat known as Mister Smoke.

The foredeck might be neutral territory, but that did not
make it *agreeable* territory. Folk gathered in their tribes, tight
as a school of fish, and every one of them filled with distrust
and suspicion.

Dolph was standing by the wind fiddles, surrounded by
friends and relatives. Petrel scowled at the older girl. "I hate her."

"Why's that, shipmate?" whispered Mister Smoke.

"Why do you think?"

"Tar bucket again, is it?"

Petrel nodded, although she suspected that her hatred was more complicated than that.

Dolph was part of the Officer tribe, which meant she had a proper place on the *Oyster*. She ate when there was food and starved when there wasn't. She didn't have to beg or steal, or live on other folk's scraps; she didn't have to hide in corners and pretend to be an idiot to avoid being kicked or spat on.

She had friends.

Petrel wriggled uncomfortably. "*I've* got friends," she whispered to the rat. "I've got you and Missus Slink."

"Course you 'ave," said Mister Smoke.

"And I saved the stranger. That makes *him* a friend, if he only knew it."

"Hmph," said Mister Smoke, his tattered whiskers twitching. "Wouldn't boast about it if I was you. Strangers is a bad bad thing."

He had been repeating those same words for most of the night, and Petrel ignored him. Despite the cold, she liked being in the lifeboat, with its albatross-eye view of the foredeck. From up here she could see things she was not supposed to see, and hear things she was not supposed to hear.

Like the voice of Second Officer Crab, for instance, drifting upward from below . . .

"We must attack Grease Alley," hissed Crab. "Immediately after this meeting, while Albie is off-balance. We must capture the boy and throw him back to the ice!"

First Officer Orca's reply was as cold as the morning air. "Are you trying to instruct me in my duties, Mister Crab?"

"Of course not, First! But this opportunity—"

"We will attack Grease Alley when the time is right, Mister Crab, and not a moment before."

"But the time is right *now*, First! We must act! To have a stranger on the ship for a moment longer than necessary is unlucky. It is— It is *untidy*!"

Petrel snorted under her breath. Everyone on the *Oyster* knew that Crab was obsessive about tidiness. When the sailing was clear and the ship's course was straight, when the Engineers were in Grease Alley and the Cooks were in Dufftown, when the toothyfish returned on the correct date and the navigation equipment worked as it should and Third Officer Hump did as she was instructed, then Second Officer Crab was happy.

But if a single one of those things was out of place, even for a moment, he would not rest until it was set right. Petrel couldn't see him, but she could imagine his blue eyes bulging with frustration.

"It is up to us, as Officers," he continued, "to show the correct way. And that way is clear. We must get rid of the stranger as quickly as possible! We *must*!"

"You have had my answer, Mister Crab," said Orca. "I should not have to repeat myself."

"But I insist—"

And with that, Orca lost patience. "I do not want a stranger on this ship anymore than you do, Mister Crab!" she snapped, raising her voice so that those Officers nearby could hear her. "But Albie will be expecting an attack. He will be prepared for it. Only a lackwitted fool would oblige him." She paused. "Only a *tidy* lackwitted fool."

Petrel heard a chorus of sniggers from the other Officers, and when she peeped over the gunwale, she saw Crab scuttling away, his face red. She pulled the sleeves of her jacket down over her hands, trying to keep her fingers warm.

On the deck below, folk were getting restless. But no one else said anything interesting until Dolph, as sharp and proud as her mam, turned to the Engineers and shouted, "Is the stranger alive or dead? What are you going to do with him? Don't go thinking you can keep him."

"We'll do wha we like with him," cried Albie's son, Skua, a muscular boy with red hair. "We're the ones who rescued him, not you."

Three boat lengths away, a small pod of whales broke the surface of the water with a groan, then dived again. The morning sea was as flat as a biscuit.

"But where did he come from?" shouted a woman who had pushed her hood back to show the slit earlobes of a Cook. "What's he doing here? It's a bad omen, a stranger on the ship."

"Bad omen?" roared Chief Engineer Albie, his red beard wagging. "Nonsense! It's a gift, that's what it is, same as the seals and the toothyfish. It's a sign of a good fat summer on its way."

Beside Petrel, Mister Smoke cocked his head. "Does Albie believe that nonsense, shipmate?"

"No, he's just pretending," whispered Petrel. "He doesn't believe in signs and omens."

Most of the folk on the foredeck however *did* believe in signs and omens, and they shouted their agreement or disagreement, depending on their tribe. Insults began to fly, most of them between Officers and Engineers.

Head Cook Krill banged on a skillet to demand attention. A dozen small bones were knitted into his beard, and an apron stretched tight across his barrel chest.

"This ain't a question to be decided by Grease Alley alone," he bellowed. "If there's a stranger on the ship, it's a *ship* problem, and it needs to be thought out by cool heads."

"First sensible thing I've 'eard all mornin'," muttered Mister Smoke.

But Albie glared at the Head Cook. "You trying to sound *reasonable* there, Krill? Fancy yourself as wiser than the rest of us, do you?"

"Wouldn't be hard." Krill showed his teeth. "And here's my wisdom. I say we throw the boy back where he came from, before he brings trouble upon us."

"I agree," said Orca, and the black and white feathers of office, sewn to her jacket, fluttered in the breeze.

"No," whispered Petrel.

"Put him back on the ice," continued Krill, "or kill him and throw him to the Maw. It's the only sensible thing to do. Even you, with your mind rotted by grease and fumes, gotta see that, Albie."

Albie's scars bristled and he said, loudly, "I've never

bothered listening to the Cooks before. I wonder why that is? P'raps—"

Krill tried to interrupt, but Albie was used to making himself heard over the relentless *thump thump thump* of the engines. "P'raps it's because Cooks ain't got no more brain than a wooden spoon!"

His face split in a vicious grin, and his fellow Engineers— men, women and bratlings—roared with laughter. Krill flushed, and raised the skillet as if he was going to throw it.

"Ooh, he's got a weapon on the foredeck," shouted Skua, and he made a great show of hiding behind Albie. "Ooh, I'm scared! Save me, Da!"

The laughter grew louder. Krill shook his skillet at the red-haired boy and muttered a string of threats.

"Be quiet!" shouted Orca over the racket. "For once, Krill is making sense. We must talk, Albie, the three of us."

She strode forward, waving the rest of the crew back to their duties. Second Officer Crab didn't move.

"I should be part of this discussion, First," he said stiffly. "It is my right."

"No, Mister Crab."

"But I am Second Off—"

"No, Mister Crab!"

"But I—"

"Are you a bratling that has to be told the same thing over and over again?" snarled Orca. "Go inside at once!"

Crab's shoulders twitched, and his lips pressed together so hard that they lost all color. But he followed the rest of the crew inside without further protest. The men and women of the fishing shift turned back to their tasks. In the lifeboat, Petrel crouched as still as a bollard, hoping the three leaders would not see her.

"This stranger," said Orca, as soon as the deck was more or less clear, "*will not* remain on my ship. Get rid of him, Albie."

There was a sour taste in Petrel's mouth. *Don't listen to her, Uncle,* she thought.

"It's only common sense," rumbled Krill. He nodded towards the fishing shift. "What do they do if they pull up something that's all bones and bile? Why, they chuck it straight in the digester, that's what. Get rid of the boy."

"Get rid of him," said Orca, "or face the consequences."

Albie shook his head in mock sorrow. "You two can give me all the orders you want, and it won't make a shred of difference. The captain's the only one *I* take orders from. You get the captain telling me to throw the boy back and I'll do it, quick smart."

Petrel's breath hissed between her teeth. Like the crew's outdoor clothes, the story of the *Oyster*'s captain had been passed down from generation to generation, and patched and mended until no one could remember what it used to look like. Some folk said there had never been a captain. Others said he had been killed two hundred years ago, when the crew split into warring tribes and the ship's log was burned.

But most folk, including Petrel, believed that the captain was merely asleep, and that one day, when they needed him most, he would wake up. No one had ever seen him, of course, and there were endless arguments over where on the ship his sleeping body might lie. But they knew he was there somewhere, and it comforted them.

Petrel suspected that neither Orca nor Albie believed in the sleeping captain. Krill did, however, and he bridled at the Chief Engineer's words.

"You think you're so clever," said Krill. "Captain's not going to wake up for a storm in a soup bowl like this. He's sleeping till a *real* disaster comes, and you know it. But I tell you what, you keep that boy and I'll cut off your rations. See how pleased your folk are with you when they ain't got enough to eat."

"We didn't have enough to eat all winter dark," replied Albie. "And what little we got was barely edible." He jerked a thumb at the fishing shift. "But toothies'll be running soon—can't be more than a day or so away—and you can't stop us catching *them*."

"We won't cook 'em for you!"

"Then we'll eat 'em raw!"

The two men stood nose to nose, the breath streaming out of them in angry puffs. Above their heads the wind turbines cranked, and the song of the wind fiddles wove through their rage.

"Ice and fog, Albie!" snapped Orca. "You're as stubborn as a glacier. But it won't do you any good." And she spun on her heel and marched away. Krill followed her.

Albie spat thoughtfully over the rail and shouted to one of the Engineers on the fishing shift. "Any sign of the toothies, shipmate?"

The woman shook her head. "It's just tiddlers, Chief. Good for bait and not much else."

"Hmm," said Albie, and he fell silent.

Petrel didn't move a muscle, didn't even breathe. It was a dangerous thing to catch the Chief Engineer's attention; she had known that for years. Her mam had been Albie's sister, but that fact did not soften him towards Petrel. If anything, it made him worse.

Beside her, Mister Smoke cocked a cautious ear, then nodded. Petrel let out the breath she'd been holding. Her uncle was leaving at last.

She waited until he had disappeared inside the ship, then she climbed out of the lifeboat and crept after him.

She knew that Albie mistrusted strangers as much as the rest of the crew. She also knew that if he saw a chance to annoy Orca, he would take it. Which meant that he might hang on to the stranger, or he might throw him back to the ice, and there was no telling which way he would turn, or when.

If Petrel wanted to see the frozen boy, she had better do it soon.

CHAPTER 4

AS HARMLESS AS A SEAL PUP

When the boy woke a second time, his head was clear.

I am on the ship, he reminded himself.

He lay very still, his eyes flicking from one side of the small room to the other. He was in a sort of rope cot suspended from the ceiling. The walls around him were a patchwork of rusty iron, and a single light burned above the door. Somewhere nearby, the machines rumbled and thumped in a steady rhythm.

The boy knew all about machines. *They weaken us. They make people lazy and soft and corrupt; they steal our souls . . .*

The mere thought filled him with revulsion. But it set him thinking too. Because if the machines were so close to where he lay, the demon must also be close.

His heart raced, and he remembered the night, four months ago, when he had been dragged from his dormitory and brought before the Inner Circle of Devouts.

At first he had thought he was in trouble. He had stood

barefooted on marble floors beneath the Citadel spire, surrounded by men in silken robes. Men who ruled the world. Men who did not seem to notice he was there.

But then, suddenly, Brother Thrawn had loomed up in front of him, looking so severe that the boy braced himself for a whipping at the very least, and perhaps even a stint in the punishment cells.

Instead, to his astonishment, the Circle's leader praised him. "You are the best Initiate we have had for years," Brother Thrawn said in his flat voice, "and we have a task for you. A mission."

The boy's heart thumped, but he knew better than to show any emotion. He kept his eyes fixed on the floor and murmured, "Thank you, Brother."

"It is the culmination," said Brother Thrawn, "of three hundred years' work." He cleared his throat, and all conversation in the marble room ceased. "You have heard us speak of the *demon*?"

A prickle ran down the boy's spine. "Yes, Brother. The Abomination."

Brother Thrawn nodded approval. "We have always suspected that the creature escaped the Great Cleansing, along with its imps. But we did not know how it escaped, or where it had concealed itself. Generations of Devouts have sought the truth. They have scoured the world, searching for hidden documents. They have traced rumors and folk tales. They have risked their lives, just as you will soon risk yours."

The boy kept his face blank. But inside he was glowing with excitement. This was his chance to win a Name and become part of the Circle! Risk his life? He would do it a hundred times over for such an opportunity!

"And now," continued Brother Thrawn, "the courage of the searchers has been rewarded at last. One of them has found an old sea chart. Another has found a diagram. A third has found a hidden diary. Things that mean nothing if taken separately, but put them together and they tell us all we need to know . . ."

There was a sound at the door, and the boy dragged himself back to the present. A man entered—a savage with scars carved into his cheeks and elaborate knots tied in his red beard. The boy sat up quickly, and the rope cot rocked from side to side.

"So you're awake," said the man, dragging a rickety chair up to the cot and sitting down with his legs splayed.

"Yes," said the boy, thinking, *Now it begins.*

"Good, good," said the man. "Let's have some introductions. This ship's the *Oyster*. I'm Chief Engineer Albie, and"—he waved a casual hand at the rumbling and thumping on the other side of the door—"I'm the one who keeps that lot running."

The boy was astonished that even a savage would confess to such a thing. But he gave no sign of his surprise. "You serve the machines?" he said quietly.

"Don't know about serve 'em." The man laughed. "They serve me, p'raps. Do what I tell 'em most days."

Which was almost as bad, as far as the boy could see. Without moving his lips, he whispered the First Discipline under his breath, to protect himself from contamination.

"That's me explained," said Albie, smiling. "Now what about you? Let's start with your name."

"I cannot remember my name," replied the boy.

It was the first lie he had told in many, many years. Lying was not permitted in the Citadel—it was on the list of forbidden things, directly above dancing. But lying to savages and demon-worshippers was different. The boy had Brother Thrawn's ex-press permission to lie for the greater good, to play his part in cleansing the world of evil and returning it to a state of perfec-tion, where all creatures lived in civilized harmony, uncorrupted by machines.

He had practiced his lies under Brother's pitiless gaze, until he could say them without flinching.

"Do not tell them anything at first," Brother Thrawn had instructed him. "They will not value what comes easily. Make them wait. Make them think you are coming to trust them, and then *they* will come to trust *you*. And when you lie, do it well. Do not let us down."

The boy must have lied well enough, because Albie nodded and said, "Brain's addled, no doubt, by the ice. But I expect it'll come back to you." He coughed and scratched his chest. "Don't mind me," he said. "There's a bit of boat fever going round and I've caught the tail end of it. Let's try a different question. How did you get on the ice in the first place?"

"I cannot remember."

That was another lie. The boy could recall every moment of his voyage south, with the waves mounting up behind the sailing ship—a ship that had seemed enormous when he first boarded it, but which was now shown to be puny and insignificant. He could remember the wind howling, and the crew battling the elements, and the fighting men of the Circle huddled around the iron stoves, sharpening their axes in anticipation . . .

"It's just," said Albie, "that we don't see a lot of *strangers* down this way. In fact"—and now there was a hardness in his voice— "we don't *ever* see strangers. And there's folk on the *Oyster*— not just Cooks and Officers, but my own folk—who don't like it. Suspicious, they are, and I don't blame 'em. From the look of you, you're as harmless as a seal pup. But looks aren't everything. You can understand us wondering, can't you?"

"Yes," said the boy.

"Good, good," said Albie, all friendly again. "I expect your memory'll come back after a bite to eat."

And a few minutes later, after sending for some food and assuring the boy that he was among friends, he left.

The boy immediately climbed from his rope bed and tried the door, but to his immense frustration it was locked. He ate the hard biscuits and the slimy green paste, telling himself that Albie would not keep him confined for much longer. After all, the Chief Engineer had said he was among friends . . .

But when Albie came back, several hours later, he asked the same questions. And it was not long before his friendliness gave way to shouting.

"You must've come from *somewhere*! So tell me again, bratling, *how* did you end up on that berg?"

"I do not remember."

"Course you don't. *Course you don't!* I should've left you there to freeze to death. In fact"—Albie leaned forward, showing his teeth—"it's not too late even now. Won't be the same berg, of course, but frozen is frozen, no matter where it happens. Eh? *Eh?*"

The boy was not used to loud voices. The Citadel, where he had lived for most of his life, was a place of study and reflection. There were no raised voices, no arguments or foolish emotions. According to Brother Thrawn, emotions were wasteful things. Ignorant people wallowed in them, instead of dedicating themselves to purity and discipline.

But this man was worse than ignorant. He shouted and swore and smiled and frowned all in one sentence. "Maybe you're not sure of us; is that it?" he cried. "Well, the feeling's mutual; we're not sure of you either, and we won't be, until you give us a bit more information. You see, I can smell intrigue five decks away"—he tapped the side of his nose, his eyes hard—"and you reek of it. Intrigue and plots—"

"Wait!" said the boy, judging that the moment had come to reveal a little more of his story. He put his hand to his forehead. "It—it is coming back to me! There was a . . . a shipwreck—"

He broke off as the door flew open and a hulking young man with red hair and a few hopeful scrapings of beard entered.

"Everyone's talking about the stranger, Da," said the

redhead. "Everyone wants to see him." He grinned, and jiggled from foot to foot. "I even caught the Nothing girl sneaking round. Taught her a lesson, I did."

Albie grunted. "What about Braid and Duff? What are they up to?"

"Not a peep out of Krill. But word is, Orca's waiting for us to lower our guard, then she's gunna hit border three, and try and snatch the stranger."

The Chief Engineer stood up. "We'd better move him then, just in case."

And the next thing the boy knew, he was being hustled out of the cabin and towards the clanking machines.

He had thought he was prepared for anything, but still the machines took his breath away. In a daze he stumbled between huge metal hot-smelling *things* that towered above him and seemed to be made entirely of noise. When he shrank from them, Albie's son roared with laughter and dragged him closer, until the noise beat around his head like Brother Thrawn's fists. The boy whispered the First Discipline and tried not to let his horror show.

No wonder these people are such savages, he thought. *They are surrounded by vileness. And these machines are not even the worst of it!*

A pipe hissed at him, as if it could read his mind. The metal grating beneath his feet rattled. Albie's fingers dug into the boy's arm, and it was all he could do to keep walking.

"He didn't like that, Da," said Albie's son, grinning. "Didn't like our babies. Didn't appreciate their little song."

Albie did not answer. He was muttering to himself, "Put him in the brig, I reckon. Orca won't get him out of there."

The boy jogged between the Chief Engineer and his son, trying to clear his mind of the dreadful machines so that he could take note of his surroundings. They were passing through some sort of living quarters now, with cots and nets and rope ladders hanging down in every direction, and the stink of fish oil and unwashed bodies.

People were chattering in groups. Between them, skinny half-naked children scrambled up and down the rope ladders, squealing at the tops of their voices. Babies chortled and cried. It was a different sort of racket from the machines, but the boy's lip curled in disgust.

Look at them, he thought. *What do they know of discipline and virtue? They have machines on their ship! They have a demon! And do they care? Are they trying to rid themselves of these impurities? No, of course not. Brother Thrawn was right; they are savages and cowards, and they deserve to die.*

Albie pushed through the crowd, lifting rope cots out of the way with a brawny arm and greeting any questions with a grunt.

His son, however, smirked and sang out at the top of his voice, "Here's the stranger, shipmates, see? Ain't he a feeble-looking thing? Hardly worth fighting Orca for. And no use talking to him, neither, 'cos he's a dummy."

"You shut your gob, Skua," said Albie mildly, "or I'll shut it for you."

Skua fell silent. But his words had done their damage. Before the boy had taken another three paces he was surrounded by gaping mouths and wide, astonished eyes. There were too many people and they pressed him too close, picking at his clothes with fingers that stank of fish. Some of the smaller children began to cry, as if the *boy* were the strange one. As if *he* were the demon-lover.

After the horror of the machines, it was almost too much for him. He wanted to push them back, to shout at them, *Do not stare! Get away from me!*

His training saved him. He reminded himself that Initiates of the Circle did not shout. Initiates of the Circle were like the Citadel spire, rising clean and superior into the sky, even while the storms of the ignorant raged below. The boy gritted his teeth and bent his mind to the Spire Contemplation, which had never failed him yet. Before long his thoughts began to trace the familiar shape, and the people around him faded a little, as if he had set them behind glass.

Savages, he thought. *Savages and cowards. Barely human.*

By the time the small procession came to the brig, the boy had himself entirely under control.

That is, until Albie pushed him into a small cell with a bucket in one corner, saying, "I've got things to deal with, bratling, but when I return I'll want to hear more about this shipwreck. I'll want your name too. Names are important. A name tells me where you stand in the world, and whether I can trust you or not. You've got until the second dog watch tomorrow to remember yours. If you won't give it to me by then, it's back onto the ice with you."

The carefully constructed pattern of the Spire

Contemplation fell to the deck like broken glass. The boy's stomach tightened.

He was willing to lie about any number of things, knowing that he was doing the will of the Circle. But there was one thing he was determined *not* to lie about, and that was his name.

Initiates like the boy and his fellows did not *have* a name, not until they had carried out some noble deed. Winning a name and taking their place in the Circle of Devouts was all they talked about. It filled their days, and their nights too, sliding into their dreams like a bright flame, and every single one of them yearning towards it.

Brother Thrawn was no fool, however. He had known that the boy's lack of a name might arouse suspicion among the savages.

"Hold them off for as long as you can," he had said. "Leave holes in your story so that your name is not the only thing missing, and fill those holes in gradually. If you are clever, you will be able to kill the demon before they press you too hard on the matter. But—"

Here he had fixed the boy with a granite stare. "But if it comes to the point where it threatens the success of the mission, then you must give yourself a name."

The boy had nodded, of course; no one ever said no to Brother Thrawn. But secretly he had promised himself that things would *not* come to that point. That he would not *have* to invent a name; that he was clever enough to win through without it.

As he listened to the footsteps walking away from his prison, he gritted his teeth and renewed his secret promise.

"I am the best Initiate for years," he whispered fiercely. "I will *never* accept a name I have not earned!" And he set out to inspect the cell, knowing that he could not afford to wait for Albie's trust.

Instead he would escape. He would find the demon and kill it. And then—*then* he would summon the bright cleansing axes of the Circle to destroy the ship and everyone on it.

CHAPTER 5

SECRETS . . .

"I COULDN'T GET NEAR HIM," SAID PETREL, LATER THAT NIGHT. "Albie's got him locked up tight as tight."

"And a good thing too," said Mister Smoke.

"What's the matter with your head?" asked Missus Slink, craning her neck. "Is that blood?"

Petrel touched her scalp gingerly. "Skua chucked a wrench at me. His aim's getting better."

"Hmph," said Missus Slink. "Let's have a look."

Grumbling quietly, Petrel lay facedown on the hard deck of the workshop. Small paws patted her scalp, and she winced.

"Hurts, does it?" asked Missus Slink. With every movement her old joints creaked, and the tattered green ribbon she wore around her neck brushed Petrel's ear. "He's sliced you right open. Needs stitches."

In Petrel's other ear, Mister Smoke said, "So what's Albie gunna do with the stranger, shipmate?"

"You tell me, Mister Smoke, and we'll both know."

"Hold still, girl," said Missus Slink. "Don't jump around so much."

"Ow," said Petrel, as something stung her scalp. "What's that?"

"Grog," said the rat. "Make sure the wound's clean before I stitch it." She dabbed at Petrel with tiny paws, muttering under her breath. "There's always something. Stitch the scalp, scrape the turbines, patch the for'ard sea valves— No, I forgot, the valves are your job, Smoke."

A tiny needle appeared in her paw. "Hold still," she warned again, and Petrel felt a pricking sensation that made her squawk.

"Scalps is easier than valves," said Mister Smoke.

"Rubbish," said Missus Slink, as the needle dived in and out. "Valves don't talk back. Three stitches should do the trick. Seal gut, who'd've thought I'd end up using seal gut? Mind, it's better than seaweed, which I tried a while back. Was it seaweed? I can't recall."

"What are you talking about?" asked Petrel.

"Never you mind," said Missus Slink. "There now, that's done."

Petrel probed the tiny, neat stitches with her finger. There was no sign of the needle now, which didn't surprise her. She had known the two rats for as long as she could remember, but there were mysteries about them that she had never got to the bottom of. Sometimes they answered her questions, sometimes they didn't, and there was nothing she could do about it.

There was nothing she could do about the strange boy,

either, no matter how much she wanted to see him. She rubbed her eyes and stood up. "I'm hungry. Ain't eaten since yesterday."

"Hang on, hang on," said Mister Smoke, squinting up at her. "What about the stranger?"

"I told you, I can't get near him. And Albie'll do more than slice my scalp open if he catches me hanging round the brig."

"But you're the one 'oo found the boy," said Mister Smoke. "That means you got a responsibility to look out for 'im."

Petrel stared down at the rat. "Why are you so worried about him all of a sudden, Mister Smoke? You said strangers are bad."

"And so they are. But don't you want to know where 'e came from?"

"He fell from the sky."

Mister Smoke made a rude snorting noise.

"Hungry," said Petrel, and she marched out of the workshop.

Mister Smoke limped after her, with Missus Slink hobbling in the rear. "You should go back and talk to the boy, shipmate," said Mister Smoke, his nose twitching.

"Course I should," said Petrel, not meaning it. "Your leg getting worse, Mister Smoke?"

"You should ask 'im questions. What's 'is name? Where'd 'e come from? How'd 'e end up on that berg? Was 'e alone, or were there folk with 'im? If there were, where are they now? Get some answers."

"You trying to get me into trouble with Albie?" said Petrel.

The rat's eyes gleamed. "Answers."

"No."

"Answers!"

"Why can't you be nice?" hissed Petrel, her irritation growing. "If I had to be friends with a rat, why couldn't it be a *nice* rat?"

"He's a law unto himself," said Missus Slink gloomily. "I'm not saying he's wrong, mind."

Mister Smoke began to sing in a sandpapery voice, "Answers answers answers. Answers answers answers—"

Petrel bent down and scooped him off the deck.

"Oy," he said, wriggling. "Lemme go!"

"No, you listen, Mister Smoke," said Petrel, slipping into the shadows and squatting down with Missus Slink beside her. "You know what Albie said, last time he caught me poking my nose into his business? He said I was as useless as feathers on a fish, and he might just do the whole ship a favor and chuck me overboard. So I'm not going near that brig, not for anything."

The rat stopped wriggling. "Thought the boy was your friend. 'Cos you saved 'im from the ice."

Petrel scowled. "When did I ever have friends, 'cept for you and Missus Slink?"

"All the same—"

"And besides," continued Petrel, "I tried to see him once. Not gunna risk my life trying again."

Mister Smoke blinked thoughtfully. "Maybe there's an easier way," he said. "A safer way."

"What do you mean?"

The old rat cocked his head to one side and peered at Petrel. "You think you know this ship? You think you know every bit of 'er?"

"Careful, Smoke," said Missus Slink. "You're getting perilously close to things that shouldn't be talked about."

Petrel looked from one rat to the other. "What sort of things?"

"Never you mind," said Missus Slink firmly.

But Mister Smoke winked, and whispered, "Put me down, shipmate. This needs a bit of negotiatin'."

The two rats retired to the corner. Petrel did her best to overhear their muttered conversation, but the clatter of the engines drowned out all but a few words.

". . . got to find out . . . ," said Mister Smoke.

". . . a sacred trust."

". . . have to bend . . ."

"No!" said Missus Slink.

Mister Smoke persisted, ". . . need answers . . . just in case . . ."

Whatever argument Mister Smoke was making, it eventually brought Missus Slink up short. She wrinkled her nose. "I can't see how . . ."

". . . honorary . . ."

". . . mmm. Possible . . ."

They turned and inspected Petrel with sharp eyes.

Despite what she had said, Petrel *did* want to try again, if she could only do it without risking her life. After all, the boy wasn't a part of the crew any more than she was. Maybe he *would* be her friend, if she could just talk to him.

At last the rats came to an agreement. Missus Slink was not entirely happy, but she seemed resigned. "Girl," she said, before

Mister Smoke could open his mouth. "Will you dig out those answers for us, if we get you close to the stranger?"

Petrel nodded eagerly.

Missus Slink's claws tapped against the deck. "This is serious business, mind. There's no telling anyone what we're going to show you. Not even if they've got a knife to your throat. Not even if they're dangling you over the side, and the Maw's gazing up at you from below, all agape for a tasty meal."

Petrel gulped.

Missus Slink turned away, saying, "Ha, she can't do it."

"I can!" said Petrel quickly. "I— I'm used to keeping secrets, Missus Slink. My whole life's a secret, and there's no one else on board who can say that."

Mister Smoke chortled. "She's got you there, Slink. She'll do." He scrambled up onto Petrel's knee. "So, give us your promise, shipmate."

Petrel shut her eyes, and opened them again. "I promise. I won't say anything to anyone. Ever."

"Good," said Mister Smoke. "You is now an honorary rat, and a servant of the sleeping captain."

"Tsk!" said Missus Slink. "We never agreed on that last bit."

"She can't be one without the other," said Mister Smoke. Then he leaped down from Petrel's knee, saying, "You come with us, shipmate."

As they made their way for'ard, they hardly saw a soul. It was just coming up to midnight, and any Engineers who weren't working or asleep were sticking close to quarters in case of an attack. The whole ship felt jittery, the way it did when the weatherglass was dropping fast and the pipes rattled with storm warnings.

"How much farther, Mister Smoke?" asked Petrel.

Mister Smoke nodded towards the for'ard store cabins. The door of the second one was ajar, and when Petrel put her head around it she saw a pile of driftwood and whale bones. They filled the cabin from deck to overhead, crammed so tight that she could barely see between them.

"How am I sposed to fit in there?"

"Maybe you won't," sniffed Missus Slink.

"How far do I have to go?"

"Right to the back," said Mister Smoke. "There's a cupboard."

He scrambled up onto the nearest bit of driftwood and launched himself into the pile. Missus Slink followed him, and the two rats disappeared. Petrel edged into the dark cabin after them.

It was a tight fit, even for someone as scrawny as she was. She squeezed between the bits of wood and bone, crawling over the top of some of them and underneath others, and hissing whenever a bone-end jabbed her in the ribs. "Stupid thing, get out of my way!"

At last, bruised and panting, she reached the far wall. She was right up high by then, on top of the pile, and she had to fumble downwards to find the cupboard. There it was—she could feel the top edge of the door. And there, all ragged fur and whiskers, was Mister Smoke.

"You won't do any good up there, shipmate," said the rat.

Which meant that Petrel had to wriggle down, like a seal sliding off a rock, only not as graceful.

The cupboard door was open far enough for her to squeeze through the gap. She twisted and squirmed until she was the right way up, then drew in a deep breath.

"What now?" she asked, but she was talking to thin air. "Mister Smoke? Missus Slink? Where are you?"

She heard the scrabble of claws, and Mister Smoke said, from somewhere in front of her nose, "Whatcha waitin' for? Get a move on, shipmate."

"All right, all right," said Petrel, and she put her hands out and fumbled blindly towards him.

There was a ragged hole in the back of the cupboard, but it did not lead to the cabin on the other side of the bulkhead, as it should have done. Instead, it opened into a cramped tunnel.

Petrel drew in a sharp breath. This was a fine secret! She had never even suspected that such a tunnel existed.

"Where does it go?" she whispered.

"Where *don't* it go might be a better question," said Mister Smoke.

"Will you show me? Are there other places where I could get in and out?"

"Mebbe."

"I could creep along inside the bulkhead and watch Dolph, and she'd never know I was there," whispered Petrel. A fierce glee took hold of her. "I could watch *Albie*!"

"Enough chatter, shipmate. Come on, keep your 'ead down and don't lag behind."

The tunnel was not made for humans. It was narrow and cramped and pitchy dark most of the way, although every now and then there was a crack where light seeped through from a cabin or a passageway. Petrel wanted to stop and peer through those inviting cracks, but the rats hurried her on.

She felt as if she were crawling through the innards of a whale. The familiar rumblings of the ship were magnified and strange, and the darkness seemed to pulsate around her. At one point she had to stop and breathe deeply before she could continue.

Still the tunnel spun out ahead of her. Her knuckles scraped against the decking. She bumped her elbows and her nose, and flakes of rust stuck to her face like snow.

And then suddenly Missus Slink was whispering in her ear, "Nearly there, girl. Hush now. The brig's just ahead of us."

"You come and ask those questions," said Mister Smoke. "Slink and I'll grab 'old of the answers as he gives 'em. Come on."

"No, wait," hissed Petrel. Now that the moment was so close, her heart was beating right up in her throat. "What if he won't talk to me?"

"Course 'e'll talk to you. Why wouldn't 'e?"

"I don't know. My mouth's gone all dry. What if I can't talk to *him*?" Petrel bit her lip. It was true; her mouth *was* dry. She couldn't remember the last time she had spoken to anyone except the rats. But that wasn't her only reason for saying what she said next. "Maybe you and Missus Slink should stay back here. Not sure if I can do it with you listening. Not sure at all."

Missus Slink and Mister Smoke muttered to each other, so quiet that Petrel couldn't pick out a single word. The ship gurgled and crunched. Petrel knelt in the darkness of the tunnel, thinking about the questions *she* wanted to ask the boy; questions that were far more interesting than the ones the rats had in mind.

At last Missus Slink turned back to her and said, "Go on then. But remember everything he says. Don't lose a word of it."

"I won't," said Petrel. And she crawled towards the brig.

CHAPTER 6

LIES . . .

THE BOY PICKED STUBBORNLY AT THE PATCH OF RUST ON THE wall behind his cot. His fingers were scraped and sore, but he did not even think of giving up. He had already made a small hole. All he had to do was keep working until it was big enough to climb through.

And hope that Albie didn't come back too soon.

He had no idea where the hole would take him, or how he would find his way unnoticed through the corridors of the ship to the place where the demon was hidden. But he would do it somehow.

He dug his fingers into the rusty iron, wiggling bits of it back and forth. "I am going to beat you," he said to the wall.

To his horror, the wall replied. "Boy," it whispered.

His first thought was of the demon and its imps, and he took an involuntary step backwards.

"Come here," whispered the wall. "I want to talk to you."

With a stab of relief the boy realized that it was not the voice of a demon after all. Nor was it an imp.

It was a girl.

His mind raced. Should he reply or stay silent? What did the girl want? Was it a trick? A trap? Had Albie sent her?

It seemed very likely.

But surely, thought the boy, *I can outwit a savage girl, no matter who sent her. Perhaps I can even persuade her to help me. It would be far quicker than trying to dig my way out through the rust . . .*

"What do you want?" he said.

"Come here," whispered the girl. "Come close so we're not yelling at each other. That guard of Albie's has got sharp ears."

The boy crept back to the wall, trying to pinpoint the direction of her voice. "Where are you?"

"Nowhere," whispered the girl.

The boy put his eye to the hole he had made. There was nothing but darkness on the other side, and the oily stink of the ship's crew. He supposed the girl must be standing in an unlit corridor.

"What do you want?" he said again.

"Your name for starters. Mine's Petrel."

"I cannot tell you any more than I told Albie," said the boy. "I do not remember my name."

He braced himself for an onslaught of questions, but instead, Petrel whispered, "I'm not surprised. It's hard to remember anything when Albie's shouting at you. He's the worst shouter on the ship, worse than Orca even. Course, she doesn't really shout. She just goes all quiet and nasty, but it *feels* like shouting, 'cos

56

it pierces right through you and you end up feeling no bigger'n a shrimp."

Her husky voice was soothing, and the boy was still tired from his ordeal on the ice. But he knew better than to let down his guard.

"Crab's just as bad," whispered the girl. "Only he's all buttoned up and trim, even in midwinter, which is not a trim sort of time. Now Skua's a shouter like his da. Lots of bluster and noise, only not so dangerous as Albie. You can get away from Skua if you're tricksy enough, but hardly anyone gets away from Albie unless he feels like letting you go—what's your name?"

The question was thrown in so neatly that, if the boy had not been expecting some such ruse, he might have answered truthfully.

But for all his tiredness, he was not fooled. With a sigh, he said, "I told you, I do not remember."

"That's the strangest thing I ever heard," whispered Petrel. "*Why* don't you remember? Did the ice take it? Did it freeze inside your head and break into pieces? Did a gull swoop down and—"

The boy interrupted her. "I do not know."

There was a moment's silence, as if Petrel was thinking. Then she whispered, "What's it like in the sky?"

"*What?*"

"In the sky, where you come from. What's it like?"

For all the seriousness of his mission, the boy almost laughed out loud. *How absurd these savages are,* he thought. *How ignorant!*

At the same time, this was an opportunity he could not afford to miss. He gathered his wits and whispered, "It is beautiful in the sky. The food is plentiful. Everyone has full bellies every day of the year—"

A stifled groan from behind the wall.

"It is warm," said the boy, "even in winter—"

Another groan. The boy grinned nastily. *I have hooked myself a fish. Now I shall reel it in.*

Aloud he said, "There is so much I wish to tell you. But . . . I cannot."

"Why not?"

"Because I am a prisoner, and Albie has threatened to throw me overboard if I do not remember my name. How can I bear to think of my beautiful home in such circumstances?"

"Oh."

It was the smallest of sounds, but the disappointment in it was all that the boy could have wished.

"Of course, if someone should free me from this cell," he whispered, "I would be so grateful that I would tell her anything she wished to know. *Anything.*"

Total stillness greeted his words; he could almost hear the girl thinking. He knew he could not afford to trust her, even if she helped him escape. The whole thing might be a trick. She might be planning to deliver him to the demon. Or straight back to Albie.

But she will not succeed, he thought. *I am too clever for her.*

At last the girl said, "Maybe I could—" She stopped, and

the boy held his breath. But when she continued, all she would say was, "I'll have to talk to someone."

"Not Albie!"

"Don't be stupid," she said.

The boy had to press his lips together to keep from snapping back at her. *You are nothing but an ignorant savage! How dare you call me stupid?*

When he could trust himself to speak, he whispered, "The second dog watch. When is that?"

"Is that when Albie's going to chuck you overboard? Don't worry, that's not for hours. We've got plenty of time."

The boy thought he heard her move. But it seemed she was not quite ready to go. "You poor sad thing," she whispered, "forgetting your name. How about I give you one to tide you over?"

"No," said the boy quickly.

Petrel ignored him. "Fin. That's what I'll call you."

"No. *No!* You cannot just *give* someone a—" He slammed his mouth shut on what he had been about to say.

"Finnnnnnn." The girl sounded pleased. "Now you've got something to tell Albie next time he asks. He can't object to a name like Fin. It could be anything, Officer, Engineer or Cook. Mind you, I wouldn't be surprised if he decides to chuck you overboard anyway. He's not a man to change his mind, once he's set his course."

And with that she was gone, leaving the boy shocked beyond belief. She had given him a name! She had *forced* a name on him, when he had neither earned it nor wanted it!

He closed his eyes. A muscle in his cheek twitched. "I will not answer to that name," he whispered. "You cannot make me."

And he went back to digging at the wall, determined to find his own way out of the cell, and to have nothing more to do with the girl.

Nothing whatsoever.

"WELL?" SAID MISTER SMOKE, AS SOON AS THEY WERE OUT OF the tunnel. "You gunna tell us them answers, or are you savin' 'em for midsummer?"

Petrel's spirits were rising and falling like a storm wave. She had talked to the boy! What's more, the boy had talked back to her, just as if she was a real person. *He* didn't think she was worthless. *He* did t think she should've been thrown to the Maw years ago.

That was the white-flecked peak of the wave. But after it came the trough. The boy was in trouble. Petrel wanted to save him, but she'd never be able to get him out of the brig by herself, and she was quite sure that Mister Smoke and Missus Slink wouldn't help her.

Not unless she could come up with a very good reason.

Which was why, instead of answering Mister Smoke's question, she mumbled, "Hungry. Gotta find something to eat." And took to her heels.

Cook territory, or Dufftown, occupied the *Oyster*'s middle decks, with Braid above it and Grease Alley below. The Commons ladderways passed through Dufftown, so that Engineer folk could climb up to the outside decks for their fishing shift or to mend the wind turbines, or perhaps just to see the sun, there being no portholes in Grease Alley.

But if one of those Engineers—man, woman or bratling—should try to set foot in Dufftown, they would find themselves face-to-face with a dozen hostile border guards.

Petrel was not an Engineer. She was not a Cook either, or an Officer. She was nothing, and the guards knew it. So even though they were jittery, they did not try to stop her. Instead they scowled as she scuttled past, then went back to cursing Albie, who was endangering the whole ship with his stubbornness.

Because it was the middle of the night, there was none of the usual bustle in the *Oyster*'s galley. In fact, Petrel could only see a single Cook, bent over a grinding machine with her back to the door. It was Squid, the daughter of Head Cook Krill.

Petrel sidled into the room, her eyes fixed on the tray of hard biscuits two benches away. She would rather have had fish, of course, or seaweed broth, which was thick and hot and satisfying. But the winter had been a hard one and biscuits were better than nothing, even though they were so tasteless that folk said they must be made from ground-up whale bones, with maybe a bit of salt added.

Squid was muttering to herself, too low for Petrel to catch the words. The grinding machine made a ratcheting noise, then fell silent again. Petrel ducked under the first bench, then under the second. The biscuits were just above her. Silently, she reached upwards . . .

She had stolen food from the galley countless times before

and never been caught. But perhaps the excitement she felt at having talked to the boy—at having *named* him—had changed her. Perhaps she was no longer quite as small and unnoticeable as she had been. Whatever the reason, as her fingers touched the edge of the tray, a hand grabbed her wrist.

Petrel tried to jerk away, but Squid had a firm grip. "What's this?" said the young woman. "Someone out of bed when they shouldn't be? Someone I know, maybe? No, don't recognize this grubby hand. Who are you, bratling? Come out and show yourself."

Squid had never been one of Petrel's tormentors, and even now she did not sound angry. Still, Petrel trusted no one but herself. She braced her feet against the leg of the bench so she could not be dragged out against her will.

"What's the matter?" asked Squid. "You think I'm going to eat you? Not likely. Imagine Da turning up first thing in the morning, while I'm still licking my chops. 'What've you been eating?' he'd say." She copied Krill's growl perfectly. "And then I'd have to confess," she continued. "I'd open my mouth and point to the bits of gristle wedged between my teeth. 'See that, Da?' I'd say. 'That's an intruder I caught last night.' And wouldn't he belt me. 'I've told you before,' he'd bellow. 'You're not to eat the Officers!'"

It was such nonsense that Petrel wanted to laugh. But she did not move or speak.

Squid sighed loudly. "I've got work to do, you know. I can't wait here all night. Come out and let's have a look at you."

There was no hint of violence or cruelty in her voice. She

just sounded curious. And besides, tonight was . . . different. Slowly Petrel let herself be dragged out from underneath the bench.

Squid was big, with muscular arms like her father, and a broad face. When she saw Petrel, she snorted with surprised laughter, "Ha! It's Miss Nothing." Then she walked around the smaller girl, inspecting her from every angle.

"Folk reckon you're simple," she said. "You don't look simple to me."

Quickly Petrel adopted the foolish expression that had kept her safe for so long. Squid laughed again. Then she said, "Your mam was an Engineer, wasn't she? You know anything about fixing grinders?"

Petrel didn't move, didn't even blink. But inside . . .

Hardly anyone except Dolph ever mentioned her mam. Or her da. Petrel knew little about them except that they had done something terrible; something that had rubbed off on Petrel so thoroughly that none of the tribes wanted her.

"No?" said Squid. "Ah well, it was worth a try. You look a lot like her. Not that I *knew* her exactly, what with her being Grease and me being Duff. But we exchanged a word or two on the afterdeck. Course, that was before—"

She broke off, embarrassed. "Aye. Well. Biscuits, is it? Take three. No, take four in case you get peckish. Glory be, it's getting late, Da'll have my guts for gravy if I don't get this grinder working by morning."

And she thrust four large biscuits into Petrel's hand and hurried away.

It was an even-more-thoughtful-than-before Petrel who crept past the border guards and back down the ladderway to Grease Alley. She had already eaten one of the biscuits, though it was so hard that her jaw ached from chewing, and so lacking in flavor that she thought it was probably true about the whale bones. But it was filling, and that was enough.

"Squid met my mam," she whispered to herself. "Spoke to her on the afterdeck. She met my mam!"

It was like pressing on a bruise to see if it hurt. Petrel pulled a face, wondering what the Head Cook's daughter wanted from her in exchange for the information and the biscuits. She must want *something*, but Petrel couldn't imagine what, so she tucked the whole thing away in a quiet corner of her mind, to think about later.

By the time she squatted beside the rats, Mister Smoke was almost dancing with impatience. "You gunna give us them answers?" was the first thing he said to her. "Or is it more excuses? You need a nap first, mebbe? Or a game of cards?"

"Steady, Smoke," said Missus Slink. "She's gotta eat, you can't deny that. They don't last long if they—"

"This is what the boy said," interrupted Petrel. "First he said he'd forgotten his name. So I gave him one. Fin, that's what he's called now."

"That's a start," said Mister Smoke, "though not much of one. What about the other questions? They're the big ones. Where did 'e come from? Who was with 'im?"

"Oh, he wouldn't tell me any of that," said Petrel, not wanting to admit that she had skipped the rest of Mister Smoke's questions and gone straight to her own. "I asked and asked, and he clamped his mouth shut and wouldn't say a word. He's afraid of Albie, that's the thing. Wants to get away from him; wants to get out of the brig before it's too late. If we get him out, he said, he'll answer a *hundred* questions, all true and proper."

"Get him *out*?" said Missus Slink in appalled tones. "I hope you told him you'd do no such thing."

"Weeeell—"

Missus Slink gave a little *humph* of displeasure.

"If Albie chucks him overboard," said Petrel, "you'll never get your answers."

"If Albie chucks him overboard we won't *need* answers," said Missus Slink.

"Unless," said Petrel, with great cunning, "*another* boy falls out of the sky. Better get the answers from this one, just in case."

A second *humph* from Missus Slink. But Mister Smoke cocked his head and said, "You got a point there, shipmate. She has, Slink, you gotta admit it."

The rats looked at each other. The fur on their backs was as ragged as their whiskers, and for the first time in her life, Petrel found herself wondering how old they were, and what would happen to her when they died. She would be completely alone . . .

"Oh, please," she said. "*Please!*"

"I spose we could keep a watch on the boy," said Mister Smoke.

"A constant watch," said Missus Slink. "Day and night. Never let him out of sight." She glowered at Petrel. "Never let him out of *ratty* sight."

"Thank you," whispered Petrel, and if she had thought for a minute they would let her, she would have lifted the rats up and kissed their noses.

Instead, all she did was bow her head and say, very formally, "Thank you, Missus Slink. Thank you, Mister Smoke. I'll get those answers for you, see if I don't."

CHAPTER 7

ESCAPE!

It took the remainder of the night to set up a distraction for the brig guard. First Petrel stole two pairs of outdoor trousers and a couple of jackets and gloves, picking them off bone pegs while their owners slept. Then she crept around all her hidey-holes collecting certain treasures that she had hidden in case she might need them one day.

She brought back a broken saucepan, a bit of rope, the remains of a chain, and a feather that looked very much like the ones on Orca's jacket. She tied the saucepan to an overhead pipe halfway between the brig and Albie's cabin, right in the heart of Grease Alley.

"This'll make 'em jump," she whispered to Mister Smoke, who was crouched on top of the pipe next to the rope.

"You sure you know what you're doin', shipmate?" asked the rat.

"Course I do. I told you, I'm gunna get Fin out. And maybe

pay Albie back for all the times he's shouted at me." Petrel grinned at the thought.

"That's a good thing, is it, shipmate? Payback? You don't think it'll make things worse?"

"Not for me, Mister Smoke. If it makes things worse for the rest of 'em, I don't care."

She tucked the chain and the feather into the saucepan. Then she stood back and eyed them. "You gunna help me, Mister Smoke?"

"What if it don't work?"

"Then I'm sunk, and so's Fin."

"You need a backup system. Gotta have backup. And if it's not there to start with, you gotta build it. Just in case."

"Too late for that now," said Petrel. "Are you gunna help me, or not?"

"Somethin' tells me I shouldn't, shipmate. But seein' as you is an honorary rat . . ."

A tiny knife appeared in Mister Smoke's paw, and he tested it against the rope, snipping through the first few fibers.

"Wait for the word," said Petrel, "or I'll have wasted all that creeping around. This ain't the sort of trick I can pull twice." And she hurried towards the brig, where Missus Slink was waiting for her.

Many of the lights in the *Oyster*'s passageways had broken years ago, but the ones that still worked were always on, powered by the spinning of the wind turbines above the bridge, which fed into a bank of batteries. So there was no question of Petrel trying to get close to the brig guard without being seen.

Instead, Missus Slink did a reconnoiter at deck level, and came back with the news that the guard was wide-awake, sitting upright in his chair with his fingers tapping out an uneasy rhythm on his knee.

"He's worried about Orca, I bet," whispered Petrel.

Missus Slink nodded. "Border guards are edgy too. Expecting an attack day or night."

"Good," said Petrel. "That's what we want."

There were hardly any hiding places in the passageway that led to the brig. But Petrel had learned to climb before she could walk, and she was as nimble as a cockroach. Using nothing but the bolts and hooks set into the bulkhead, she swarmed up to the overhead pipes and tucked both herself and the outdoor clothes on top of them.

"Pssst!" she hissed to Missus Slink, who was squinting at her from below. "Go!"

The rat hobbled away, her green ribbon wagging. Petrel clung to the pipes, wondering how long it would take Mister Smoke to slice through the rope, and if their trick would work, and what she would do if it didn't.

All that talk about backup. Maybe I should've thought of TWO plans, just in case!

The crash, when it came, was all she could have wished for. Chain and saucepan hit the deck with a clang that echoed through the passageways. To ears that were already on the alert, it must have sounded very much like an attack.

Somewhere not too far away, the fighting shift shouted as they leaped into action. Petrel held her breath. Then, to her delight, the brig guard dashed past beneath her, gripping his pipe wrench and swearing under his breath.

Petrel grabbed the jackets and trousers, swung down from the overhead pipes and ran towards the brig. There was the key, on the wall of the guard room. She snatched it off its hook and raced to the cell.

"Fin," she whispered, scratching at the bars. "Fin!"

She heard a gasp. "You!" And there was the boy, right in front of her, his face pale and set.

Petrel slid the key into the lock and turned it. The door swung open.

"Come on!" she hissed, beckoning to the boy.

His eyes narrowed, but he stayed where he was.

"Do you want to escape or not?" whispered Petrel. "'Cos this is your only chance!"

To her relief, that got him moving. He crept through the door and she thrust a jacket and trousers at him.

"What are these for?" he said.

Petrel didn't reply. She was already wriggling into the second jacket, and pulling the trousers up.

Fin copied her as quickly as he could, which was not quick at all. He had no idea how to fasten the jacket, and Petrel had to do it for him. She pulled the hood over his head so his face was hidden, then she stood back and inspected him.

"What are we—"

"Shhhhh!" said Petrel.

She had known from the beginning that she would not be able to take the boy back the way she had come. The distraction would not fool Albie for long, and the first thing he would do, when he recognized the trick for what it was, was head for the brig.

Which meant Petrel and the boy must go in the opposite direction, through one of the old cargo bays. It had probably held stores once, but now, like most spaces on the *Oyster,* it held shipfolk. They slept in family groups, with their neighbors above, below and on every side, and their fishing knives and outdoor clothes strung up beside them. There were no walls except those made of sealskin, and no floors except whalebone and netting, so that everybody knew everybody else's business, and what affected one person affected them all.

The idea that Petrel might be able to drag the stranger unnoticed through such a crowded space was so ridiculous that she wondered if she had gone winter-mad.

But there was no other way out, not if they didn't want to run straight into Albie and his fighters.

Petrel put her finger to her lips again, "Shhhh!" and crept towards the hatch that led to the cargo bay.

This was the moment when timing *really* counted. She thought she had got it right, but as the two of them waited beside the hatch she listened for the sound of Albie's running footsteps and chewed her knuckles until they hurt.

"What are we waiting—"

"*Shhhhhh!*"

And then it came, just as she had hoped—the blessed sound of the fishing siren. It whooped through the ship like a summons, three times. Petrel braced herself. But to her amazement, the siren whooped again. Just a single loud note, but everyone on board knew what it meant.

The toothies, thought Petrel. *The toothies have come!*

Her timing couldn't have been better. She grabbed Fin's hand and pulled him through the hatch. All around them, folk were rolling out of their hammocks. It wasn't just the fishing shift, not today. Even the bratlings of six or seven winters were pulling on their outdoor clothes and climbing the nets to the next deck. Within half a minute, Fin and Petrel were indistinguishable from the folk around them.

Except for Fin's climbing.

He couldn't have made himself more conspicuous if he had tried. With Petrel prodding and pushing him, he managed to reach the top of the net. But then the two of them had to hop across a dozen whale ribs, shimmy up one rope and down another, and crawl under a hammock full of babies.

It wasn't that Fin was particularly clumsy. He just wasn't used to a pathway that consisted of nets and ropes and whalebones. Folk were beginning to stare.

There was nowhere to hide and no time to get to the other side of the cargo bay. So Petrel did the only thing possible. She slid the nearest fishing knife from its sheath and, concealing her actions with her body, sliced through the rope that held the babies' hammock.

There was a net directly below, and the babies tumbled into it, unhurt. But the shock set them to screaming at the tops of their voices, and in the chaos that followed, Petrel dragged Fin up another level.

Below them the babies wailed inconsolably, and nets and whalebones shook as their parents rushed to comfort them. Petrel kept her head down, and motioned for Fin to do the same. And it was as well she did, because before she could even begin to think of what to do next, a man shouted, "This rope's been *cut!*"

Between one breath and the next, the atmosphere in the cargo bay changed. "My jacket's missing," cried a boy. "And my trousers."

"And mine!"

Petrel groaned. She should have stolen the clothes from a different part of Grease Alley. Why hadn't she thought of that?

But it was too late now. Men and women were unsheathing their fishing knives and peering at their neighbors, trying to see beneath the concealing hoods. Bratlings bounced across the nets from one jacketed figure to another, shouting, "Who's that? Grease or intruder? Show your face!"

Fin grabbed Petrel's hand. "How do we get out of this?" he hissed.

Petrel looked around frantically. If she was caught, and Albie discovered that she had freed the boy, she would be dead within the hour.

That thought was enough to break the self-imposed lock on her throat. She took a deep breath, and pointing in the direction of the brig, she shouted, "Braid! Look! It's stinking *Braid!*"

It worked. Half the folk in the cargo bay surged towards the brig, shouting with fury and almost trampling each other in their desire to get at the invaders. The other half swore and made threatening gestures, but then they sheathed their knives, finished lacing their jackets and began to climb towards the Commons ladderway. The toothies had come, and everyone was hungry.

Petrel and Fin climbed too. With their faces turned from their companions, they scrambled up the nets, then onto the Commons and up again, saying nothing to each other. Ugly words spun around them, as folk vowed revenge on the intruders. There was even talk of a reprisal attack on the foredeck, despite it being neutral territory, but that was quickly squashed.

Petrel stayed as close to Fin as she could, kicking him whenever he hesitated. But the Commons ladderway was easier than the nets, and besides there was such a press of folk on every side that the boy's lack of shipboard experience hardly showed.

That is, until they stepped through the hatch and out onto the foredeck.

Everyone stopped then and checked their jackets, putting on gloves and pulling ice masks over their faces. Fin and Petrel copied them. But when someone handed Fin a fishing line, the boy stared at it as if he had never seen such a thing in his life.

Most folk got on with their own business, baiting their hooks and throwing their lines into the water. But one or two of them looked back as if they were wondering what was wrong . . .

Petrel pinched Fin's arm, hard. "Fish," she hissed. "Fish or die."

CHAPTER 8

THE FISHING SHIFT

THE FISHING LINE WAS WOUND AROUND A SLAB OF BONE, WITH a vicious hook and a lump of metal at the end. The boy had no idea what to do with it. What's more, he did not want to waste his time fishing; now that he was out of the brig, he wanted to be in the belly of the ship, hunting the demon.

Still, he knew Petrel was right. If he was to avoid recapture, he must play out this charade for a while at least.

Soon, he promised himself. And he stumbled to the rail.

There were birds everywhere, huge black-and-white creatures that swooped and dived at the deck. The sky, so big that it made the boy dizzy, loomed above him. All about the ship were icebergs, as unforgiving as death itself.

Petrel threaded a lump of gristle onto the boy's hook and pushed him closer to the rail.

"Quick!" she whispered. She threw the end of her own line outwards. The boy braced himself and did the same.

Far below him, the sea rolled past, as gray as a corpse. The deck heaved. Up and down. Up and down. The boy hoped that nothing would take his hook, but it was no more than a few seconds before he felt a jerk on the line, and something tried to drag it out of his hands.

The fish was heavier than he had expected and it took a good deal of his strength to pull it all the way up the side of the ship to the rail. There it stuck and would have stayed, but for a man who cried, "Hold it!" before grabbing the fish with a hooked stick and hauling it on board.

It fell flapping to the deck, blunt nosed and ugly, and the boy had to force himself to stand still while a woman sliced its head off with a sharp blow and tossed it into an icy bin. Blood and snow and fish heads spattered the deck around the boy's feet. A bird swooped past him, its wings almost brushing his hair.

Petrel held out another lump of gristle.

With clenched teeth, the boy threaded the bait onto his hook. Then, determined not to arouse suspicion, determined not to be recaptured before he had destroyed the demon, he tossed his line over the side again.

The next hour quickly descended into a nightmare of ice, hooks, aching muscles and sore hands. But only for the boy. The savages who lined the ship's rails on either side of him, shoulder to shoulder in some places, didn't seem to notice the discomfort. They laughed as they threw their hooks into the water, and whooped through their ice masks as they hauled up their catch. The smaller children chased each other around the deck with fish heads, screaming, "Toothy! Toothy!" Fish rose up the side of the ship in the hundreds, struggling and flapping. It was like a festival—

Except for the tensions. The boy saw the almost-brawls out of the corner of his eye, and heard the threats and accusations that punched through the laughter.

"Look at 'em," Petrel whispered, as she rebaited her hook. "Grease thinks Braid stole you, with a bit of help from Duff-town. Braid's denying it for all they're worth, and so's Duff. *They* reckon Albie must've got careless, and they're blaming him for everything. If we weren't on the open deck, there'd be blood spilt by now."

She hissed with enjoyment. "Look at old Crab! I reckon he's just heard the news. Doesn't he look as if he's about to burst his boiler?"

The boy nodded, though he had no idea who Crab was, or what a boiler looked like when it was about to burst. He did not care either. The only thing that mattered was to get back inside the ship. To find the demon. To destroy it.

"When can we stop?" he whispered.

"Not for ages yet." And Petrel tossed her line back into the water.

From that moment on, only fierce determination kept the boy going. He worked in a trance, pulling the fish up, throwing his line down. Pulling the fish up, throwing his line down. Pulling the fish—

It was midmorning when the weather changed. It seemed to happen between one heartbeat and the next; the horizon disappeared and the wind rose. Birds tore across the sky. The ship began to plunge up and down like a child's toy.

The boy grabbed hold of the rail, then let go when he realized that everyone else had merely braced themselves and kept working. A fish flapped against his foot. His stomach lurched. Something at the back of his throat tasted foul.

He swallowed and looked down at the deck, but that made it worse. There were fish heads everywhere, sliding back and forth with the motion of the ship, their eyes staring at him. There was blood too, more than he had realized. It washed around his feet, red and viscous, and he could not escape it.

His stomach heaved, and he grabbed for the rail again. A bird flashed past, like a premonition of disaster. A sheet of spray sliced up towards him.

"What's the matter?" hissed Petrel.

"Going—to be—sick!"

"No! Not in a little sea like this! You'll give us away! Both of us!"

The boy could see the panic in Petrel's eyes, and knew that it was reflected in his own. He must *not* be sick! He must not give himself away!

But all the willpower and training in the world could not stop what was coming. He felt as if he were about to vomit up every meal he had ever eaten.

There was a flash of movement, and something thumped against his arm.

At first, the boy did not realize what had happened. All he knew was that Petrel was dragging him away from the rail.

"What's the problem, shipmate?" asked one of the fish hookers.

Without a word, Petrel pushed the boy's sleeve up. The man nodded and said, "Take him to sick bay."

The boy stared at his arm. It was starting to hurt now, and he could see blood. *His* blood. It was such a shock that he stopped feeling sick. "You *cut* me," he said to Petrel, as she dragged him towards the hatch.

"Shhhh!" Petrel pulled the hatch open and bundled him inside.

"But—"

"Be quiet," she snapped, "or I'll cut you again!"

The boy was exhausted and badly shaken, and oh, how he longed to snap back at her! But he pressed his fingers to the wound and said nothing.

I should be GLAD she cut me, he told himself. *I am inside again. I can search for the demon!*

And so, as he and Petrel climbed down through the ship, he tried to work out where he was, tried to remember the ancient tattered diagram that he had learned by heart. It was not easy. The stairs were so steep that he felt as if he risked his life with every rung. There were people everywhere, and hardly a moment passed when Petrel was not dragging him one way or another to avoid them, or whispering, "Can't you go faster than that?" or shoving him across a whalebone floor and into a labyrinth of pipes.

The boy felt as if the ship were playing with him, as if the *girl* were playing with him. By the time he stumbled off the final ladder, he had lost all sense of direction, and knew only that he was far below the waterline and that the walls around him were thick with rust and grease. The engines rumbled on such a deep note that he could feel it in his bones.

Petrel pushed him through one last hatch into a dimly lit room. She tore off her outdoor clothes, then she turned on the boy without warning.

"You nearly got us killed!" she hissed. "Staggering around the foredeck like a sick penguin." She shook her head in disgust. "Don't know why I bothered getting you out of the brig in the first place."

The morning, with all its torments, spun around the boy, and for a moment he felt his own temper rising . . .

No, stop it! Torments do not matter. The girl does not matter. Nothing matters except the demon!

With an enormous effort, he managed to smile apologetically. "I am sorry—" he began.

But even as he spoke, the pipes around him started to clang, so loud and insistent that the boy was deafened. He jammed his hands over his ears, but still he felt as if he were in the middle of a storm, and the ship tumbling down around him.

"What is happening?" he cried.

"It's a message," shouted Petrel over the noise. "For the whole ship."

"What does it say?"

"Murder . . . disaster . . . mutiny . . ." The dreadful sound stopped, and Petrel stared at the boy, her mouth agape.

"What is it?" he said.

Petrel swallowed. "First Officer Orca's been murdered! Someone just found her in her cabin with her throat cut. And whoever's sending the message swears—they *swear* that it was you who did it!"

CHAPTER 9

MURDER!

DOLPH, ONLY CHILD OF FIRST OFFICER ORCA, STOOD AT THE door of her mam's cabin and could not speak.

This isn't happening, she thought. *It's not possible. Other folk die, but not Orca. Not Mam.*

At her shoulder, Second Officer Crab murmured, "A dreadful shock! Dreadful! For all of us."

Dolph didn't want to talk to Crab, didn't even want to look at him. She kept thinking that her mam would stride into the cabin and take command of the situation. Fix things. Make them better.

Except nothing could make *this* better.

A shiver ran through Dolph. Her heart was boiling over with fury, grief and love, and she didn't know which one to grab hold of. Which one to give voice to.

Crab cleared his throat. "Her last thought was for the ship, did you see?"

He pointed, and Dolph's unwilling gaze followed his

gesture to where Orca's hand rested on the deck. Her fingers were coated with her own blood, and bloody marks on the floor showed where she had scrawled something before dying.

"Obviously she didn't want the *Oyster* torn apart by suspicion," murmured Crab. "She didn't want us looking in the wrong direction for her killer."

Dolph tried to focus. She shook her head and wiped her eyes. She made herself look at the last message from her mam, a single word written in blood.

STRANGER

Second Officer Crab was nodding to himself. "She was a great First Officer," he said softly. "Quite possibly the greatest the *Oyster* has ever known. As such, we will honor her in death as we honored her in life. We will hold her funeral first thing tomorrow morning. And then—" His voice rose. "And then we will find the stranger and throw him overboard!"

"Yes," said Dolph, finding her voice at last.

And with that, all her grief and uncertainty seemed to vanish, and the only emotion left inside her was hatred.

It took Petrel a moment to catch her breath. But when she did, she was furious. "How could you be so *stupid*?" she demanded. "Did you think they wouldn't come after you? Did you think you could walk right into the middle of Braid and murder the First Officer, and no one would—"

"Stop!" cried Fin. "I do not know what you are talking about!"

"You do!"

"No! I did not murder anyone! When could I have done it? I was locked up until you freed me!"

Petrel didn't believe a word he said. As she glowered at him, the pipe messages started up again, carrying shock and anger from every part of the ship. Not a single person in Grease Alley or Dufftown had liked Orca when she was alive, but that no longer mattered. With one fell act all the blame and hostility of the foredeck had vanished. This wasn't a case of tribe against tribe. This was the crew against murderous strangers. The ship against the rest of the world.

"Well, everyone thinks it was you," snapped Petrel, listening to the messages. "And they don't like it one bit! It'd be bad enough if *Albie* had crept in and done the deed. That'd set Braid against Grease worse than ever, but at least it'd be something folk could understand." She glared at the boy. "Not like this. You're a stranger, and you've no business murdering anyone!"

"I did not do it!" said the boy.

"Why are they saying you did, then? They must have good reason."

"I do not know their reason! But I could *not* have done it. I was in the brig."

"You must've sneaked out somehow, then sneaked back again."

"But I did not! I promise you! I— When did this murder happen?"

Petrel listened again. "No more than a half turn of an hourglass ago."

"There, you see? I was with you on the open deck, fishing."

"So you were . . ." As her anger died, Petrel began to think more clearly. She pulled a face. "Hmph. Don't spose you could've done it, not really. You'd never have got all the way up to Orca's cabin without being caught, not by yourself."

She tapped the boy's arm. "But Crab's not gunna worry about that. *He'll* be First Officer now, and he'll be after your neck. So will everyone else."

"Then you must tell them!"

"Ha, they wouldn't listen to *me*! Specially not when there's blood to pay back. Any minute now they'll declare Truce, so they can hunt for you. Which means—"

She glanced around the abandoned workshop with its single entrance. "Which means we can't stay here." She grabbed her outdoor clothes. "If they trap us, you're a goner and so am I. Come on."

They hurried back down the walkway side by side. "Nowhere's gunna be *really* safe," whispered Petrel, "not with the whole crew in a fury. I reckon we'll have to move from hidey-hole to hidey-hole, and try to keep one step ahead of 'em."

Fin nodded, his face pale. "Do you know where to find these—these hidey-holes?"

"Course! There's no one else knows the ship like I do."

It was not an idle boast. Petrel had learned many things in her short life. She knew how to survive loneliness, and how to make more-or-less warm clothes out of rags and feathers. She knew instinctively when night was about to end, and when the sun would rise above the horizon. She knew the *Oyster* from stem to stern, and could tell exactly where she was on the ship, even in pitchy darkness.

It was this last knowledge that helped her now.

The passage she led Fin to—listening every step of the way—had lost all its lights generations ago, and was as black as midwinter.

Petrel grabbed the boy's hand and pulled him along, whispering, "Watch your head. There's a couple of pipes sticking out. Here's the first . . . and the next. Now keep right to the side 'cos there's a hole in the deck . . . there, we're past it."

Near the end of the passage was an old rope locker. It was long and narrow, and half filled with bits of broken machinery, and there was another locker above it, and two more on the other side of the bulkhead.

What no one except Petrel had realized was that rust and time had turned four separate lockers into one, and that if an outcast girl and a hunted boy squirmed past the broken machinery, they would find themselves in a room of sorts, with several exits. There was even a little light, seeping through cracks from the deck above them. It was cramped and uncomfortable, but right now safety mattered a lot more than comfort.

Petrel rolled her outdoor clothes into a bundle and tucked them in a corner. Then she squatted on the rusty floor, with nuts and bolts scattered around her, and said, "Show me your arm."

The boy peeled back his sleeve, and Petrel winced. The cut was deeper than she'd thought. She handed Fin a not-very-clean rag to wrap around it, and said, "I'd better go and find a needle to sew you up. And something to wash your arm with."

She rummaged in the corner and brought out a battered cup with a lid. Then she crawled to the sill, whispering over her shoulder, "Don't you wander off while I'm gone! Your life won't be worth living if they catch you."

"I will not wander," said Fin. And he lay down on the floor of the locker and closed his eyes.

Where am I gunna get a needle and thread? wondered Petrel, as she crept back along the passages. *It's no use asking Missus Slink. She doesn't approve of Fin.*

Neither, clearly, did anyone else on the ship. The toothies had come, and folk *should* have been happy. But instead, they ground their teeth, swearing that they would soon find the stranger, and when they did they would kill him.

Petrel skittered through the upper reaches of Grease Alley with her heart in her mouth. But today, not even Skua bothered with her. Everyone had more important things to think about than the Nothing girl.

At least they haven't started a proper search yet, she thought, as she climbed the Commons to Dufftown. *Which is just as well, seeing as Fin's down there on his own and won't know where to run if they come for him.*

The Dufftown border guards were as absorbed as their Grease Alley counterparts, and Petrel scuttled past them unnoticed. As she approached the galley, the smell of fried fish hit her, rich and compelling.

She peered around the hatch. The galley was always the hottest part of the ship, apart from the engine rooms. But now it burned with anger as well as fish oil. Dozens of Cooks hurried back and forth with trolleys and baskets, talking furiously to each other. Dozens more gutted, filleted and fried, their faces grim, their knives flashing.

Head Cook Krill stood, sharp-eyed, on a little platform in the middle of it all. "Burner four for Braid!" he shouted. "Come on, snap to it! Murder or not, folk must be fed!"

Several Cooks rushed to burner four, flipped the cooked fish into baskets, piled the baskets onto a trolley and rolled them to the mechanical hoists, muttering all the way.

"Did Grease's fish come down?" shouted Krill. "Or did Albie decide he prefers 'em raw?"

"I don't think Albie's too bothered about fish right now," replied a woman.

"Course he is," cried the Head Cook. "He can't hunt for the murderer on an empty stomach! Are they down?"

The woman nodded.

"Good," said Krill. He spun around. "Burner two, you're done."

Petrel licked her lips and wished for the thousandth time that she belonged to one of the tribes. Not because she needed them or liked them; she didn't need anyone, and she certainly didn't *like* anyone except Mister Smoke and Missus Slink. But the fact was, while the cooked toothies would go up the hoist to Braid and down to Grease Alley, there would be none for Petrel, not unless she begged for them. Or stole them.

Squid was attending to one of the burners, sleeves rolled up and hair dragged back from her face. She was one of the few people who didn't look angry. As Petrel watched, she flipped a dozen fillets over and wiped her arm across her forehead. Then she raised her hand. "Burner three for Braid," she shouted.

"Burner five, you're ready," cried Krill, spinning around on his toes. "Six, get a move on with those baskets!" His voice rose to a bellow. "And belay that muttering! Right now our job is to feed the ship. When we've done that, you can mutter all you like!"

A dozen barrels rolled past Petrel, filled to the brim with raw fish. Petrel crept after them, her pulse pounding; she crept right into the heart of Dufftown, hoping the noise and the bustle and the fuss over Orca's murder would keep folk from noticing her.

Squid was already cooking the next lot of fillets. When she saw Petrel, tucked in small and silent behind her, she smiled and said, "Hello, Miss Nothing. We don't usually see you here in the middle of the day. I spose you're hungry?"

Petrel didn't move. But her mouth watered.

"Hang on a bit then," said Squid, and she turned back to the burner and flipped the toothies over.

Krill's bellow had stopped the muttering for now, but the anger still sizzled from one side of the galley to the other. Petrel licked her lips, wondering how quickly she could get out of here. Wondering what Squid would want in exchange for a piece of fish. Some mockery, maybe, to take folk's minds off the murder? Whatever it was, Petrel wasn't about to turn down a feed.

Behind her a hard voice said, "What's that bratling doing here? She's not Duff. You, Nothing Girl. Get out."

Petrel sighed. She should have known it was too good to be true. But before she could scurry away, Squid grabbed her arm and frowned at the man who had spoken. "Leave her alone. She's doing no harm."

"She doesn't belong here," said the man, his arms full of baskets. "Who knows what she's up to? And besides, she's in my way."

"Then walk around her," snapped Squid, "and don't make such a fuss—"

"Burner three," bellowed Krill.

"Oops!" said Squid, turning back to the fish. She raised her hand. "This lot for Grease Alley!"

But when the trolley came, she kept back two large fillets, saying, "These are burned. Better not send *them* to Albie, not with a Truce in the offing."

The basket carriers hurried off to the hoists. Squid grabbed a bit of seaweed paper, wrapped it around the two remaining fillets (which were not burned at all), and gave them to Petrel. "Here," she whispered.

Petrel was stunned. Two whole fillets! Two *enormous* fillets! It was almost enough to make her forget why she had come.

But not quite. She tapped Squid's arm, and made sewing motions.

"A needle?" said Squid, raising her eyebrows. "Is that what you want? What for?"

Petrel didn't answer.

"You got secrets, Miss Nothing? Course you have. Spose

you want thread too?" Squid dug in her pocket and handed over a sliver of bone with a hole drilled in one end, and a length of thread spun from seaweed. Then she gave Petrel a gentle shove and whispered, "Now get out of here. And be careful. Folk are angry and frightened, which makes 'em behave worse than usual."

Petrel was too hungry to go far. She slipped out of the galley and squatted in a quiet corner. Then she tore a piece off one of the toothy fillets and shoved it in her mouth so fast that the sweet juice ran down her chin. She groaned with pleasure and licked her fingers, and tore off another piece.

The fillets were huge, and she was full even before she had finished the first one. She sat there for a moment, thinking about Squid, who had handed over the toothies and the needle far too easily. She hadn't tried to squeeze information out of Petrel. She hadn't offered her the fish, then snatched them away at the last minute, which was one of Skua's favorite tricks. She hadn't done anything.

And that was a puzzle.

Maybe she's just worried about the murder, thought Petrel. *Or maybe she's trying to soften me up for something. Ha! I'll take all the toothies she wants to give me, but I won't trust her, not me.*

With that settled, she considered the remains of the fish. She should hide what was left for tomorrow. Somewhere on the afterdeck, in the cold, so it wouldn't spoil. Behind the aft crane, maybe.

Then she remembered Fin.

Petrel wasn't used to thinking of other folk, and at first she hugged the second fillet to her chest and told herself that the boy could find his own food.

Except, of course, he couldn't. Everyone was hunting for him, and besides he was as useless as a baby. "Stupid sky folk," she muttered, enjoying a rare sense of superiority.

She scrambled to her feet. Maybe she'd hide *half* the fish, and give Fin the other half.

With the fishing shift over for the day, the afterdeck was almost deserted. Petrel hid half a fillet behind the crane, then ran back down through the ship, down and down and down. By the time she reached Grease Alley, her heart was thumping wildly. She'd been gone longer than she had intended. Truce had not yet been officially declared, but the search was already underway.

It gave Petrel the shivers to see folk poking into every corner and ransacking lockers and sea chests. She ran faster, sliding around corners in her ragged shoes, ducking past angry Engineers with her face as blank as she could make it.

But still she was too late. When she came to the lockers at last, and crawled inside, they were empty. The only sign of Fin was the rag she had given him, lying limp and useless on the floor.

CHAPTER 10

THAT IS NOT MY NAME

The boy waited until he was sure Petrel had gone. Then he crept out of the locker.

He knew the risk he was taking. But he would not let danger deter him, or exhaustion, or the knowledge that nearly everyone on the *Oyster* thought he was a murderer and was hunting for him. According to Brother Thrawn's ancient diagram, the demon was hidden in the very bottom of the ship, which meant that the boy was in the right place and must not waste the opportunity.

He crept through the narrow noisy spaces, trying to make sense of what he saw. Trying to connect it to the markings on Brother Thrawn's diagram.

Everything was strange and dilapidated. The walls were clammy, the air was foul, and there were machines of one sort or another everywhere the boy looked.

Some of them clanked and growled. Others were silent, and he suspected that they were dead, but still they made him uneasy. What if they weren't dead? What if they were about to spring to life and steal his soul? He had heard of such things—the Initiates whispered about them late at night, whispered about the treacherous nature of machines, and how they could catch the unwary and change them forever.

"I will not be caught," whispered the boy fiercely. "I will not be changed!"

And he crept onward.

He was not sure when the black rats began following him. At first he thought his senses were playing tricks on him, causing the shadows to scuttle and squeak like vermin. He reminded himself of Brother Thrawn's words—*Imagination is for weaklings and fools*—and kept going.

But then the imp appeared.

The boy caught only a single glimpse of its gray body, with a flash of green around its neck, but that was enough. His skin crawled, and his every instinct warned him that, although the creature looked like a large rat, it was something far more sinister.

Brother Thrawn's voice echoed in his ear. *According to the diary we found, the demon is asleep. But its imps are awake, and they are as vile as their master.*

This imp seemed to have some control over the rats. The *real* rats. The black rats. In its presence, they grew bolder, and before long they left the shadows and began to dash at the boy with high-pitched cries.

The boy loathed rats. There were none in the main part of the Citadel, but the punishment hole, which was underground and lightless, swarmed with them. They made him feel sick. They made him wish he had stayed in the lockers where Petrel had left him . . .

"No!" he whispered, despising himself for his weakness. "I wish no such thing!" And he gritted his teeth and shuffled forward.

The wall was damp and horrible under his fingers, but he thought he knew where he was now. He could picture Brother Thrawn's diagram, which showed a hatch somewhere near here, in the floor.

And there it was! The boy felt a fleeting sense of achievement. But as soon as he bent over and tried to lift the hatch cover, the black rats surged around him, leaping and bumping against his bare hands until he jerked away with a cry of disgust.

He made himself try again almost immediately. "I am no longer three years old," he whispered, "and this is *not* the punishment hole. I will not be stopped by a few rats!"

And with that, he grabbed the hatch cover and threw it to one side. Then he dropped through the hole, with the black rats pouring after him.

The space below the hatch was not made for standing upright. The boy had to bend his knees and duck his head, and even then it was a tight fit. He forced himself to stumble forward, with the rats pressing against him from every side.

It was like trying to wade through mud—through *living* mud—and it made the boy whimper in protest. But he kept going, feeling his way along the wall, judging his path by how furiously the rats tried to stop him.

The farther he went, the bolder they became. *The imp is driving them,* thought the boy. *I must be getting closer to the demon!*

That thought gave him courage and he pressed on. The rats nipped at his ankles and scrambled up his legs to his knees. When that did not stop him, they changed tactics, climbing the wall and flinging themselves at him. One of them managed to cling to his shoulder, and he felt its filthy teeth brush his ear . . .

With a sob of disgust, he grabbed it with both hands and threw it as far as he could. Then he plunged furiously through its mates, lashing out with his feet and hissing, "Go away! Get *off me!*"

It made no difference. The rats grew more frenzied than ever, until he was sure that they would pull him to the floor and kill him.

He groped frantically for the wall, for something to hold him upright, and found another hatch. He scrabbled at it with one hand, flailing at the rats with the other. But the hatch did not have a handle. There was no way of opening it.

Not from this side, anyway.

This is it! he thought. *The demon lies behind this door!*

He felt a great flurry of triumph—followed immediately by a disappointment so immense that he wanted to howl. What was the use of finding the right door if he could not open it?

The rats were falling back now—perhaps the imp had realized he was helpless. The boy's arm throbbed and he wanted to kick something.

He stood very still and listened.

The darkness seemed to magnify the relentless clatter of the engines, and the scrape of ice on the hull. But beneath those noises, the boy thought he could hear the imp's claws on the deck. They made a different sound from the *real* rats. Sharper. Cleverer. More metallic.

The boy clenched his teeth. He could not yet reach the demon, but he *could* destroy one of its minions . . .

Without warning, he threw himself at the imp. He was so sure of the direction, and so full of fury and frustration, that he held nothing back. He grabbed at the creature, caught it in his fingers—and fell onto his sore arm.

He *did* howl then. His fingers spammed. The imp was gone. And the boy was left alone in the darkness.

As he lay there, panting, the steady reverberation of the engines seemed to change, and take on a mocking tone. At first the boy did his best to ignore it. He was starting to feel sick again. Not nauseous this time, but thick-headed and dopey, as if his skull were filled with sawdust. His arm hurt, and so did his throat and chest.

The sound of the engines changed again—and now it seemed to form a word. *Finnnn*, rumbled the engines. *Finnn, Finnn, Finnn.*

"That is not my name," whispered the boy. "I do not *have* a name!"

Still the engines rumbled, *Finnn Finnn Finnn*. And the ice, scraping against the hull, joined in. *Fffin, Fffin, Ffffin.*

The boy gritted his teeth. This was a test, he told himself, and nothing more. In fact, the whole ship was a test. Everything about it unsettled him—including Petrel. When he had been given this mission he pictured himself being calm and clever, no matter what happened. But instead he felt as if he was losing control . . .

He took a deep breath and bent his mind to the Spire Contemplation. Then he stood up and fumbled along the wall, searching for the all-important hatch. He would try again. He would *not* be beaten!

But the imp had turned him around somehow, and the hatch was nowhere to be found. What's more, his head felt thicker than ever, so that he could hardly think straight.

With a groan he bent down and groped along the floor, hoping to find a weapon of some sort, in case the imp came back. The darkness was so profound in this part of the ship that he could barely find his own fingertips, but he eventually tripped over an iron device. It was narrow, and curved at the end like a crescent moon, and he knew that it was something to do with machines. He did not want to use a machine-thing, in case it corrupted him. But he *did* need a weapon . . .

As he hesitated, weighing the device in his hand, he thought he heard footsteps. He stiffened. Had someone discovered his presence? Were they after him? Who could it be? Albie? Skua? The *demon*?

It was a terrifying thought. The demon was supposed to be asleep, but perhaps all his bumbling around had woken it. Perhaps it was coming for him, right now!

The boy clutched the iron device, wishing that his throat and chest did not hurt so much. Wishing that his head was clearer. According to legend, the demon could kill with a glance. It could destroy whole cities. It could boil the blood in a man's veins . . .

And then the footsteps were upon him, and it was not Albie or Skua or the demon after all. It was Petrel.

She put her face right up to his in the darkness, so that the boy could feel her hot breath. "I've been looking everywhere for you!" she said. "I thought Albie'd got you, and no wonder. I told you to stay put, Fin!"

"That is not my name," said the boy automatically.

"I don't care. What d'you think you're doing down *here*?"

The boy grasped at the first excuse he could think of. "I— I thought I heard someone searching for me, so I had to move. I got lost." He shivered. "And there were rats, dozens of them. They attacked me."

"You're lucky it was just rats," said Petrel. "The whole ship's in a fizz, and getting worse by the minute. Albie's seething, Cooks are sharpening their knives, Officers are just about frothing at the mouth. I nearly bumped into Crab on the afterdeck. Never seen him acting so daft, washing his hands in the snow over and over again. And it's all 'cos of you murdering Orca!"

"But I did *not* murder her!" cried the boy, trying to ignore the fuzziness in his head.

"Doesn't matter," said Petrel. "Everyone *thinks* you did, and that's what counts."

Above all things, the boy hated feeling helpless. But that was how he felt now. Helpless and alone. *These savages are mad,* he thought.

He tried to recall Brother Thrawn's voice, but it was drowned out by the subterranean sounds of the ship, the distant scurry of rats and the beating of his own pulse.

It does not matter if they kill me, he told himself. *As long as I can first destroy the demon, I will die knowing that I have helped cleanse the world of evil.*

The thought was not nearly as comforting as it should have been.

"I brought you something to eat," said Petrel, when they were back in the lockers.

Fin stared at her and said nothing. And when she unwrapped the package of fish, he merely picked at the sweet toothy flesh with his left hand. In his other hand, he clutched something and would not put it down.

"What's that you've got?" asked Petrel. "An old spanner? Where'd you find that?"

The boy didn't answer. His face was paler than ever.

"I thought you'd be hungry, Fin."

"That is not my name," said the boy.

"I *said,* I thought you'd be hungry."

"No, I—" Fin stared at his greasy fingers. "I need a cloth."

"What for?"

The boy set his teeth and said very slowly, "To—wipe—my—hands."

He was almost as annoying, thought Petrel, as Mister Smoke. What's more, his eyes had gone all blank, as if he were peering down at her from a great height, which made her feel small and ugly.

"Wipe 'em on your clothes," she said.

"I am not a savage!"

"No," snapped Petrel, "you're just plain foolish. What do you think keeps the cold out? Grease, that's what. Helps keep things waterproof too. So you be glad of those mucky fingers of yours, and wipe 'em all over your clothes, like everyone else does."

Fin looked for a moment as if he might snarl back at her, but then he clamped his lips together and did as she suggested.

"Now," said Petrel, "wriggle over here where there's a bit more light and show me your arm."

"Why?"

"I'm going to sew it up, that's why."

She took out Squid's needle, and Fin's eyes widened. "It does not need sewing."

"Course it does. I should know. I'm the one who cut you." Petrel grinned. "You scared?"

"No!"

"You are. You're afraid of a little needle." She jabbed it at him, and he flinched. "No use being scared," she said. "There's lots of things worse than needles. Knives and fish hooks and pipe wrenches, and that's just the start of it." She shook her head in mock sorrow. "Maybe I should tell Albie where you're hiding. *He'll* put you out of your misery quick enough—"

That shook him. The blank wall of his face cracked open for a second, and Petrel could see the real boy behind it. The boy who *was* afraid, but would never admit it, not even to himself.

She almost laughed. But she was not a cruel girl, and fear was fear, after all. So instead of laughing she said, "I wouldn't, not really. Don't be scared."

By then, of course, the crack in the wall had closed, and the boy was as blank as ever. "Scared?" he said distantly. "I do not know what you are talking about." And he rolled up his sleeve and thrust his arm under Petrel's nose.

When she saw the wound again, Petrel's anger died instantly. "Ooh, I bet that hurts."

Fin said nothing, but there was a thin line of sweat on his forehead. Petrel took the lidded cup from her pocket and poured icy water over his arm. "Grog'd be better," she said, "but I ain't got any, so I fetched this from the afterdeck. You can drink the rest, if you want." The boy took the cup and finished off the water.

"Now hold still," said Petrel, "or I'll sew up the wrong bit of you."

It was strange and horrible, poking the bone needle through the boy's skin. Petrel winced with every stitch, and so did Fin, his eyes squeezed shut and his other hand gripping the old spanner so hard that his knuckles were white. But he didn't yelp, which made Petrel think better of him, and neither did he complain about the ragged stitches, which were nowhere near as small and neat as Missus Slink would have made them.

Instead, when she had finished, he dragged his eyes away from the wound and said, "The rats— They will not come in here, will they?" He glanced at Petrel and added quickly, "I am not afraid of them."

Petrel wanted to laugh again, but she didn't. "No, they won't come in. Not while we're here."

"What about the crew? The Engineers?"

Petrel yawned. She'd been up all night and all day too, and she was suddenly exhausted. "The Truce ain't official yet, so Albie'll still have his fighters on guard, just in case. Plus he has to keep the engines and the digester running, which takes a good few folk. *And* there's more hidey-holes in Grease Alley than in Dufftown and Braid put together. I reckon we're safe down here till after Orca's funeral."

"When is that?"

"Tomorrow morning. We'll move then." And Petrel yawned again, made herself as comfortable as she could on the lumpy floor, and closed her eyes.

The sounds of the ship soothed her, as always. The slow rumble of the engines. The gurgle of the ballast pipes. The creaking and groaning of the iron hull as it plowed the ocean.

Don't spose Fin can help being annoying, thought Petrel. *He's a bit like that orphaned penguin chick Krill caught last summer. All it did for the first week was snap at folk and squawk its head off. But Krill didn't give up on it, and after a while it followed him around as if he was its mam.*

She opened her eyes and said kindly, "Don't worry, Fin, I'll look after you."

"That is not my na—"

"It was me who saved you, right back at the beginning. That

means I've got a responsibility for you. You were gunna die on that berg. If it weren't for me, you'd be lost."

"Albie rescued me," said Fin, "not you."

"But I'm the one who told Albie you were there."

The boy didn't believe her; Petrel could see it in his face. "You should be grateful to me," she said, annoyed with him all over again. "And grateful for the name too, seeing as how you forgot yours!"

But that, it seemed, was the wrong thing to say. Fin's expression darkened, and he turned away from her and refused to utter another word.

CHAPTER II

FEVER

THE BOY DID NOT THINK HE WOULD SLEEP. Not with bits of rusty iron jabbing at his back, and the whole ship hunting him. But he closed his eyes anyway, and when he opened them again an unknown amount of time had passed, and he ached all over, as if he had been beaten. His head was so heavy and thick and sore he could hardly lift it.

He wondered if the imp had cursed him. Or perhaps Petrel had poisoned him. Such a possibility should have filled him with alarm, but for some reason he could not muster the energy to worry about it.

Petrel was still asleep, curled up against the wall with her mouth open. *She is a fool*, thought the boy.

But then, unwillingly, he found himself thinking about her dark hair bent over his arm, and the care she had taken with his stitches. Someone else had taken care of him like that once. Someone whose face he could not quite remember . . .

He shoved the thought back into the locked recesses of his

mind, where it belonged, and told himself that of course Petrel had taken care. After all, she was the one who had cut him in the first place.

On the pile of broken machinery, something moved. The boy stiffened. It was the imp, the one with the green ribbon! The one he had tried to kill!

A dreadful coldness crept over him. He tried to think, which was not easy with his head so sore and jumbled. He gripped the spanner.

But the imp was still making its way across the machinery when the dreadful coldness turned to a dreadful heat. The boy blinked, and blinked again. *That is odd,* he thought. *The creature is dancing.*

It ought not have been funny, because the Circle of Devouts did not approve of dancing. But it *was* funny. *Hoppity hop,* went the imp. *Hoppity hop.* The boy wanted to wake Petrel and tell her about it, but when he tried to raise his hand it would not obey him.

That brought him to his senses, for a moment at least. *There is something wrong with me,* he thought. *The creature is not dancing, it is coming to kill me. And I cannot lift a finger to fight it.*

The imp, however, merely inspected him. It began at his toes and examined him inch by inch, all the while muttering to itself as if it were taking notes.

What if it can read my mind? thought the boy, and he tried desperately and unsuccessfully not to think about the sailing ship that had brought him here—the ship that even now was following the *Oyster,* waiting for the boy to kill the demon. Waiting for the signal to attack . . .

The wrongness took hold once more. The boy hardly noticed when the imp left him. He thought he heard the *tick tick tick* of its claws heading towards Petrel, but it might just as easily have been his heart beating too fast, or Brother Thrawn's cane tapping the desk in front of him.

Petrel woke up and crawled past him, whispering to the imp as if they had known each other for years. The boy tried to be angry with her. How could she befriend a servant of the demon? How could she betray the human race like that?

Perhaps, whispered his fevered mind, *she does not know what the imp is. Perhaps she is just ignorant.*

But then Brother Thrawn was leaning over him, saying, "Ignorance is no excuse. Most people *choose* to be ignorant. *And* to be poor and lazy and dirty. It is only right that we should be severe with them."

To his astonishment, the boy found himself protesting. The people on the *Oyster* might be poor and dirty, but they were not lazy. The fishing shift worked extremely hard, he had seen that for himself.

Which was confusing, because hard work was virtuous, and the crew of the *Oyster* was definitely *not* virtuous . . .

The boy groaned and tightened his grip on the spanner. "I must move," he whispered. "I have a mission to carry out. I must move. I *must!*"

Mister Smoke was waiting for Petrel in the darkness outside the rope locker. But it was Missus Slink who began the attack.

"That boy," she said, "went poking around where he had no business to poke around. *And* he launched a vicious assault on my person."

"Don't be cross with him, Missus Slink," said Petrel. "He's scared of rats, that's all."

Missus Slink's voice was stiff with offense. "'That's *all*'? I say he's dangerous, and those who want to get rid of him are right."

"No!" said Petrel, who was not yet ready to give up on Fin, despite his foolishness. "We have to get those answers, don't we? You were the ones who were so keen. You were the ones who wouldn't rest till I got 'em."

The rats were silent for a moment, as if they were talking in some way that Petrel couldn't hear.

"There's things that matter more than answers, shipmate," said Mister Smoke. "We can't 'ave the boy pokin' round the ship, no matter what."

Petrel had never heard him sound so serious and determined. But she was determined too. "Well then," she said, "I'll stay with him! All the time. Then he *can't* assault anyone and he *can't* go poking round, 'cos I'll stop him."

"And how're ya gunna eat, with a stranger hangin' round yer neck like a sea anchor?" asked Mister Smoke. "Can't take *'im* up to the galley to beg for scraps. Can't take 'im anywhere, specially now Orca's been done away with. Everyone's on the lookout for 'im."

He was right and Petrel knew it. But she said, "Can't you

give him one more chance? Please? I'll question him. I'll start right now. I'll get those answers, you'll see."

Without waiting for a reply she wriggled back into the locker. "Fin," she hissed, squatting next to the boy. "Wake up. How did you get on the ice?"

"What?" said Fin, opening his eyes and blinking up at Petrel. In the thin light that trickled down from above, his face looked gray and blotchy.

"How'd you get on the ice?" she repeated. "You said you'd tell me."

The boy nodded vaguely. "I did—say so."

"Are you all right?" asked Petrel.

"No— Yes— Did you poison me?"

Petrel stared at him.

"It was to be expected, I suppose," continued Fin. "They told me there would be—" His eyes changed, as if he had just realized where he was and who he was talking to. He swallowed. "I did not mean—"

"I reckon you're sick," said Petrel.

"No." Fin turned away from her and closed his eyes.

Petrel watched him for a moment, then climbed back out to where Missus Slink and Mister Smoke were waiting. "He's sick," she said into the darkness.

"All the more reason to be rid of 'im," said Mister Smoke. "Don't want sickness on the ship. Throw 'im off before it spreads, that's my advice."

"No!" cried Petrel, dismayed.

"Has to be said, shipmate."

"No, it doesn't. Go away. I don't want to talk to you." And Petrel squirmed back past the machinery and sat beside Fin, taking care not to bump his sore arm.

"Don't worry," she whispered, "I won't let 'em throw you overboard. You're not *really* sick, are you? This is prob'ly the worst of it already. You'll be up and skipping around by the end of the middle watch. And then it won't be just *me* against the rest of the ship. It'll be both of us."

BUT BY THE END OF THE MIDDLE WATCH, IN THE EARLY HOURS of the morning, Fin was no better; in fact, he was considerably worse. His teeth chattered and he shivered uncontrollably, even though he was still wearing his outdoor clothes.

At first Petrel's main worry was how she would move him if the searchers came. But it was not long before she began to wonder if he might die.

Death was commonplace on the *Oyster*, especially in winter. Folk perished from the cold or the lack of food or the unseen coil of a fishing line that snatched them up and dragged them overboard before they could cry for help. They got hit on the head by falling ice or a pipe wrench. They ventured onto the wrong deck and were found hours later at the bottom of a ladder with their neck broken.

None of those things were Petrel's concern. She didn't care what happened to the crew.

But she was beginning to care, just a little, about Fin.

He had been dreaming on and off, and in his dreams, something was chasing him. He panted and yelped. He cried out and clenched that old spanner in his fist and tried to fight back. Once he wept.

Petrel watched helplessly. Just a few hours ago she had thought of the boy as a sort of pet, like Krill's penguin. But now . . .

She knew what it was like to be hunted. *She* knew what it was like to be filled with terror, and to hide her real self so carefully that it only came out in dreams.

"Maybe we're not so different after all, you and me," she whispered.

She wished she'd been nicer to Fin before he got sick. She wished she'd been able to clean his arm with grog before she stitched it.

"P'raps you *are* poisoned," she said to the boy. "That fish knife was a dirty old thing. P'raps the fever started in your arm and now it's got hold of the rest of you. Let's have a look."

She tried to roll Fin's sleeve up, but he thrashed so wildly that she had to stop.

"All right," she said. "Don't yelp at me, I won't touch it. Not now, at any rate."

It struck her then that perhaps it wasn't too late for the grog. She didn't really know how fever worked, but surely if she cleaned the wound properly, the way it should've been cleaned in the first place, it would make a difference?

"Trouble is," she said to the unconscious boy, "Krill makes

his grog out of secret ingredients, and keeps it locked up so tight that no one can get near it. I spose I could ask Missus Slink or Mister Smoke to steal some . . ."

But she already knew they would refuse.

"I bet Squid could get it," she said. "She's the one who gave me the toothies and the needle. Don't know why she gave 'em to me; don't know why she'd give me grog either, or how I'd ask for it."

She sat back against the wall, thinking. She didn't want to leave the boy alone, not with everyone hunting for him. She didn't really want to ask Squid for the grog either. There was something about the young woman that made Petrel uncomfortable. She almost wished that Squid *had* mocked her or pinched her or snatched the toothies back at the last minute. It would have been easier to understand. Easier to hate.

"Trouble is," Petrel said to Fin, "there's no one else."

She gazed down at the boy. *It was me who saved you. That means I've got a responsibility.*

Petrel hadn't meant those words when she had said them to Fin; she was just copying Mister Smoke. But now she thought about them. She thought about Krill's penguin chick, which had pined away in the end, and died. She thought about the witless silence she had woven about herself for protection, and what might happen if she broke that silence . . .

In the end, she drifted off to sleep, and didn't wake up until the rattle of pipes called the crew to Orca's funeral.

"It's morning already," she said to Fin, and she inspected

the boy closely, hoping to see some sign of improvement. But the fever had dug its claws deep, and he groaned and shivered worse than ever.

"Reckon you're gunna die if I don't do something soon," whispered Petrel. And with those words, she came to a decision.

She crawled to the second exit, feeling suddenly breathless. "Don't worry, Fin," she said over her shoulder. "No one'll find you while I'm gone. They'll all be too busy seeing Orca off." She crossed her fingers, hoping that she was right. "And Squid's sure to be at the funeral. As soon as it's over I'll grab her. I'll get some grog from her. I'll— I'll even *talk* to her, if I have to. I will, I'll ask her properly and she'll give me some grog and I'll fix you."

CHAPTER 12

THE FUNERAL

THE DAY OF THE FUNERAL WAS BLEAK AND THE SEA WAS GRAY and flat. On the afterdeck of the *Oyster*, Dolph stood guard over the sealskin-wrapped corpse of her mam. She held herself very straight, the way Orca had taught her. Somewhere in the distance a gull mewed, plaintive as a lost child.

Funerals were dramatic affairs on the *Oyster*. But a murdered First Officer's funeral was more dramatic than most. The entire crew was there, gathered on the afterdeck in their best outdoor clothes, which mostly meant the same outdoor clothes they wore every day, but adorned with feathers and sharks' teeth.

Out of respect for the dead, no one was talking. But everyone was furious, and everyone was uneasy.

And so they should be! thought Dolph. She wanted to scream at Albie, *Why are you up here, instead of hunting for the stranger? Why did you let him escape? Why did you save him from the ice in the first place? Why why why?*

Several paces away, Second Officer Crab—

Of course he was officially First Officer now. But Dolph refused to even think of him that way. The one time she had tried, it stoked her rage to such a terrifying degree that she had been afraid she would die of it.

Several paces away, Second Officer Crab was beginning the funeral service. His words drifted past Dolph like melting bergs.

". . . in the name of the sleeping captain . . . flesh to flesh . . . water to water . . . commit her body to the creatures of the deep—"

At that, a ripple of anxiety ran through the gathered crowd, and everyone took a step away from the rail. Only Dolph stood firm. She eyed the sea and waited. Behind her, one of the ruined lifeboats began to shake in its cradle. The Maw was coming.

Dolph's legs shook almost as much as the lifeboat, but she didn't move, not even when the sea below her turned as black as the polar night, and the water boiled and surged.

Something roared, deep and sullen, like a glacier tumbling into the ocean. Dolph gripped the sealskin that covered her mam's corpse. The Maw's massive head broke the surface of the water with a sound like the end of the world. Its huge jaws opened.

Quickly, Second Officer Crab and Third Officer Hump stepped forward. With Dolph, they lifted the sealskin parcel onto the rail and tipped it until Orca's body slipped from its wrapping and fell down, down, down—

Vast teeth, as big as pistons, snapped at the corpse. Crab and Hump leaped backwards, but Dolph shut her eyes and stayed where she was, clinging to the rail. She didn't open her eyes again until she heard the smack of the huge body against the waves and knew that the Maw had vanished back to wherever it had come from, taking her mam with it.

There was a stunned silence. Then Crab said loudly, "We all know what we must do now."

The Second Officer was not a strong speaker. His voice was thin, and he had an irritating way of pinching his words off at the end, as if to keep them as neat as possible. But today everyone listened to him keenly.

"We must find this stranger," said Crab, "and throw him off the ship."

Mam is dead, thought Dolph, and the sea below her had never looked so dark and deep.

"Until then," said Crab, "Truce is declared. All fighting between the tribes will cease. How the boy got away from Albie does not matter. Payback for old crimes does not matter. What matters is the hunt for the boy."

Mam is dead.

"But we will keep this hunt tidy," said Crab. "Braid will search Braid. Dufftown will search Dufftown. Grease Alley will search Grease Alley. There will be no trespassing on each other's territories, but between us we will find this stranger. This villain. This *murderer.*"

Mam is—

There was a roar of agreement from the crew, and they began to disperse, some to fishing shift, others to the engines and the galley and the bridge. But most of them went to continue the search.

Crab, Albie and Krill left together, talking among themselves as if they had never even thought of fighting. Dolph leaned against the rail and watched them go. As the hatch closed behind them, she turned back to the sea.

"Mam," she whispered, "Second Officer Crab wants the hunt for your murderer to be *tidy*." The word had never sounded so absurd. Dolph clenched her teeth. "Don't worry, Mam, *I* won't be tidy. I'll hunt that boy down. I'll trespass on Dufftown, and I'll trespass on Grease Alley, and no one will stop me. No one will dare. I'll find the stranger and I'll throw him overboard myself!"

PETREL CAUGHT UP WITH SQUID ON THE COMMONS. The young woman was deep in thought, and when Petrel touched her arm, she jumped.

"Oh, it's you, Miss Nothing!" she said, putting her hand on her heart. "For a moment I thought maybe it was the stranger, come to slit my throat. I'm getting as bad as the rest of the crew."

She smiled, but then her smile became a grimace. "I wish they'd settle down a bit, don't you? It's a terrible thing, what happened to Orca, but folk don't make sensible decisions when they're angry. And I'm not sure that Crab's up to the job of controlling 'em—"

She broke off. "Don't spose you care one way or the other, do you, Miss Nothing? What d'you want? You hungry? There's plenty of toothies, but you'll have to wait a bit, Da turned the burners off for the funeral."

Petrel hesitated. Now she was here, she was not at all sure that she was ready to give up her silence. She opened her mouth and shut it again. She stared at Squid's feet.

Then she thought of Fin lying feverish in the rope locker while Albie hunted for him, and she looked up—and tipped her hand as if she was drinking.

"You thirsty?" asked Squid.

Petrel shook her head and tipped her hand again.

"Well, if it's not thirst, I don't know what—"

Petrel cradled her arm protectively, the way Fin had done. Then she made a sewing motion.

"You've hurt yourself, is that it?" said Squid. "Is that why you wanted the needle? Show me."

A quick shake of the head. Another tip of the hand, but instead of drinking, Petrel pretended to pour something over her arm.

"Ah," said Squid, her eyes sharp. "You want some grog to clean the wound."

Petrel nodded, relieved that she wouldn't have to talk after all.

"Hmm. Not sure if I can get it. Da keeps it locked away and hardly even trusts himself with the key—the stuff's so hard to make. Have you sewn the wound up yet?"

Another nod.

Squid looked thoughtful. "Spose I could ask him for half a cup. But, first, let's just check—"

And before Petrel could move, the young woman had grabbed her by the wrist and pushed up her sleeve.

There was no wound, of course. "Now, why doesn't that surprise me?" said Squid, still hanging on to Petrel's arm. "What are you *really* up to, Miss Nothing?"

Petrel didn't answer. She was wondering how soon she could escape. *I shouldn't've left Fin by himself,* she thought. *Not while he's helpless. What if someone finds him while I'm gone?*

Squid dragged her away from the ladder and lowered her voice. "You see, I've been thinking, which is just as well, 'cos no one else seems to be. Do I believe there's a stranger? Aye, I do, though I haven't seen him. Do I believe he escaped from Albie's brig? Aye, again. Do I believe that Krill and Orca were responsible for that escape, like the Engineers were saying before the murder? No, I don't."

Petrel glanced up at her, then stared at the deck again.

"I would've known about it," said Squid firmly. "Da can't keep secrets from me. So. If Braid and Dufftown didn't help the stranger, how did he escape? By himself?" She shook her head. "I can't see it. No one gets away from Albie that easily. Which means someone must've helped him. But who? Someone from Grease Alley? Nope, too risky. If Albie found out he'd have their heads stove in and their corpses over the side before they could draw breath."

Petrel tried to wiggle free, but could not.

Squid didn't seem to notice. "You know what I think?" she said. "I think someone *else* helped him. Someone who's worried. Someone who wants grog for a wound she hasn't got."

Petrel froze. *Squid's going to shout now,* she thought. *She's gunna tell the whole ship that I know where Fin is. That I freed him in the first place. This is the end of me, this is!*

But instead of shouting, Squid shook Petrel's arm gently. "Am I right? Where is he? What've you done with him?"

Still Petrel did not answer. Squid sighed and sat down on the deck, pulling the younger girl with her. "I didn't see you at the funeral, so maybe you don't know how angry everyone is. It's like a sort of winter madness, only winter's gone and there's no excuse. Now, I know you don't want to tell me where you've hidden the boy. So let me ask you an easier question. Did *you* kill Orca?"

"No!" The word was out of Petrel's mouth before she knew it.

Squid grinned. "You can talk, then? I thought maybe you could. You've got more secrets than anyone knows, haven't you?"

Startled, Petrel stared at her, but Squid was serious again. "Did you have anything to do with Orca's death?"

"Course not," mumbled Petrel, looking away.

"That's what I thought, Miss Nothing," said Squid, with considerable satisfaction. "Hang on, I can't keep calling you that. What's your name? You've got one, haven't you?"

A long pause. *I don't trust her. I don't! But she hasn't shouted yet. So maybe . . .*

"Petrel."

"Well then, Petrel, could that boy have got to Orca without your help? Without *someone's* help?"

"No, of course he couldn't! He didn't *do* it. He swore he

didn't—" Petrel clapped her hand across her mouth. But it was too late.

"Aha," said Squid.

"You tricked me!"

"No, I didn't. *I* don't think he killed Orca. I think he's taking the blame for someone else's nastiness. Don't know whose, mind. But that's not the question, right now. The question is, are you going to trust me?"

Petrel chewed her knuckles. Of course she wasn't going to trust Squid! Years of bitter experience had taught her that *no one* could be trusted. No one except herself.

But if she didn't do something soon, Fin would die.

I could pretend to trust her. And keep my eyes open, so I see when she's about to turn on me. That's when I run, and if Fin's better, he can run with me. And if he's not better—

"He's sick," she said. "I think it's his arm, gone bad."

"Might be," said Squid. "Will you take me to him?"

Once again, Petrel didn't answer straightaway. *It's like one of those dreams,* she thought, *where I'm climbing nets. Every time I get to the top, and I think the hard bit's over, another one pops up in front of me, even steeper than the one before.*

Then she thought, as she did in the dreams, *But I've gone this far. Not much use turning back now.*

"He's in Grease Alley," she whispered, hoping desperately that she was doing the right thing. "But you can't see him. Border guards'll never let you past."

Squid nodded slowly. "You're right, but . . . What if Head Cook Krill sent a gift to Albie, as a symbol of the Truce? Maybe a couple of extra-large toothies, cooked in Krill's special sauce that no one outside Dufftown has ever had the pleasure of tasting? Would that be enough to get me past the border?"

"Might be."

"Then let's give it a try. And if it works, young Petrel, then it's up to you to take me to the boy."

CHAPTER 13

HIS TREACHEROUS MEMORY

Hot. Cold. *Hot.* Cooooooold. The boy shivered and burned and shivered again. He had never felt so ill, not in all his life.

He groaned, and someone knelt beside him. He wasn't sure who it was. A girl, maybe. She rolled his sleeve up and said, "See, that's where I sewed him. He wouldn't let me near it earlier."

Someone else touched him with cool fingers. "Doesn't look as if it's gone bad. No red streaks. You did a good job with those stitches."

The boy drifted off for a bit, though he knew he shouldn't. Brother Thrawn did not like it when the Initiates daydreamed. Besides, the boy had a mission to carry out.

"I am trying, Brother," he muttered. "I am getting close. Please be patient. Do not go away and leave me here . . ."

"What's he talking about?" said a voice nearby.

"Don't know. He's been mumbling all night. None of it makes sense. Squid, if it's not his arm, what is it?"

"Not sure. Let's see his chest."

"Do not go away and leave me here," whispered the boy again, and the words cracked open a door in the hidden tracts of his memory. His treacherous memory.

He tried to fight it, but he was too weak. Under the heat of the fever, the door swung wider. The girl bending over him became a woman with tears pouring down her far-too-thin face.

"It's for the best, my love," she whispered, though her arms, wrapped tight around him, said something else entirely. "There's no food, not for us poor folk. At least in the Citadel you'll eat."

The boy could not bear it. "No," he cried out loud. "*No!*" And he tried to sit up.

"Shhhh, lie down," said a voice. "It's all right, you're sick, that's all. Don't be scared, Squid'll fix you."

"Look at this rash," said a second voice. "You know what I think? He's got boat fever."

"But no one gets this sick with boat fever. Squid, are you *sure* it's not his arm?"

"I'm positive."

"Will he get better?"

"Who knows? Where does he come from? Has he told you?"

"No," whispered the boy, as the illness gripped him tighter. "Do not tell. Must not warn the demon . . . it will blow us out of the water if it suspects . . . cannot send a man . . . send a boy . . . it will never suspect a boy . . ."

And then the woman with the thin face was bending over him again, only she had a different voice, and she said, "What are you talking about, Fin?"

"That is not my name," whispered the boy. "I do not have a name, Mama, not yet . . . they took away the one you gave me . . . but I am going to earn a new one . . . soon . . . when the demon is destroyed . . . when the ship is—"

A fit of shivering overtook him, and he broke off. Someone said, "We need to bring his temperature down. We need to find out what he's talking about too. I don't like the sound of it, Petrel. I think I'm going to have to tell Da."

"What? No, you can't!"

"You heard what he said. It's something to do with the ship. Maybe something that affects the crew. Don't you want to know what it is?"

"I don't *care* what it is. I don't care about the crew!"

There was a long silence. Then one of the voices said, "You know, not everyone agrees with what was done to your mam and da."

"Bit late for that now," said the other voice bitterly.

"Aye, I spose it is."

Another long silence.

Then, "Petrel, Da *has* to be told."

"He'll throw Fin overboard!"

"No, he won't. I'll talk to him first, make sure he sees the sense of it. Da's no fool, and he can tell good meat from bad. I wouldn't be surprised if he's already realized that the boy couldn't have killed Orca."

"What if he doesn't see the sense of it?"

"Listen, everyone's searching for the boy. If he stays here, Albie's going to find him sooner or later—"

"I'll move him."

"How? Where? Look at him. He's really sick, he needs proper care. He'll be warm in Dufftown and he'll have plenty to eat. Don't worry, you can come with him. I know he's your friend."

Deep in the boy's memory, the once-loved voice murmured, "You'll be warm in the Citadel. You'll have plenty to eat. You'll make friends."

The boy's face convulsed. With the small part of his mind that was still aware, he told himself that this was not a memory at all, but the fever playing tricks on him. Or perhaps it was the demon, crawling into his mind.

"Go away," he whispered. "Go away, demon." And he closed his poor frozen heart off from the past, as he had learned to do so long ago, and forced himself to dream of nothing but duty and hard work and the virtue of destruction.

IT WAS THE MOST DIFFICULT DECISION PETREL HAD EVER FACED. "How would we get Fin up to Dufftown?" she said. Then she quickly added, "I'm not agreeing, mind, I'm just wondering. Can't carry him; Engineers'd grab him before we got to the ladders."

"Mm. And Da can't come down and get him. Border guards'd never let *him* past, no matter what he gave 'em."

They both fell silent. Fin tossed and moaned, but did not speak.

"Maybe—" said Petrel slowly, wondering why in the name of blizzards she was even *thinking* about the idea. "Maybe there *is* a way. Not sure yet. You go and talk to your da. Make sure he promises not to hurt Fin, and promises not to tell anyone about him either. And when you've got those promises, all proper and solemn, send me a rattle through the pipes in Cook code."

"You know Cook code?" Squid looked surprised.

"Course I do," said Petrel.

"I should've guessed. All right, let's see. I'll say something like . . . *The soup is safe for eating.*" Squid shuffled away from the boy. "The whole of Dufftown'll think I've gone mad."

"Fin will get better, won't he?" asked Petrel.

"Hope so," said Squid. "Hope we can fillet out whatever he's talking about too." She frowned, then her face cleared. "As for me, it's back past the border guards. They'd better've liked that extra bit of sauced toothy I gave 'em, eh?"

"Can you find your way?"

"I think so. If I get lost I'll shout for help." And with a wave she was gone.

Petrel bent over the feverish boy. "Am I doing the right thing, Fin?" she whispered. "Am I? I don't know. These are strange days, and I can't see where they're going."

"No," said Mister Smoke. "No no no no no. Understand me, shipmate? I say no. No no no—"

"And so do I," interrupted Missus Slink. "No no no—"

"I heard you the first time," said Petrel. "But listen to me—"

"No no no—"

Petrel put her hands over her ears. The only way to get Fin up to Dufftown unnoticed was to carry him through the bulkhead tunnels. If the rats had agreed straightaway, she might have had second thoughts. But their refusal to even consider the matter brought out all her stubbornness.

"He won't know where he is," she said. "He's too feverish. And I won't tell Squid or Krill. They'll think I sneaked him past the border guards somehow."

"No no no—"

Petrel hadn't told Mister Smoke and Missus Slink about Fin's ravings. They already distrusted the boy, and she didn't want to make things worse. But now she had no choice.

"He's— He's been saying things," she said. "Something about a demon, and about the ship. Squid says we have to take him to Krill."

The relentless chorus broke off, and beady eyes peered up at Petrel. "Demon?" said Missus Slink.

Petrel nodded.

"Ship?" said Mister Smoke.

"Aye. He said something like, he doesn't have a name 'cos someone took it, but he's going to earn a new one soon when the demon is destroyed and the ship is—"

"'The ship is' what?" said Missus Slink sharply.

"Don't know. Fever took him before he finished. Why's he talking about a demon?"

The rats looked at each other. "How's your memory, Slink?" said Mister Smoke. "You got records of a demon in there?"

"My memory is all rust and fish oil," replied Missus Slink, "and getting worse every day. I've got suspicions, but nothing solid."

"Me too," said Mister Smoke.

"So maybe the girl's got a point."

"Maybe she 'as."

"I could blindfold him," said Petrel quickly. "Just to be sure."

The beady eyes inspected her once more. "And not tell a soul?" said Missus Slink. "Not even if they hang you by your heels over the side—"

"Not even then," interrupted Petrel, who was fairly sure that Squid at least would not hang her over the side of the ship.

"Then you 'ave our permission," said Mister Smoke.

It was some time before the message came through. Petrel sat beside Fin, wiping the sweat from his face and whispering reassurances that he didn't seem to hear. She wondered if he would say something that made sense of his previous mutterings about the ship. But although the boy groaned and moaned, and his eyelids flickered as if he were trapped in a nightmare, he did not speak again.

The longer Petrel sat there, the more worried she became. *What if Albie finds us before Squid's message comes through? What if Squid can't persuade her da that Fin didn't kill Orca? Or what if Krill only PRETENDS to be persuaded, so he can get his hands on the stranger?*

Petrel had never feared the Head Cook the way she feared Albie and Orca, but still Squid's da was a huge and powerful man. Once he had his hands on Fin, there would be little Petrel could do to protect the boy . . .

It was almost evening when the pipes rattled out their

seemingly innocent message about soup. "That's it," said Petrel, and Missus Slink immediately hobbled away.

Petrel unwound the scrap of sealskin that she had been using as a scarf, and tied it over Fin's eyes. "It won't be for long," she whispered. "And it's prob'ly best that you can't see what's happening."

If Fin *had* been able to see, he would have been horrified. Because Missus Slink was back already, and with her she brought a horde of rats, black and lean and clever. They scrambled over the broken machinery, then stood on their hind legs and inspected Petrel and Fin with quivering noses.

Petrel had never seen so many rats gathered in one place. She didn't mind them, not like Fin did, so she stayed where she was while they sniffed her.

"You're going to help us, ain't you," she whispered, though she knew they couldn't understand her, not the way *her* rats did.

They understood Missus Slink though. At a signal Petrel did not hear, they swarmed around Fin and began to wriggle underneath him. There were so many of them, and they pushed so stubbornly, that they raised the boy right off the rusty floor, until he looked as if he were floating on a sea of tiny legs.

"Be careful with him," said Petrel. "Don't drop him."

"You mind *your* business, shipmate, and we'll mind ours," said Mister Smoke, as he limped past Fin's head, nudging and poking the rats into place. When he came to the spanner, which was dragging on the floor, he said, "You'd best take that orf 'im, it'll make too much of a racket."

Petrel eased the spanner out of Fin's grasp. Then she grabbed her outdoor clothes, and tucked the spanner in her own trouser pocket.

"We'll go that way," said Mister Smoke, nodding towards the back exit, which was not as cluttered with machinery parts as the front. "Is it clear? Don't want Engineers trippin' over the cargo. Snap to it, shipmate."

"It's clear," said Petrel, peering out into the passage beyond, and the light at the far end. "What—"

She stopped. Fin was moving, rippling across the floor towards her, with one hand wavering uncertainly out to the side.

"Get that arm, Smoke," said Missus Slink, who seemed to be overseeing the expedition, and Mister Smoke chivvied the errant rats until they trotted back towards their fellows, and Fin's arm was where it should be.

The sill of the rope locker was the worst bit. The rats heaved and strained, and some of them fell back, and then they heaved again, and Fin's head flopped and his shoulder banged against a worn-out piston, and Petrel gasped.

But then Missus Slink and Mister Smoke rearranged the rats somehow—Petrel couldn't see the difference, but things immediately became easier—and Fin's body rose up and over the sill, wriggling and wobbling and jerking like a fish on a hook, and down the other side into the passage.

Halfway down the passage, the boy began to groan. "Shhh!" whispered Petrel, who was trotting a little way ahead, watching out for Engineers. "It's all right, Fin, we're taking you to Dufftown."

She had no idea if he heard her, but he grew quiet again,

and there was no sound except ordinary ship noises, and the patter of a thousand tiny feet.

The entrance to the tunnels was not the one Petrel knew about. This one was right down at deck level, and hidden in a dark corner, so that it looked like just another bit of rusted-out bulkhead.

With Missus Slink guiding them, the rats eased Fin through the gap. One of his jacket strings caught on a jagged piece of iron. "Wait," cried Petrel, and she dragged the string loose.

When the boy was right inside the tunnel, and only his toes visible, Petrel crawled in after him, pushing her outdoor clothes in front of her. "You ready, shipmate?" muttered Mister Smoke, from somewhere up ahead.

"Aye," replied Petrel, and the expedition began to move again.

It was a strange journey. The rats, pattering along in front of Petrel's nose, had a rank, musty smell. They kept up a constant squeaking, just on the edge of her hearing, and she found herself wondering if they were arguing with each other, and if they had tribes like shipfolk, and fought among themselves for power and territory, and which one was rat-Albie and which was rat-Orca.

Something tickled at her memory, something about one of the Officers. What was it? She had a feeling it might be important . . .

But then the tunnel sloped upward, quite steeply, and Petrel had to grab hold of Fin's feet to make sure he didn't slide off the rats' backs.

The boy had fallen completely silent by this time, so much so that Petrel began to worry. *What if he's dead? What if I'm following a corpse through the tunnels?*

"Mister Smoke," she whispered. "Is Fin all right?"

"Course 'e is," came the rough answer. "Now, hush. We is passin' through tricky territory."

Petrel hushed, and a moment later heard sounds on the outside of the bulkhead, the sort of hostile mutterings that folk might make as they searched the ship for a murderous stranger.

That set her to worrying again. *Did I make the right choice? What if I should've kept Fin a secret, even from Squid?*

After all, the searchers *mightn't* have found him in the rope locker. And the boy *might* have got better on his own. Then Petrel could have taught him to creep around the ship the way she did, until the crew eventually gave up their hunt and forgot about him.

It's safer, being forgotten.

Petrel didn't feel safe now, not with Krill somewhere up ahead, waiting for her, *thinking* about her. She didn't like folk thinking about her. She didn't like folk thinking about Fin, either. She wondered if she should tell Missus Slink and Mister Smoke to turn back before it was too late.

But what if they *did* turn back, and Fin died? Or Albie caught him?

Better Krill than Albie, thought Petrel, and she kept going.

At last, after a particularly long and difficult upward slope, Missus Slink brought the formation to a halt. Petrel felt a familiar tapping on her hand.

"You still with us, shipmate?" said Mister Smoke. "Reckon you can do a bit of maneuverin'?

"What do you want me to do?" whispered Petrel.

"First up, squeeze past the cargo. There's a bit of decking just above 'is 'ead. Push that outta the way, then grab 'old of said cargo and haul 'im outta the tunnel. We'll 'elp where we can."

It wasn't easy, squeezing past Fin and the rats. Petrel had to breathe in, and scrape along the tunnel wall, making herself and her bundle of outdoor clothes as small as possible. Even so, she bumped against the rats, who squeaked in protest.

"Sorry," she whispered. "Sorry, didn't mean to, 'scuse me, sorry."

The bit of decking came away easily. Petrel crawled up through the hole, and found herself on the same level as the galley, but considerably farther aft, and surrounded by enormous silent vats.

It was a part of Dufftown that she knew well. Folk said the vats used to grow food, many years ago, to feed the crew through the winter months. Petrel didn't really believe it; she couldn't imagine how those big empty tanks could grow anything. Nowadays Krill used them for storing the lightweight hunting sleds, and Petrel sometimes slept in the spaces between them.

She stood up and glanced around, but there was no sign of any Cooks.

"Quick," she said, bending over the hole in the deck, and she reached down and grabbed Fin under the arms.

Petrel was strong for her size, but she couldn't lift Fin by herself. She hauled and dragged at the limp body. Below her the rats pushed and shoved and squeaked. At an instruction from Missus Slink, some of them leaped out of the hole and joined forces with Petrel, grabbing the boy's clothes in their yellow teeth and pulling for all they were worth.

He's gunna have some bruises when he wakes up, thought Petrel.

As soon as the boy was entirely clear of the tunnel, the black rats whisked away. Missus Slink peered up at Petrel. "Remember, not a word about how you got here."

"Just find out as quick as yer can what the boy's mumbling about," said Mister Smoke.

"Wait," said Petrel. "I'm not sure—"

But the two gray rats were already gone, and the bit of decking screwed neatly into place behind them.

Petrel sat there for a moment, catching her breath and brushing bits of rust and cobweb off Fin's clothes. Then she took the iron stub from her pocket, found the nearest pipe, and banged out, in Cook code, *To Squid. Food vats.*

With that done, she squatted on her heels beside Fin, feeling a bit like a toothy that was about to be thrown on the burners.

Squid and her da must have been waiting for the rattle, because Petrel heard their voices only a few minutes later.

"I don't believe for a moment she could've got him past the border," Krill was saying, in what he probably thought was a whisper. "Not with the guards on high alert."

"Don't shout, Da," said Squid. "I told you, she's clever. And if she's not here, why did she send a message saying she—"

They rounded the corner, and Krill's great bulk ground to a halt. "I'll be skewered," he said. "The boy's here."

"So's Petrel," said Squid unnecessarily.

The Head Cook's eyes narrowed and he strode forward. "How'd you get him here?" he rumbled, scowling down at Petrel. "You're a runty little thing. You didn't carry him all the way up from Grease Alley by yourself, that's for sure."

Squid elbowed him. "Don't bully her, Da. It's her business how she brought him. It's a secret."

"Don't like secrets," growled Krill. "Especially if they mean strangers can come and go without me knowing about it." He leaned closer to Petrel. "Does Albie know these secrets of yours? Does Orca— I mean, Crab?"

Petrel's immediate reaction was to duck her head and look stupid. Anything else felt too dangerous. It didn't matter that Squid knew she could talk, and had probably told her da. Petrel was sure she could out-stubborn both of them.

It's safer, being ignored.

Krill however was not willing to ignore her. He bent right over, so his beard almost prickled Petrel's face, and said, "I'm taking a mighty risk here, you know that, don't you, bratling? If Braid and Grease knew I'd given refuge to Orca's murderer, they'd be down on me like an avalanche."

Petrel felt a surge of anger. But she might yet have stayed silent, if her eyes hadn't fallen on Fin, pale and helpless at her feet.

Can't protect him if I'm witless, thought Petrel. *Can't protect him if I don't talk.*

It was enough. Before she could lose her nerve, she took a deep breath, glared up at the Head Cook and said, "Fin didn't murder Orca, and don't you try and make out he did!"

Krill was clearly taken aback. He straightened up, knotting his bushy eyebrows and glancing at Squid.

I've done it now, thought Petrel, her legs beginning to shake. *He'll prob'ly kill me, and maybe that's just as well. I can't go back to small and silent after this!*

"I told you, Da," said Squid.

"Mmph," grunted Krill. Then he bent down again and effortlessly scooped Fin up in his arms. "Lead the way," he said to Squid. "We'll put him in my cabin." To Petrel he said, "Coming, bratling?"

And he strode off, taking Fin with him.

CHAPTER 14

YOUR DA WAS A TRAITOR...

THE HEAD COOK'S CABIN HAD AN ENORMOUS HAMMOCK SLUNG across the middle of it, and a sea chest on the floor beneath the porthole. Krill laid Fin in the hammock. Then, with a nod to his daughter and a deeply suspicious glare at Petrel, he left, locking the door behind him.

Blizzards, I'm glad he's gone, thought Petrel, and she sank down onto the sea chest, still clutching her outdoor clothes and wondering if maybe she *was* witless after all. She couldn't think of any other reason why she would've let herself be trapped in a cabin with no way out.

But then Squid laughed. "I think Da likes you."

Petrel shook her head and mumbled, "He prob'ly thinks *I'm* a murderer too."

"You wait," said Squid.

Five minutes later, Krill was back with a second hammock, and five minutes after that he was back again, with a cup of water and a plate of toothies, cooked to perfection.

He frowned at Petrel. "How old are you, bratling?" he growled.

Petrel, who had no idea how old she was, merely shrugged. But she watched that plate with a hungry eye.

"She's twelve, Da," said Squid. "You know that as well as I do."

"She doesn't look twelve," grumbled Krill. "She's too small, never been fed properly."

And he thrust the plate at Petrel, who grabbed it and began to eat before he could change his mind.

Krill turned back to his daughter. "Try to get some water into the boy," he said. He passed her the cup, then took a key from his pocket and held it between finger and thumb. "And keep this close. I wouldn't be surprised if she"—he nodded at Petrel—"tried to slit your throat and make a run for it, like her killer friend."

Petrel stopped eating and narrowed her eyes at the Head Cook. She was beginning to suspect that all his gruffness was on the surface. There was none of the bone-deep nastiness that made Albie so dangerous.

I don't trust him all the same, she thought. And she mumbled, through a mouthful of fish, "If I want to leave, nothing'll stop me."

Krill reared back in mock surprise. "Scrawny *and* fierce," he said, and suddenly Petrel could see the similarity between him and his daughter.

She ducked her head and kept eating, but her mind was following odd pathways. She didn't look up when Krill left, saying, "That boy utters another word, I want to know about it." Or when Squid wrestled Fin's outdoor clothes off him, sponged his face and arms to bring his temperature down, and persuaded him to drink a little water.

Petrel was thinking about her own da, of whom she knew nothing, not even his name. She had thought about him many times before, but he had always seemed impossibly distant, like sunlight on a far-off berg, and she had never been able to imagine what he looked like.

Now she found herself wondering if he had been big and gruff like Krill. *Maybe Squid knew him,* she thought. *Maybe she'd tell me about him if I asked.*

But then again, maybe she wouldn't. And besides, Petrel didn't *want* to ask. With a sniff, she put down the empty plate and went to help with the sponging.

That day was one of the strangest Petrel had ever known. Outside the cabin, the crew was scouring the ship for Fin, and that betrayal was only a word away.

But for the first time Petrel could remember, she was well fed, comfortable and warm, which made it hard to stay wary. She had to remind herself frequently that she must not trust the Head Cook and his daughter; that they could turn against her at any moment, and she must be ready to run when they did.

She worried at first that Squid mightn't let her out of the cabin. But instead of keeping a tight hold of the key, as Petrel would have done, the young woman hung it on a hook beside the sea chest.

First time Squid looked away, Petrel snatched the key off the hook and backed towards the door.

Without turning around, Squid said, "Make sure you shut the door behind you. We don't want anyone looking in."

Which left Petrel with a dilemma. She wanted to leave, mostly to prove to herself that she could. But what if Fin disappeared while she was gone? What if Squid had another key and was just *waiting* for her to leave? What if this was the point of betrayal?

In the end, she stayed where she was. But she kept the key in her pocket, and she was the one who unlocked the door when Krill came back halfway through the watch with a bowl of carefully strained fish soup, to see, he said, "if Orca's killer can be persuaded to eat."

Petrel flared up at that, and said sharply, "I never heard of Orca being taken by surprise before. Maybe someone *poisoned* her before they cut her throat. Maybe it's dangerous to take food from the hand of a Cook."

Krill glowered at her, and said, "You ate hungrily enough, bratling. I didn't see you refusing my fish."

"But I'm not a killer, am I?" said Petrel.

Squid laughed and said, "You mustn't mind Da. He's got a strange sense of humor."

"Sense of humor or not," said Petrel, "I want to see him take a spoonful or two himself before it goes anywhere near Fin."

To her astonishment, Krill nodded. "A sensible precaution," he rumbled, and he slurped several mouthfuls of soup through his beard, then stood huge and solid in the middle of the cabin, rubbing his belly.

"That's not bad," he said, which made Petrel hungry again, even though she had just eaten.

After all that, Fin was not interested in the soup. He lay pale and restless, with his fair hair spread out on the pillow and one arm dangling from the hammock. His eyes were closed, and he panted for breath.

"Has he said anything yet?" asked Krill.

"Not a word, Da," said Squid. "Do you think it's trouble, all this talk of demons and suchlike?"

"I reckon so." Krill rubbed his face. "Albie should never have picked him up off the ice."

"But—" began Petrel.

Krill held up an enormous hand. "But what's done is done. What I want to know now is, where did he come from?"

"He fell from the sky," Petrel said quickly. "He told me so."

"*Snow* falls from the sky," said Krill, scowling, "and ice, and even a bird on occasion. But a boy?" He shook his head. "No, there's another explanation somewhere, and it's got me worried. According to the old stories, there's nothing north of here but madness. So what if *that's* where he comes from? Eh?" He walked to the door, then turned and glared at Petrel. "What if he comes from somewhere north? And what if he's brought a bit of that madness with him?"

Krill's parting words sent a shiver down Petrel's back, and she felt more reluctant than ever to leave the cabin. But in the end she had to, especially after drinking all the soup. "I'm going to the head," she muttered to Squid.

"You'd better give me the key in case Da comes back," said the young woman.

"No, I won't be long." And Petrel darted out of the cabin and locked the door behind her before Squid could stop her.

She ran to the nearest head, peed as quickly as she could, and ran back again, worrying all the way. Because there *might* be another key, and the Head Cook and his daughter were sure to turn against her sooner or later . . .

But when she unlocked the cabin door, Fin was still there, and so was Squid, as calm and unbothered as ever.

That first day marked out a pattern. Krill visited at regular intervals with more food than Petrel had ever seen in her life. Each time, just before he left, he asked if Fin had said anything more about the ship, and when the answer was no, he scratched his beard and looked worried.

Squid mostly stayed in the cabin, taking care of Fin with a gentleness that Petrel did her best to copy. At night the young woman went to her own cabin, and Petrel slept in the second hammock, which Krill had slung above the sea chest. She did not rest easy, but woke every few minutes, convinced that someone had opened the door and was about to snatch Fin from under her nose.

On the second day, the boy's fever worsened. Squid and Petrel hovered over him from dawn to dusk, wiping his poor hot face and arms, and trying to persuade him to drink a little more water.

Krill, when he visited, still said things like, "How's Orca's killer getting on?" and "Has the murderous boy said anything yet?" But Petrel was growing used to him, and could see that he was almost as worried about Fin as she was.

She could see, too, how proud the Head Cook was of his daughter, and that sent a twinge right through Petrel's heart, because no one was proud of her, or ever likely to be.

At the end of the second day, she tucked the two sets of outdoor clothes inside the sea chest, along with Fin's spanner. Then she put the key back on the hook and left it there.

That night, Fin tossed and shivered and cried out for his mam, whom he called "Mama." Petrel crouched beside him, whispering, "Hush, Fin, hush!" and putting the covers back over him whenever he threw them off.

Squid came in several times, and on the last occasion she stayed. There was nothing much either of them could do, but Petrel was glad for the company.

It was a long, wearisome night, but towards the end of it, Fin quieted a little. The moon shone low and bright through the porthole, and Petrel felt as if she and Squid were in another world, far away from the *Oyster*. A world where important questions might be asked. And answered.

Without looking at Squid, she whispered, "You knew my mam."

"We spoke once or twice, that's all," came the low-voiced reply.

"What about my da? Did you speak to him?"

"No. Never."

Petrel let out a sigh. Then she said, "What were their names?"

Squid didn't answer the question straightaway. Instead, she eyed Petrel and said, "No one's ever told you?"

"If they had, I wouldn't be asking."

"Spose not." The young woman stood up and bent over Fin. "He's sleeping a bit more easily. That's a relief."

She sat down again. "They prob'ly shouldn't have done what they did," she began, and Petrel knew they were back to talking about her mam and da. Her skin felt suddenly hot, and she wondered if she had caught Fin's fever.

Your da was a traitor and your mam was mad.

"But neither should they have been punished so severely," continued Squid. "Da spoke against that punishment at the time, and so did a few other folk. Trouble was, it came at the end of a long, hungry winter, when there'd already been a hundred or so deaths from starvation, and more looming every day. It was a bad year for the tribes—not enough food, and everyone suspicious of everyone else."

"What did they do wrong?" whispered Petrel.

Once again, Squid didn't answer the question, not directly. "Your mam's name was Quill."

"Quill," murmured Petrel, turning the sound on her tongue, and liking the way it was soft and sharp at the same time.

"And your da was—"

"Was what?"

"He was called—um—Seal."

Petrel sat bolt upright. "But that's an Officer name!"

"Aye."

"But— But my da can't have been an Officer. Mam was Grease. You can't mix Grease and Braid, that's just wrong, that's—" She stopped.

Squid's face was calm in the moonlight. "They loved each other. Da says it's happened once or twice before, but in those cases there were no babies, and besides they happened in fat times, when no one minded as much. The year we're talking about was different. Folk were starving, and Seal was passing food to you and your mam, food that belonged to Braid. The tribes wouldn't stand for that, even though he was Orca's brother."

"Orca's *brother*? My da?" Petrel felt as if all the breath had gone out of her and would never return.

Your da was a traitor . . .

It made a horrible sort of sense. No wonder Dolph hated her.

Petrel leaned back against the wall, trying to take it all in. She almost wished Squid hadn't told her. She felt as if the story had laid some sort of claim on her; as if she must behave differently in response to it.

I'm half Braid, half Grease!

She wriggled uncomfortably. It was like being half penguin, half fish. It was impossible.

And yet . . .

"Orca's brother and Albie's sister?" she whispered.

"That's right."

"So—couldn't Orca and Albie have saved 'em?"

Squid laughed, but there was no humor in it. "They were the ones who shouted loudest against your parents. Da reckons

146

it's the only time he's known the two of 'em to agree on anything. Like I said, that was a bad year, and some folk thought maybe Albie and Orca were part of what was going on. And you know Albie; as soon as he realized *he* was in danger, he started crying out for his sister to be killed, and Seal with her. Orca was a step behind him, but she caught up soon enough. She wanted *you* killed too, but Seal and Quill begged for your life, 'cos they loved you. And in the end, folk felt bad about killing a bratling."

"Not enough to take me into one of the tribes," said Petrel.

"Da would've taken you, but Albie wouldn't let him. You were only two winters old and Albie thought you'd die, I spose, and the disgrace and suspicion would die with you. Instead, you just—disappeared."

Mister Smoke, thought Petrel. *And Missus Slink. They must've looked after me until I was old enough to look after myself.*

And she wondered what it had been about that small bratling that had made the two old rats think her worth saving.

Outside the porthole, the moon was sinking below the horizon. Petrel stood up and pressed her nose to the glass.

Half Braid, half Grease.

She shook her head at the wrongness of it. And yet . . .

Squid seemed to understand that Petrel didn't want to talk anymore. The young woman touched Fin's forehead and said, "I think the fever's just about gone. He'll be good in a day or so. Then we'll find out the truth." And with that, she left.

Petrel locked the door, climbed into the second hammock and curled in a ball. She fell asleep almost immediately. No one disturbed her, but she woke herself once, whispering, "Half Braid, half Grease."

The idea shocked her all over again. It was impossible, it was wrong, it was—

It was better than being nothing.

When she woke the second time, she felt warm inside as well as out. It was such an odd sensation that at first she couldn't work out what it was. When she did, she wanted to laugh at herself for being such a fool. But something stopped her. The memory of Squid's kindness, perhaps. Or Krill's gruff concern. Or the slowly dawning realization that they *weren't* going to betray her.

Petrel rolled over in her hammock so she was facing Fin. "You know what?" she whispered, though she knew he couldn't hear her. "I *do* belong. I belong to the ship more than anyone! Mister Smoke and Missus Slink don't care about tribes, and neither did Mam and Da. They loved each other, and they loved me. Folk say they disgraced the ship, but where's the disgrace in feeding your own daughter?"

The warm feeling grew. "That's me, Fin," she said. "Quill's daughter. Seal's daughter too. Mam and Da. They loved me."

And with those astonishing words, she closed her eyes and went back to sleep.

CHAPTER 15

SOME MAY CALL US CRUEL

THE SHIP WAS IN A PURPOSEFUL MOOD. It was there in everyone Dolph met—the same furious intensity, the same sense of comradeship and anger. Officers she had barely spoken to in the past gripped her hand and said, "We'll find him, never fear. He'll regret the day he murdered your mam!"

This feeling went from bow to stern, and from the heights of the wind turbines to the depths of the bilge. The first time Dolph stepped off the Commons ladderway into Grease Alley, she was anticipating trouble. But the border guards merely nodded and let her pass. Behind her back, they murmured, "How dare he? How dare the stranger attack *us*?"

Dolph had never in her life expected to walk through Grease Alley without having to fight every inch of the way. But today no one tried to stop her, not even Skua. They thought she was searching for the stranger, and so she was. But she was searching for someone else too.

Because Dolph had been thinking. How could a stranger

have found his way right into the middle of Braid, and killed Orca, who was the cleverest person her daughter had ever known, and one of the wariest? It didn't make sense.

Now if the *stranger* was the one who had died, Dolph could've understood it. But the other way around?

Impossible.

Which meant the boy must've had help. Someone to show him the trip-ups and traps in both Grease Alley and Braid. Someone to guide him from the bottom of the ship to the top. Someone to ease him into Orca's cabin as slick and sly as a rat.

And who was the slickest, slyest rat Dolph knew? Who was the only person on the ship to know her way around Braid as well as she knew it around Dufftown and Grease Alley?

The Nothing girl.

"If I find her, I'll find the stranger," Dolph whispered, and she fingered the knife in her pocket.

She knew the sort of places that the Nothing girl made her nests—Dolph had chased her out of them often enough. And so, while the Engineers tore open lockers and poked behind the digester, Dolph climbed into darker corners, looking for scraps of cloth and whispering through her teeth, "I'm going to find you, Nothing Girl. Going to *find you.*"

But for all her efforts, there was no sign of either the girl or the stranger. And so, after three days, Dolph turned her attention to Dufftown.

WHEN THE BOY WOKE AT LAST, STRIPPED OF BOTH FEVER AND nightmares, he was dreadfully weak. All he wanted to do was lie still in his rope cot. But weakness was dangerous for an Initiate of the Circle. If the other Initiates knew that one of their members was weak, they would beat him, to prove their own strength.

It was harsh but fair. As Brother Thrawn said, "Weakness does not win wars. And never doubt it, my friends, we are at war for the soul of humanity."

The boy tried to sit up, but his limbs felt as if they belonged to someone else. He fell back with a cry of helplessness—and beside him, in a second cot, someone stirred.

It was Petrel. She tumbled to her feet, peering at him and rubbing her eyes. "You awake?" she asked. "Got your wits back, or are you still rambling?"

Without waiting for an answer she touched his forehead with a cool hand. "Fever's gone. That's good. 'Twasn't your arm, in case you're interested. 'Twas boat fever, that's all, only you had a whopping great dose of it, worst I ever saw."

As she spoke, she held a cup to the boy's lips, and wiped his mouth when he had finished drinking. "You hungry?" she said. "Dufftown's bursting with food, so ask away if you want something." She laughed. "There's fish, fish or fish."

The boy stared at her. There was something different about her, something he couldn't put his finger on. "What are you—?" It hurt him to talk, but he tried again. "What are you doing?"

"Looking after you, that's what. You warm enough?"

The boy shook his head, then nodded, confused by her words. In all his years in the Citadel, no one had ever looked after him.

"Kindness is a mistake," Brother Thrawn had said in one of his regular sermons, "and you will find none of it here. Should we smile at those who commit crimes against society? Should we pat them on the shoulder and send them on their way to commit *more* crimes? Should we *soothe* them, and *tolerate* their foolishness?"

He made *soothing* and *tolerating* sound so dreadful that the boy joined with his fellow Initiates in roaring, "No! No!"

"No, indeed," said Brother Thrawn. "Some may call us cruel—"

Which was true, the boy knew it. He had been called cruel on several occasions.

"—but we know the truth. We are like surgeons, cutting away the rotten flesh so the body can grow healthy. And if the rotten flesh complains, do we listen?"

"No!"

Those enthusiastic voices seemed oddly distant now. The boy knew he should despise Petrel for her kindness, but he could not. His fever seemed to have burned something out of him, though he was not yet sure what it was . . .

He wondered how long he had been lying there. Half a day, perhaps?

"How long was I sick?" he asked.

"Three days."

For all his weakness, shock brought the boy to a sitting position. "Three *days*?"

"Told you it was a bad case," said Petrel, with considerable satisfaction. "Mostly boat fever comes and goes so quick you

152

barely know you've got it except for the rash. But it clung to you like a limpet shell."

The boy hardly heard her. He had wasted *three days*! While Brother Thrawn and his Devouts trailed after the *Oyster* in their wooden sailing ship, risking their lives to make the world a better place, the boy had wasted *three whole days*!

He groaned aloud, and Petrel said, "You feeling bad still? You should lie down—"

A knock on the door interrupted her. Petrel unlocked it, then stood in front of the boy protectively. "He's awake," she said, "but only just. And he's not feeling too perky, so don't you go bothering him."

"You're as bad as my daughter," said a deep voice, and an enormous hand picked Petrel up and moved her to one side.

The same hand pressed the boy back in his hammock, and he could not resist it. He saw a massive chest, and a beard with bones plaited in it, and fierce, intelligent eyes above the beard.

"That's Head Cook Krill," called Petrel from somewhere behind the man. "Don't worry, he's not as mean as he looks."

"Oh, but I am," rumbled Krill, "if the circumstances require it." He leaned over the boy, scowling. "You've got questions to answer, lad. Quite a few of 'em."

"Not now!" said Petrel, squeezing around the side of him. "Look at him, Krill, he can't even sit up properly. And he hasn't had anything to eat for three days."

Three days, thought the boy savagely. *I am a fool! I am not worthy of the trust they placed in me!*

"But is he going to answer my questions," said Krill, "even when he's fed?"

"Course he is," said Petrel, nodding furiously at the boy.

"Let's try him out then," said Krill. At Petrel's instant protest, he raised his hand. "I just want to hear his voice, that's all, make sure he knows how to say aye or nay. 'Cos from what I heard, all he'd give Albie was *I don't remember.* And that's no good to any of us."

He turned back to the boy. "Think of this as a test question, lad. What's your name?"

"It's Fin," said Petrel.

"You be quiet," said Krill. "He's not a baby, to be carried around all day. Let him answer for himself."

The boy set his jaw. There must be no more mistakes. No more delays. *I promised myself that I would not take a name. But that was only my pride! We are saving humanity from its own foolishness. Set against that, my pride is unimportant.*

With an effort, he dragged himself back up to a sitting position.

"Well?" said Krill, steadying the cot with one hand.

The boy took a deep breath—and nodded. "That is my name," he said, and the world around him seemed to tremble with shock. "Fin. I am Fin."

THE DUFFTOWN BORDER GUARDS WERE JUST AS SYMPATHETIC as those in Grease Alley, but less willing to let Dolph pass.

"Krill heard you were poking round," they told her. "He sends his sympathies, but he's with Crab on this one. 'Let's keep things tidy,' he says. 'Braid should stick to Braid. Our folk can search Dufftown better than anyone else.'"

Dolph nodded slowly. "Maybe he's right," she said. "Let me know if they find the stranger."

But as she climbed back up to Braid, her mind was a whirl of suspicion. When had Krill ever concerned himself with tidiness? Dolph had seen his apron so thick with soup she could've lived off it for a month.

Under her breath, she whispered, "Things have changed on the *Oyster*, Mam, but not that much."

And she headed for the other Commons ladderway, closer to the ship's bow.

Dolph was not a girl who showed her emotions easily, nor had she ever used tears to get what she wanted. Now, however, she set out to do both. She scrubbed at her eyes until they were red and puffy, and ruffled her usually neat hair. She wished she could squeeze out a few real tears, but she was too angry. This would have to do.

The border guards on the for'ard ladderway were embarrassed about stopping her. "If it was anyone but Krill who'd given the order we'd let you through," said one of them. "Everything's turned upside down as it is—one more rule broken isn't going to make a difference."

"I-I just want Mam's killer found," sobbed Dolph.

"Course you do," said the same guard. "It's only natural. No sign of him in Braid, then?"

Dolph shook her head. "Nor in Grease Alley, though Albie's got nearly everyone on the hunt. I expect Krill's the same."

The guards looked at each other. "Mm," said the second one noncommittally.

Dolph pretended not to notice. She choked out another sob and said, "I expect Krill's tearing Dufftown apart. I know he and Mam didn't get on, but when it comes to the safety of the ship, you can always count on the Head Cook."

"You can," said the first guard. He stared at his knuckles. "Mind you, he's not perfect."

"Now then, Cod," said the second guard in warning tones.

"Well, he's not, is he?" said Cod. "That wasn't a proper search, not so far as I could tell."

"Krill said—"

"I know what Krill said. He doesn't think the stranger murdered Orca."

Dolph stared at the guard, forgetting for the moment to look tearful.

"He *says* he's not even sure there *is* a stranger," continued Cod. "Thinks maybe it's some trick of Albie's. But he's wrong—"

The second guard tried to interrupt, but Cod plowed on. "—and he knows he's wrong too. Him and Squid, I've seen 'em whispering in corners—"

"You shut your mouth," snapped the second guard. "What are you thinking, spilling Dufftown business to anyone who passes?"

"She's not just anyone," protested Cod. "She's Orca's kin. She's got a right—"

"She's Braid. The ship may be turned upside down, but she's still Braid." The second guard nodded apologetically at Dolph.

"Sorry, lass, but that's the way things are. You'd best get back to your own decks. I'm sure someone'll find the stranger soon, and you'll have your revenge."

Dolph sobbed out her thanks, then scrambled back up the Commons ladderway. She felt breathless, but sharp too, like a knife blade that had been stropped against stone until its edge was thin and deadly.

"They've got him, Mam," she whispered as she hurried towards the bridge. "Krill and Squid've got him, and they're keeping it a secret! I bet they've got the Nothing girl too. But they're going to get a very nasty surprise if they think they can keep those murderers safe from *me*!"

CHAPTER 16

HALF A TRUTH

By midday, the boy had eaten a meal of fish and was strong enough to stand on his own, though his legs were still shaky. Whenever Petrel or Squid called him Fin, he answered them without protest.

But the name unsettled him. It felt dangerous. It felt like a fine thread connecting him to Petrel, and he had to fight the desire to constantly watch her in case she wove him into something he did not want to be a part of.

He had to fight his memories too, shaken loose by the fever and still lurking in the dark corners of his mind. His memories of a thin-faced woman . . .

The mission, he told himself grimly. *Nothing matters but the mission.*

He looked up at Krill, who was looming over him, hands on hips. "I will answer your questions now," he said.

Krill nodded. "Good. So what's all this about a demon?"

Fin's mouth almost fell open with shock. It was only the years of discipline that kept his face blank. "A demon?" he said mildly, though his heart was beating apace. "What do you mean?"

"Don't try and twist things round, lad. You're the one who started this, while you were feverish. 'Must not warn the demon'—that's what you said. 'It'll blow us out of the water if it suspects.' And a bit later you said something about the ship." The Head Cook puffed out his cheeks until the bones in his beard rattled. "Now I'm just a simple man—"

Behind him, his daughter rolled her eyes. Petrel frowned and fidgeted.

"—but I can smell bad fish quicker'n anyone. And *this* fish stinks." Krill lowered his head, like a bull about to charge. "So I ask you again, Fin lad. What's this about a demon?"

Fin swallowed. This was a question that Brother Thrawn had *not* anticipated! He could refuse to say anything, of course, but if he did he would probably be locked up again, and the mission would fail.

The mission . . .

It struck the boy suddenly that if the mission succeeded, Petrel would die at the hands of the Devouts, along with the rest of the crew. Petrel, who had looked after him when he was ill. Who had been kind to him—

He dragged his mind back to Krill's question. "There was a—a ship," he began, wondering what he was going to say next. Perhaps he could tell them a half-truth, something that would make them sympathize with him.

"It brought me south to the ice," he said. "The men on board were cruel; they forced me to come with them and—and—"

He jumped as the pipes behind him began to clang. But his shock was nothing compared with that of the other three.

"*What?*" roared Krill, his face crimson above the beard. "They wouldn't *dare!*" And he charged out of the cabin, with Squid hurrying after him saying, "They must've found out, Da."

As the door slammed behind them, Fin turned to Petrel. "What is it?"

"Attack on Dufftown, that's what," said Petrel, her eyes wide. "*Double* attack, from above and below, which is a nasty thing. Albie and Crab have found out you're here, I reckon, and they want to punish Krill and catch you at the same time."

Fin felt sick. "They will kill me!"

"Don't worry, Krill won't hand you over without a fight," said Petrel. "And him and his Cooks are a powerful force once you get 'em away from the burners."

Nevertheless, she looked anxious.

The pipes rattled again. "Is that another message?" asked Fin. "What are they saying now?"

"Krill's calling the Dufftown fishing shift back. That's serious, that is. Fishing shift usually stays out of the fighting."

Fin thought he could hear a dull roar in the distance, as if scores of people were shouting all at once. He stood up and began to pace from one end of the cabin to the other. "What if Krill loses?"

"Why then," said Petrel, "I reckon you're a goner. And me too if they catch me here."

"Then— Then you should go." The words were out of Fin's mouth before he could stop them.

"No." Petrel gave him a lopsided grin. "Rather stay here where it's comfy."

Fin paced up and down, clenching and unclenching his fists. The dull roar grew louder. Neither of the children spoke again, but they glanced at each other often, then looked away. Fin wished desperately that the whole mission was over and done with, and that he was back in the Citadel, where life was simple, and unsettling thoughts did not plague him.

The door flew open and Squid tumbled into the cabin, her face white. "Dufftown's in trouble," she panted. "Da wants us to get Fin away and hide him till Albie and Crab come to their senses. Might be a few days, he reckons. He's trying to barricade the galley, but he's not sure it'll hold. He says most of the attack came from the for'ard ladderway, so we should go aft."

She caught her breath. "Though they might be there too, for all I know, and if they see Fin, he's lost."

Petrel threw open the chest that sat against the wall and dragged out an outdoor jacket and trousers. "Put these back on," she said to Fin. "You'll pass for Grease as long as no one looks too close."

Fin took the clothes and began to pull them on. Petrel said, "You're the other one they'll go for, Squid. If they can grab you they'll have a powerful hold over your da."

Squid nodded. "True enough. I'll hang back, so I don't endanger you two."

"No." Petrel shook her head. "I reckon we should stick together."

"We should go to Grease Alley," said Fin quickly.

Petrel agreed with him. "Good hiding places down there, and Albie's too busy chasing Krill to think about his own territory."

She dug into the chest again and handed Fin the iron device he had found.

"If we end up anywhere near the fighting," she said, "Squid and I'll start to run, and you chase us, waving that spanner as if you want to whack us with it." Her forehead creased. "Can you run, do you reckon, without falling over?"

"I will try," said Fin, relieved to be moving at last, and in the right direction. He hefted the spanner in his fist, wondering whether he might be able to use it to force the hatch where the demon was hidden . . .

"You ready?" asked Petrel.

Squid nodded. So did Fin. Petrel opened the cabin door and peeped out. "All clear," she whispered. "Put your hood up, Fin." And she climbed over the sill.

THE FIGHTING WAS CLOSER THAN PETREL HAD REALIZED. She could hear the furious shouts and the clash of pipe wrenches and knives as Albie and his crew advanced through Dufftown.

"This way," she hissed at Fin, and dragged him in the opposite direction, with Squid hurrying behind them.

Krill's cabin was not far from the old growing vats. Petrel avoided looking at them as they passed—she had promised to keep the tunnels secret, and would not go back on that promise, no matter what.

By the time they had passed the vats, the sounds of fighting had grown fainter. But Petrel didn't trust her ears, not where Albie was concerned. She checked every corner before they rounded it, and kept her eyes peeled for Engineer-shaped wrongness. It'd be just like Albie to send two or three fighters up the aft ladderway, to lie in wait for unexpected prizes. Orca would've done the same if she was still alive, but Petrel wasn't so worried about Crab.

Which was maybe why she didn't see Dolph until it was too late.

CHAPTER 17

A PATCH OF WHITE

THERE WAS NO WARNING. One moment Petrel was leading the way past a cabin; the next, Fin yelped behind her, and she spun around to see Dolph holding the tip of her knife to the boy's neck.

"Lucky me, I've caught a Grease boy," hissed Dolph. "Wonder why he's keeping company with rat and Duff, instead of fighting like he should be?"

Petrel's heart shrank within her. "Dolph," she whispered.

"Ooh, *clever* rat. It can talk—"

Squid broke in. "Leave her alone, Dolph. Leave the Engineer alone too. He's not important. It's— It's me you want."

"Is it?" said Dolph, her knife not moving from Fin's neck. "I spose Crab'd be pleased to see you. Albie, too. But maybe I've got other plans. Maybe I'm curious about this Grease boy."

Petrel's mind was awhirl, her fear of the older girl all mixed up with the brand-new knowledge that they were cousins. That Dolph's mam and Petrel's da had been sister and brother.

And that one had killed the other.

But that didn't matter, she told herself, not right now. What mattered was Fin.

"He's Squid's secret feller," she said quickly. "They're love-smitten, they are, which is just plain stupid in my opinion, 'cos Krill and Albie'll have a fit if they find out, and—" She broke off as the tip of the knife flicked Fin's hood back, exposing his face.

"Then again," said Dolph, as if Petrel's words had been nothing but rat squeaks, "maybe he's *not* Grease. Maybe he's something a *lot* more interesting. Like a murderer."

Fin's eyes flickered from side to side. The knife pressed harder against his throat.

"He didn't do it, Dolph," said Squid. "Fin didn't kill your mam."

"Course he didn't," said Dolph. "Not on his own, anyway. He had help, didn't he, from a certain rat girl."

"What?" said Petrel, astonished at the accusation. "What are you talking about? I didn't go near your mam. You think I'm stupid? If she'd caught me anywhere near her cabin she'd have whacked me on the head and thrown me to the Maw."

"Squeak squeak squeak," spat Dolph. "You've got more words than I ever thought, Nothing Girl."

"I'm not nothing," said Petrel, stung. "I'm Braid *and* Grease, which is more than anyone else on this ship—"

"Shame!" hissed Dolph. "A walking shame, that's what you are. Maybe when Mam saw you, she stopped her hand out of disgust. Or maybe you tricked her, caught her eye in one direction while the murderer crept up in the other. It doesn't matter how you killed her—"

It was then that Fin spoke up for the first time. His eyes were white around the edges, but his voice was steady. "We did not kill your mother. It was not Petrel and it was not me. You should let me go. I have done nothing to harm you."

She won't believe him, thought Petrel. *She won't believe me either. She's all astew with anger and hatred, and she's got us fixed in her mind as the cause of it.*

Petrel was right. Dolph glared at the boy. "I reckon Albie's sorry now that he picked you up, murderer. Look what you've done to the *Oyster*! Killed the best First Officer there ever was. I reckon he'll cheer when he sees me throw you two overboard."

Something twisted in Petrel's belly. *Blizzards,* she thought, *it's not just the tar bucket, not this time!*

She wasn't worried for herself, not yet. As long as it was just Dolph guarding them, Petrel could get away whenever she wanted to, and so could Squid. But escape would be a lot harder if Dolph handed them over to Crab and Albie . . .

"You think Albie's gunna let *you* chuck us overboard?" she said. "Not a chance. He'll want to do it himself."

"No, he won't," said Dolph, through gritted teeth. "It was my mam you murdered, so I get to kill you."

Petrel rolled her eyes at Squid and Fin, hoping they'd understand. "Not if you hand us over you won't. You won't count for anything once Albie gets his hands on us."

Squid nodded. "And Crab'll want to make a show of it now

166

he's First Officer. He and Albie'll be fighting over who gets to do the deed."

"They won't!" said Dolph. "They'll see I've got first rights."

"I would not count on it," said Fin, his wits nimble in spite of the blade at his throat. "Chief Engineer Albie seems to be a man of very strong will."

Dolph glared at the three of them. "You think you're so clever," she hissed, "but I know what you're doing. All the same, maybe you're right about Crab and Albie. Maybe they *would* take over, and that's not what I want, and not what Mam would've wanted either. So we're going up to the afterdeck, just the four of us. And if either of you two"—she jerked her chin at Petrel and Squid—"try to run away, or do anything I don't like, the murderer here will have a very nasty accident."

"He's *not* a murderer—"

"Shut up, Nothing Girl! I don't want to hear another word out of your nasty little mouth!"

Petrel fell silent, and the small procession set off, with Squid leading the way. The Dufftown border was unguarded for once, and the lights that usually illuminated the Commons ladder-way were shattered, as if the fighting had come this way and then retreated. The small group climbed upwards, with Dolph holding her knife against Fin's throat to remind them to be-have.

Fear for the boy coiled and uncoiled in Petrel's belly. But there was something else there too, something that made her skin flush and her hands clench into fists.

She had been called Nothing Girl all her life, and had

accepted it as the truth. The whole of the crew thought of her as Nothing Girl. If Dolph *did* somehow manage to throw her overboard today, no one would care. Likely no one would even notice!

And that wasn't right. Because she *wasn't* nothing. She was Braid and Grease; she was Seal's daughter, and Quill's.

She wondered what her parents would say, if they could see her now. She wanted them to be proud of her, the way Krill was proud of Squid.

She raised her chin. *I'm not going to let Fin die without a fight, Mam. I bet you and Da fought for your lives. Orca killed you all the same, but I'm not gunna let her daughter kill Fin. Not if I can help it!*

And she set herself to thinking about the afterdeck.

They had nearly reached their destination when the pipes started rattling. At first Petrel thought it was messages, but if it was, they were all jumbled up and mixed together, one on top of the other as if everyone was yelling at once.

"What are they saying?" Fin called from behind Petrel.

Squid, still leading the way, shouted over the noise, "Nothing sensible."

"Shut up," cried Dolph.

"Reckon they're just banging away for the sake of it," shouted Petrel.

"I said, shut up!"

The hatch, when they came to it, had ice around its edges. "You're gunna be cold out there, Dolph, without your jacket," Petrel said, raising her voice over the clanging of the pipes.

"Maybe you should swap with Fin. He won't need his, not inside the Maw. I'm sure he'll stand nice and quiet while you change."

Dolph sneered at her. "You worry about yourself, Nothing Girl, not about me. Open the hatch."

Petrel shrugged and threw her weight against the clamp. The hatch opened with a grinding sound and the cold swooped in and seized hold of them.

"Quick," said Dolph. Like Petrel and Squid, she was already shivering. "G-get out there."

Squid stepped outside, and Petrel followed. At the urging of the knife, Fin too stepped over the sill, with Dolph beside him.

The deck was coated with a thin layer of ice, and Petrel trod carefully. *Wonder if the Maw knows we're coming. Wonder if it thinks it's gunna get a feed.*

The day was so clear that she could see for miles. There was pack ice everywhere, huge flat slabs of it that the *Oyster* swept aside with ease. An albatross hung on the air, its wingspan twice as wide as Petrel's height, and the wind fiddles sang in time with its swooping and rising. In the distance a cloud of seabirds was gathering. The beauty of it all snatched at Petrel's heart and made her more determined than ever that neither she nor Fin would die today.

"Where's the f-fishing shift?" said Dolph.

"They're all fighting," said Squid. "*Everyone's* f-fighting."

Petrel wrapped her arms around herself, trying to stop the shivering. "All b-because of Fin—at least that's where it started, but I reckon they've p-prob'ly forgotten about him by now, and they're just h-hacking away for the sake of it."

She peeked at Dolph, and said, "And you know what? They *shouldn't* forget about him. 'Cos he knows s-something important. Something about d-demons, and about strange ships. Something that's gunna affect the whole c-crew. And if you throw us over the side, you won't know what it is."

Squid blew on her fists and said, "Until maybe it's t-too late to fix it."

Dolph jabbed her knife at the boy's neck. "M-move. It's c-cold out here and I want to get back inside."

"Fin," said Petrel. "T-tell her. Tell her about the ship that brought you."

Fin nodded cautiously, wary of the knife. "It is out there now, following us. The men on board—they wish to kill everyone—"

"Why?" interrupted Dolph. "This ship, which I d-don't believe in. Why would they want to k-kill us all?"

"'Cos of the d-demon," said Petrel quickly. "That's why Fin killed your mam, Dolph. 'Cos she was a demon!"

"What?" cried Dolph.

"What?" said Squid.

"No!" said Fin, looking around wildly. "I did not!"

And in that moment of uncertainty, Petrel snatched the boy away from Dolph's knife and dived for the deck.

The icy surface helped—they skidded away from Dolph as quick as seals. Squid was already on the move, and the three of them were twenty paces away before Dolph knew what was happening.

Petrel couldn't help herself. She climbed to her feet and shouted, as she had longed to shout so many times before, "Ha! You're stupid, Dolph! Fancy falling for a little trick like that! A baby could get away from you!" And she waggled her tongue in triumph.

Dolph's eyes were black with rage. She advanced on them, knife in hand, and they quickly backed away.

" 'Twasn't true what Petrel said," shouted Squid. "Fin didn't kill your mam. Neither did she."

"I would've," cried Petrel, still triumphant, still furious. "I should've, 'cos she killed *my* mam. And my da."

Squid hushed her and shouted, "She wasn't lying about the strange ship though. It's out there somewhere."

Dolph wouldn't listen. She followed them the length of the deck, and all Squid's protests did not move her. She couldn't get close enough to hurt them, but neither could they escape her for long enough to get back inside the ship.

All of them except Fin were far too cold for safety. Petrel's fingers and nose were numb, and she was beginning to regret taunting her old enemy. "We're all gunna d-die if you don't let us back inside," she shouted. "You and Squid too."

"Don't c-care," replied Dolph, and she advanced on them again, her knife turning wickedly in her fingers.

"Come on, Dolph," cried Squid, through chattering teeth. "This is m-madness."

"Don't c-care."

Petrel stamped her feet and jumped up and down, trying to summon some warmth. But the icy air was creeping into her lungs and into her flesh and bones, and she knew that time was running out.

"Fin won't die," she shouted. "Him and m-me are the ones you really want, but he's as warm as p-penguin stew in those clothes. You should've changed with him when I told you. Soon as your hands get too c-cold to hold a knife, he's going to run inside and you'll be f-frozen on the spot."

It was not entirely true that Fin was warm. Frost was forming on his eyebrows, and without gloves, his fingers were as cold as Petrel's. But the rest of it was true, and Dolph knew it.

With a furious cry she rushed at them, skidding on the ice but staying upright. Petrel and Squid backed away, dragging Fin between them. He wasn't used to the ice, not like they were, and he slipped and spun and stumbled, so that they barely avoided the knife.

Dolph sobbed with rage, and yelled, "Make him t-take the jacket off. Make him!" But she could not reach them.

It was then that Squid shouted in a cracked voice, "Look! W-what's that?" And she pointed nor'east, where the cloud of seabirds had risen above the water.

Petrel assumed it was another trick, but she looked all the same, and saw a patch of white. She blinked. It was some distance away, but it was clearly far too neat and square to be a berg.

And if it wasn't a berg, there was only one other thing it could be.

CHAPTER 18

FIN'S SHIP

"IT'S FIN'S SHIP," CRIED PETREL, HER BREATH HANGING ON the air in a dense fog. "Look, Fin, it's your ship. See, Dolph? There's folk out there who want to d-do us harm."

Dolph scowled. "It's a b-berg." But she was clearly shaken.

"There's n-never been a berg so sharp-edged and neat," said Petrel. "That's a ship. Ain't it a ship, Fin?"

Fin stared nor'east for a long moment, his face blank. "No," he said at last. "Dolph is right. It is an iceberg."

Petrel grabbed his arm. "What's the m-matter with you? It *must* be your ship. All full of c-cruel men, you said."

But Fin pulled away from her, with that old distance in his eyes that made Petrel feel so small and ugly.

"It *is* a ship, I swear it," said Squid. "We've got to t-tell Crab. Truce, Dolph, I cry Truce. This is more important than your p-private vengeance."

The cry of Truce was a powerful one on the *Oyster*. Dolph

peered unwillingly at the square of white again, then at Fin, as if trying to see inside his head. "*He* should know if it's a ship."

"He does," said Petrel. "He's l-lying."

"Why?"

Petrel tried to shrug, but she was too cold. "Don't know. Maybe he's scared."

A flush appeared on Fin's cheek, but he did not speak.

"Dolph," said Squid, "we must tell folk. If your mam was alive—"

Dolph's eyes narrowed, but she did not move towards them. Petrel felt that tickle of memory again—something she had seen . . .

But her mind was full of the strange ship, and the memory slipped away before she could grab hold of it.

"—if your m-mam was alive," said Squid, "she'd want to know about this. She was a h-hard woman and I can't say I l-liked her, but her first thought was always for the ship."

"Crab won't know what to do," mumbled Dolph. "He's not g-got half Mam's brains."

"Put him together with Albie and Krill and they'll f-figure something out," said Petrel.

Dolph glared at her. "Still going to k-kill you. Soon as this business is finished. You and him." She pointed the tip of her knife at Fin. "Now g-get inside."

Petrel was so cold by then that she could hardly walk. Dolph and Squid were in the same condition, and they ended up, in spite of everything, holding each other upright, while Fin stumbled along beside them.

But Dolph did not let go of her knife, and as soon as they were inside the ship, and the hatch closed, she held the blade to Petrel's neck and said, "Should've grabbed you in the first place, shouldn't I? Well, I've learned my lesson. You won't get away from me this time."

Petrel hardly cared, it was such a relief to be back in the warmth. Besides, the other ship scared her far more than Dolph did. She rubbed her hands together and said, "Bet they haven't got heating like ours. Bet those cruel men are all huddled together like penguins, trying not to perish of the cold, eh, Fin?"

Fin didn't answer.

"I wish the pipes'd shut up," said Squid, and Petrel grimaced agreement, though the lack of lights meant no one could see her. The fastest way to warn folk about the other ship would be to send a rattle. But the meaningless banging continued, and any message would be drowned out before it started.

"We have to find Crab," said Squid. "Where was he, Dolph, last time you saw him?"

"Not sure we should start with Crab," said Petrel. "Despite him being First Officer." The knife at her neck twitched. It might be a Truce, but it was a fragile one, and she quickly added, "Me, I still think of him as Second. He's not a First sort of person, not like Orca."

Dolph relaxed a little at that. But her rage was still there, stored up for later, so hard and painful that Petrel almost felt sorry for her.

"Well then, maybe we should try and get to Da," said Squid. "And *he* can talk to Crab—"

Dolph snorted. "Crab's not going to listen to Krill, not in the middle of battle. He's trying to prove himself, and he won't stop for anything."

"Albie then," said Petrel, and after a moment's thought all except Fin murmured agreement.

Petrel wished she could see the boy's face. She had thought he was growing more human, but the sight of the strange ship had made him shrink back inside himself, as cold and emotionless as the ice itself. She hated to think what the cruel men must be like, to do that to him.

As they descended towards Dufftown, the sounds of fighting rose up to meet them—the howls of rage, the clangor of the pipes, the clash of weapons in and out of the passages. Petrel had no idea how they were going to find Albie. A madness had overtaken the tribes of the *Oyster,* just when they needed to be clear-headed and strong.

They'll keep fighting forever, she thought. *And that ship'll creep up on us bit by bit, and the cruel men will kill us all.*

But even as she thought it, the noise stopped.

Petrel peered downwards, but it was too dark to see anything.

"Squid?" she whispered. "What's happening?"

"Don't know," came the reply from below. "Maybe—"

Her voice was drowned out by the renewed clangor of the pipes. But this time it was no mad banging. Petrel's blood ran cold as she heard the message the pipes carried. It was a warning, an alarm that everyone on the ship, from youngest to oldest, knew and dreaded.

"Fire! Fire on board! Fire!"

CHAPTER 19

FIRE ON BOARD!

Fin was shocked at the speed with which everything changed. From the moment he had arrived on the ship, all he had seen between the *Oyster*'s tribes was hostility.

But now, as the alarm rang on and on, the girls above and below him slipped into what was clearly a well-practiced discipline. Dolph shouted, "Fire stations! I'm for the aft hoses," and squeezed past Fin, as quick as a cat.

"I'm for the pumps," cried Squid, as she jumped off the bottom of the ladderway.

The alarm stopped. A whiff of smoke drifted towards Fin, and he said, into the darkness, "Are you going with them?"

"Nope," said Petrel. "Haven't got a place on the fire crews. They don't count me, they never have."

There was silence, as if she was thinking. Then she climbed down until her feet were a couple of steps above Fin's, and their faces were on a level. "Thing is," she said, her voice soft and close, "that ship of yours is still out there."

Fin tried to reply, but the words caught in his throat. The coldness of the afterdeck had been nothing compared to the coldness he had felt when he saw the sail of the *Retribution*. It had crawled inside him, so that he felt as if he were back in the Citadel, and every part of him frozen.

He did not understand where this feeling had come from. The Citadel was a place of coolness and discipline, that was all. He had not felt frozen when he lived there. Surely. Not like this.

I LOVE my life with the Circle, he told himself. *I cannot wait to return to it and get away from this chaos!*

But the frozen feeling persisted, and it was so familiar and so unpleasant that he almost wanted to climb down the ladderway and throw himself at the fire, to be rid of it.

He forced himself to say, "I do not think they will approach. Not yet." He did not tell Petrel that the Devouts were afraid of the demon and its terrible powers, that they would not attack until they saw his signal, or until the ship was clearly in such distress that the demon must be dead.

"All the same," said Petrel, "we can't just forget about 'em. We *could* try to find Albie, but he wouldn't be able to do anything, not while there's a fire to be fought. Besides—"

She put her hand on Fin's shoulder. Even through the jacket it seemed to warm him, and it suddenly struck him that this scrawny, outcast girl was the very opposite of frozen. She was filled with life and warmth. She had cared for him when he was ill and had saved his life on the afterdeck. Maybe he could save *her* life when the Devouts came—

This is wrong, he told himself. *I should not have such thoughts.*

"Besides," said Petrel, her breath tickling his cheek, "there's someone better than Albie. *Much* better."

"Who?"

"The sleeping captain, of course!"

Every hair on the back of Fin's neck rose. She was talking about the demon! She *must* be!

"I don't know where he is," added Petrel. "Might be they've got him tucked away in Braid, in a cabin I've never found. But I don't reckon that's the case. I don't reckon *anyone* knows where he is. Which means he must be somewhere so secret that you can't stumble across him by accident. *I* reckon he's in the tunn—"

She broke off, as if she had said too much.

"The what?" asked Fin mildly, though his heart was pounding.

"Can't tell you. You'll have to stay here."

"I would rather come with you."

"Nope. It's a secret where I'm going, and I promised I wouldn't show anyone."

"To whom did you make this promise?"

"Can't tell you that either. But they're my friends."

She means the imps, realized Fin, and he hardened himself against her. "What can the sleeping captain do?" he asked, though he already knew. *It can kill with a glance. It can destroy whole cities. It can boil the blood in a man's veins . . .*

"Don't know," said Petrel. "Folk reckon he'll wake up when the ship's in great danger. This is great danger, ain't it, with a fire, and cruel men on the horizon?"

Greater than she knows, thought Fin.

"But how'll the sleeping captain know about it unless someone tells him?" Petrel's voice sank to a reverent murmur. "Imagine, Fin! I'll whisper in his ear, and he'll wake up and come storming out and fix everything! Your cruel men won't know what hit 'em!"

Fin breathed in and out, trying to calm his agitated mind. His fingers flexed around the heavy spanner. This was his best chance yet. He knew where the demon was hidden, but he did not know how to get there, not from here. Not with the lights gone and the long dark passages filling with smoke. Not without getting hopelessly lost.

What he needed was a guide, someone who knew the ship from top to bottom. Someone who might be able to open that secret hatch . . .

"Are you sure you know where to find him?" he asked.

"No, but I don't see where else he could be."

Fin swallowed. "Do you know a hatch deep in the hold, with no handle? Somewhere near where you found me, when I was lost?"

"Near the propeller shaft? Aye, I know it. It's broken, that's all."

"What if it is not broken? What if there is no handle for a reason?"

Silence. Fin could almost hear Petrel's mind sorting through the possibilities. He found himself wondering how she would react when he smashed her precious sleeping captain to pieces in front of her eyes. *It must be done*, he reminded himself. *I am making the world a better place.*

At last Petrel said, "He might be there, I spose."

"We should go and see," said Fin. "We should go together and—"

A voice from below interrupted him. "Who's that?" A man climbed towards them, carrying a lantern. "Oh, it's you, Nothing Girl. Get down to the galley. Some fool knocked over a burner during the fighting and the fire's spreading. We need all hands, even yours. You understand me?" He raised his voice and pointed, with large gestures. "Down. To. The. Galley."

No! thought Fin, realizing that his plans were about to be frustrated yet again. *Not now!*

But he could not argue with the man, could not say a word for risk of being discovered. All he could do was silently urge Petrel to protest.

Which she did. She faced the man squarely and said, "I've got no place on the fire crews."

The man was taken aback to hear her speak, but he recovered quickly. "They'll make a place for you."

"But there's a ship nor'east of here, and it means us harm—"

The lantern swung towards Fin. "What're you doing here, Engineer? You should've gone to fire stations, soon as the alarm sounded."

"But a *ship*—" said Petrel.

"I won't tell you again. Get going, both of you."

And to Fin's dismay, the man pushed them off the ladderway

and through the hatch into Dufftown, dogging their heels so they could not turn back.

Fin did not want to fight the fire. He wanted to find the demon and kill it, and be done with this confusing mission. He wanted to be back in the Citadel, where everything was clear and he understood what was happening.

Beside him Petrel muttered, "They don't listen to me. Even when I *talk* they don't listen. But I'll show 'em! I'll show 'em I'm not nothing!"

As they hurried through the passages, the smoke became thicker, and the air hotter. Fin could hear something roaring, like a wild beast that had escaped from its cage. He and Petrel glanced at each other through the smoke. The roar grew louder. When Fin brushed against the wall he could feel the heat.

A doorway loomed in front of them. "In there!" shouted the man, giving them one final shove. "Get to work!"

And they stumbled into the galley.

For Fin, it was like falling back into his fever. Everywhere he looked, patched hoses squirmed and bucked. Crew members pushed past him, their grim faces streaked with soot. The noise of the fire and the water crashing against the deck made him dizzy.

"Here!" shouted Petrel, running to the hose that had fewest people on it, and grabbing its midsection.

Fin could not stand and do nothing. This was an age-old battle—humans against the elements—and there was only one side he could take. Almost before he knew it, he had grabbed hold of the hose directly in front of Petrel.

At first, it nearly threw him off his feet. Salt water poured through it in a torrent, and spurted out the nozzle. Fin could see it, four people ahead of him. He could see the flames too, leaping up the walls as if they were trying to climb to freedom, and taking no notice of the water that poured onto them.

"Move up," cried Petrel, and Fin realized that now there were only three people ahead of him, and the fourth was running past to take a new position at the other end of the hose.

He moved up. Closer to the nozzle. Closer to the fire. It was hotter there, and the hose was even harder to control. Its patches swelled with every surge of water, as if they might burst at any moment. Fin's eyes watered from the smoke and he dared not take his hands off the hose to rub them.

The third person broke away and hurried to the back of the line. Petrel nudged Fin, "Go on!" and he moved forward again. He understood what was happening now. The fire was so hot that whoever was holding the nozzle could only bear it for a few minutes. Soon it would be his turn. And then Petrel's.

The ancient hose swelled and groaned in his hands. His mouth was full of grit. His eyes were so sore that he had to screw them up to see properly.

The second person left. Now there was only one figure between Fin and the fire. He looked over his shoulder and saw Petrel, eyes narrowed, teeth bared, clinging to the hose with all her wiry strength.

When he caught her eye, she grinned unexpectedly. "Bit warmer than the afterdeck!" she shouted.

To his surprise, Fin found himself grinning in return. It

reassured him, having her right there behind him. She was like a shield at his back—a stubborn, brave, endlessly surprising shield.

And I am going to betray her . . .

The thought came out of nowhere, and he flinched away from it and tried to work out how long the man in front of him was staying at the front of the line, clutching the wildly bucking nozzle.

It was longer than Fin could believe. Even where *he* was, one place back, he felt as if he were about to burst into flame, and the hose was so hot he could barely hold it. The smoke and the noise filled his head. He kept waiting for the leader to give in and run to the back, but the man didn't . . . and didn't . . . and didn't . . .

And then he did.

"Your turn!" cried Petrel.

Fin stepped forward and grabbed the nozzle. It was almost impossible to hold, and he had to wrap his whole body around it and wrestle it into position, and keep it there while it tried to escape. Water spurted out of it, as hard as rock and as cold as death. The noise and the smoke deafened and blinded him.

But none of those things mattered compared with the flames.

He felt as if every part of him were blistering. The hose burned his fingers; the heat scorched his face. Sweat poured from him and dried on the instant.

He thought of the crew members who had taken their turns before him. He had been taught to despise these people, had been told that they were cowards. But they were not! They were as brave as any of the Devouts. Braver perhaps.

And I am going to betray them . . .

Behind him, Petrel yelled, "To the right a bit! See where it's trying to break out?"

Fin shifted the hose to the new threat and held it there as best he could. The heat pierced him from top to bottom. It gnawed at him until his eyes were blackened slits and he could no longer see properly. He remembered the ice, and wondered why it had seemed so terrible.

"That's enough, Fin! *Fin!*"

Something bumped against him from behind. He ignored it, no longer sure where he was or what he was doing. It was not until Petrel tore the nozzle out of his hands, crying, "That's enough! Didn't you hear me shouting? You'll sizzle up to nothing!" that he realized his turn was over at last.

In a daze, he staggered to the back of the line. A man clapped him on the shoulder and cried in his ear, "Well done, shipmate. We've broken its back, I reckon. Look!"

Fin dragged his eyes open and followed the man's pointing finger. The fire was changing. It no longer roared—now it whimpered as the flames sank lower and lower. Water poured onto them with a triumphant hiss. All around the galley, men and women raised brave, hopeful faces, and cried, "Steady! Steady, it's nearly done!"

For a second or two, despite his blisters and his exhaustion, Fin was happy. They had beaten the fire! He felt proud to have been part of it, proud that he and Petrel had helped save the ship—

Helped SAVE the ship?

With a jolt, he remembered who he was, and why he was here. The happiness drained out of him, and in its place came a muddled anger. These people were demon-worshippers—how could he have forgotten? He had sworn to destroy them! He *must* destroy them, to make the world a better place!

He turned away, so he would not have to see all those hopeful faces . . . and at that moment the lights went out. Half a breath later, the life-saving water stopped—and so did the engines.

It was only once the constant rumble ceased that Fin realized what a comforting sound it had been.

CHAPTER 20

ICEBOUND

PETREL KNEW WHAT HAD HAPPENED EVEN BEFORE THE PIPE messages began. "It's the lectrics," she whispered.

All around her, others were crying the same thing. "Fire's burned out the lectrics!"

Hand lanterns sprang to life. The useless hoses were thrown to the floor, and folk tore off their jackets and began to beat at the few remaining flames. Some raced to get hammocks and sealskins and anything else that might be used to douse the fire. Others ran to new stations, knowing exactly what they must do in such circumstances. Water sloshed around their feet.

Before long, the pipes were running hot with rattles to and from the bridge.

FIRE IN STORES UNDER CONTROL.

FIRE IN GALLEY NEARLY UNDER CONTROL.

SHIP DARK. ALL LANTERNS TO MUSTER POINTS.

MAN HAND PUMPS. GET THIS WATER OUT OF THE SHIP BEFORE WE FOUNDER.

THIS IS BRIDGE. NO STEERING. REPEAT, NO
STEERING. BERG LOOKOUTS TO FORE- AND AFTER-
DECKS. ENGINEERS, REPORT PLEASE.

That last message made Petrel pause. No steering? *No steering,* in waters like these?

All around her, folk glanced at each other, appalled, then went back to beating at the flames and listening keenly as the report came through from the Engineers.

MAIN LECTRIC DAMAGE MIDSHIPS STORES DECK.

STATUS?

SEVERE.

TIME FOR REPAIR?

A DAY AT LEAST.

As soon as the flames in the galley were entirely gone, and the site of the fire had been checked to make sure it would not spring up again, nearly everyone hurried off to different parts of the ship, with a lantern for each group.

Petrel found Fin leaning against a scorched stove, his face blackened and scowling.

"Fire's burned the lectrics," she said. "We're adrift."

The boy's expression didn't change.

"Reckon it won't be long before that ship of yours sees that something's wrong and starts sneaking up on us," said Petrel. "We'd best warn the berg lookouts. Come on."

She turned away, but Fin grabbed her arm. "Wait."

There was something odd in his voice. "What's the matter?" asked Petrel.

"We must go and find the sleeping captain."

"We will, but we gotta warn the lookouts first."

"Forget the lookouts. We must go straight to the hatch I told you about."

"Lookouts, then hatch," said Petrel. "It's only sensible."

"It is *not* sensible! You are wasting time!"

The last of the lanterns was gone, and Petrel could no longer see Fin's face. "You angry about something?" she asked, puzzled.

"No!"

"You are! What is it?"

"I—" Fin sounded as if he was struggling for words, and not finding them.

"What?"

"You would not understand," he mumbled at last. "You do not—*believe* in anything."

"Course I do!" said Petrel, stung. "I believe in the *Oyster*. I just fought for her, didn't I? So did you, for that matter."

"That is not enough," said Fin, through gritted teeth.

Petrel had no idea why he was so furious. But she would not let him bully her. "Well then," she said, "I believe in the sun, when it comes back after winter dark, 'cos it reminds me there's better times ahead. And I believe in my friends—the ones you don't know. In Squid and Krill too—"

"Friendship does not count," muttered Fin. "It is obedience that matters."

It sounded like nonsense to Petrel, and she snapped back at him. "Well, here's *your* chance to be obedient. I'm gunna warn the berg lookouts, and you can just be patient while I do it."

She marched off, and after a moment's hesitation, Fin followed, blundering along in the darkness until he caught up with her.

At first, they didn't speak. Fin's anger stood between them like a wall, all the way to Krill's cabin. There, Petrel took trousers and jacket from the sea chest and quickly put them on. Then she led the way to the aft Commons ladder.

The darkness did not affect her; she could have run blindfolded from one end of the ship to the other without faltering. But it was not long before Fin stumbled and slipped, and she had to grab him to stop him falling.

He mumbled "thank you" and said something about "the punishment hole." Petrel could tell from his voice that he hated the darkness.

She hated the silence. The sound of the *Oyster*'s engines was as vital to her as her own heartbeat, and without it she felt bereft, as if she had lost her mam and da all over again.

So instead of racing ahead, the way she might have done, she waited for Fin and they went up the ladderway side by side.

They were nearly at the outside hatch when he asked an odd question. "If someone gave you a task to do—"

The anger was still there in his voice, but it was no longer directed at Petrel. She thought maybe he was mad at himself for some reason. Or maybe at the cruel men.

"If someone gave you a task to do," he said, "that would make the world a better place—"

"You mean the ship?"

"What?"

"You said the world. Only world I know is the ship. And the ice, maybe, but I can't see any way of making that better."

"Very well, a task that would make the *ship* a better place. Would you—"

"What sort of task?"

"I do not know. Just— Just think of one."

"Like us going to wake the sleeping captain?"

"No! Well, perhaps. Would you do it, even if it was going to hurt someone? Who you quite—quite liked?"

Petrel, who was thinking, said nothing. They climbed higher.

"Would you?" said Fin, sounding as if he really wanted to know.

"You're the strangest boy I ever met," said Petrel.

"But *would* you?"

"I spose so," said Petrel. "I won't let anything stop me waking the sleeping captain, not anything or anyone. Gotta look after shipfolk, even if they don't look after me. Is that what you mean?"

Fin sighed and did not answer.

Before Petrel opened the hatch, they pulled on their gloves and ice masks. Then they stepped out onto the afterdeck.

Despite the cold, it was a relief to get out of the smoky ship. Petrel drew the freezing air into her lungs and squinted nor'east. The day was almost over, and the light was failing. She could see no sign of the other ship.

"They ain't after us yet," she whispered to Fin.

Men and women in outdoor clothes were scattered around

the *Oyster*'s rail, watching for the bergs that rose above the water, and for the more deadly ones that lurked below. They took no notice of the two bratlings until Petrel tapped an Officer woman on the arm.

"What is it?" said the woman, without taking her eyes off the water.

"There's a ship nor'east of us," said Petrel. "You can't see it right now, but it's there."

The woman turned and peered at her in astonishment. But then her face changed and she said to her neighbor, "It's the Nothing girl."

"What does she want?"

"How would I know? Some witless game she's playing."

"'Tisn't a game," said Petrel. "We saw a ship! It's coming after us, and—"

"Times like this, they should lock her up," said the woman, talking right over the top of Petrel as if she wasn't there. "Keep her out of the way." And she went back to her vigil.

Petrel turned to the woman's neighbor. But before she could utter a word, the neighbor said, "Times like *this*? What are you talking about? When was there ever a fire, before the stranger came on board? When did we ever lose steering?"

"Never," growled the first woman, still watching the sea. "The stranger was bad luck from the beginning. Orca said so—"

Petrel and Fin faded back toward the hatch. "You were right," whispered Petrel. "We should've gone straight to the sleeping captain. They're not gunna listen to anything *I* say."

As she opened the hatch, she heard the Officer woman

mutter, "At least the bergs won't be a problem for much longer. Look at that pack ice. We'll be icebound before we know it."

With the engines dead, it was already colder inside the ship. Petrel and Fin climbed back down the Commons ladderway with pipe messages rattling nonstop around them.

CREW KEEP TO INNER DECKS WHERE POSSIBLE, TO CONSERVE HEAT.

DAMAGE ON STORES DECK WORSE THAN FIRST THOUGHT. ESTIMATE SEVERAL DAYS' REPAIR TIME.

LOOKOUTS REPORTING. PACK ICE ALL AROUND SHIP.

Petrel wished she knew where Mister Smoke and Missus Slink were. Had they been hurt in the fire? Or were they secretly helping to mend the lectrics, scurrying back and forth with bits of wire, and joining them together with quick twists of their clever paws?

SHIP ICEBOUND. FOG CLOSING IN.

GET A MOVE ON, ALBIE.

DOING WHAT I CAN.

ABANDON BERG WATCH. PRIORITY OFFICER INSPECTION OF ALL DECKS, I REPEAT, ALL DECKS.

GET THOSE HAND PUMPS WORKING FASTER.

The crew members that Fin and Petrel passed were piling on their outdoor clothes and everything else they owned, until they were twice as wide as normal, and almost unrecognizable. Babies were being carried to the very middle of the ship, where they would be placed in a huddle, like penguins sheltering from a blizzard, with adults all around them for warmth.

Petrel knew it was no use stopping anyone, no use trying to warn them. No one had time or energy to listen to a Nothing girl, especially when she was talking about something as far-fetched, something as *ridiculous* as a strange ship.

"Sleeping captain's our only hope," she said to Fin. "Do you reckon *he'll* listen?"

Fin didn't answer. He seemed to have withdrawn into a world of his own—not the distant, superior world that Petrel hated, but a place of confusion and anger, overlain with a desperate determination.

Petrel thought he was probably remembering the cruel men, and bracing himself for the nasty task of fighting them, so she left him alone and answered her own question. "Don't know, do we? But we have to try."

Grease Alley was nowhere near as busy as Dufftown, but there were folk there all the same, hurrying through the passages with lanterns in their hands and serious looks on their faces. Some of them carried babies and small bratlings. Others checked panels and switches to see if the fire damage had come this far. There was water everywhere, spilling down from the galley and being forced out of the ship as fast as the hand pumps could work.

The usual separation of tribes had broken down completely. Petrel saw Duff helping Grease, and Grease helping Braid. She and Fin walked into their lantern light and out of it, over and over again, and no one recognized them or tried to stop them.

"Not much farther," she whispered to Fin. "Down another

deck and then aft a bit. Remember the last time I brought you this way? The toothies were running and your arm was bleeding."

It seemed like weeks ago. Everything was different now.

Everything's worse, Petrel told herself. *Ship's icebound, no engines, no steering, and the cruel men of Fin's are coming after the* Oyster *like sharks after a wounded whale. AND no one'll listen to me!*

But being ignored was nothing new. "At least there's two of us," she whispered to Fin. "It's better than being alone."

Still Fin said nothing.

As they reached the top of the next ladderway, with a lantern coming towards them along the passage, Petrel thought she saw a gray shadow dive into a cabin.

"Mister Smoke," she hissed. "Is that you? We're going to find the sleeping captain. We have to wake him—"

And then the folk with the lantern were upon them. They were Braid, Petrel thought, though they were so rugged up that it was hard to be sure. One of them, farther from the lantern light than the others, stared at the children as they passed. Petrel urged Fin down the ladderway. They must not be stopped now. They must find the sleeping captain and tell him—

"That's them," came a familiar voice from above.

It was Dolph.

Petrel didn't even turn around. "Run!" she hissed, and she grabbed hold of Fin and dragged him into the darkness.

CHAPTER 21

WE HAVE CAUGHT THE MURDERER

IF PETREL HAD BEEN ALONE, SHE COULD HAVE EVADED HER pursuers easily. She had been running from Dolph all her life, and this was no different. But Fin slowed her down.

He tried not to. He ran as fast as he could, but he didn't know the ship the way Petrel did. He didn't know where to dive into a side passage, where to climb, where to duck under a railing.

Petrel thought of leaving him. As she hauled him around corner after dark corner, with the lanterns flickering behind them and their shadows leaping in front, she told herself that she should let go of his hand. Let Braid have him. *She'd* be all right. If the cruel men came, she'd hide, as she had always done. They'd never find *her*. And once they were beaten off, as they surely would be, she'd go back to her old life, lurking around the edges of the tribes, grabbing food and warmth where she could.

And being alone.

Footsteps pounded behind them, closer and closer. "Grab them! I want both of them," cried a man.

"Through here," hissed Petrel, and she dragged Fin through a hatch and slammed it behind them. It flew open again almost immediately.

"There they are," shouted Dolph.

Petrel could hear her own breath rasping in her throat, so loud that it almost drowned out the endless rattle of pipe messages. She pulled Fin around one corner and pushed him around another. She thought of loneliness and friendship. She put on a last desperate burst of speed, and Fin ran beside her, blindly into the darkness, trusting her to save him—

The lanterns caught them. Feet rushed up behind them, and rough hands grabbed them and spun them around, shouting, "We've got 'em!"

"Leave us alone," cried Petrel, as she struggled and kicked. "We ain't done nothing!"

Beside her, Fin was fighting too, but there were three men holding him, and they would not let go.

Someone trod hard and deliberately on Petrel's foot. She bit back a cry of pain, but didn't stop struggling until her arms were held so tightly that she could not move.

"Got you now, Nothing Girl," murmured Dolph in her ear. "Got you for good."

Petrel didn't answer. Her eyes were fixed on another lantern, which was approaching more sedately.

"So," said First Officer Crab, coming to a halt in front of Fin. He was panting a little, but his eyes were as trim and cold as ever. "We have caught the murderer."

"The murderers," said Dolph. "It was both of 'em."

"Ah." Crab inclined his head. "Perhaps you are right. The boy could not have done it without—"

"'Twasn't us," interrupted Petrel. "'Twasn't either of us. Dolph, tell him about the other ship."

"Be quiet," said Crab.

"Tell him!"

"It was a lie," said Dolph, glaring at Petrel. "*I* didn't see anything but bergs. It was a trick to get away from me." Her expression changed to one of satisfaction. "But you didn't. Not in the end."

"*Think*, Dolph," said Petrel desperately. "Fin had to have got on that berg somehow—"

"A whale brought him," said Dolph.

"Don't be stupid," said Petrel. "'Twas a ship. And we didn't kill your mam, I *swear* it, on the head of the sleeping captain—"

No one on the *Oyster* swore lightly on the head of the sleeping captain, not even those who didn't believe in him. Petrel thought she saw a flicker of doubt in Dolph's eyes, and she pressed on, "—which means someone else must have killed her. It might've been anyone. It might've been Crab—"

She said it wildly, grasping at the first name that came to her. But as the words left her lips, the memory that had been tickling at her for days came into focus, bright and clear, showing her what she had seen but not understood.

Crab on the deserted afterdeck, washing his hands in the snow. Washing them over and over again, as if he could not get them clean . . .

Petrel gasped. "'*Twas* Cra—"

A gag was thrust into her mouth, silencing her. She wriggled, but it was hopeless. Someone gagged Fin too, and any hope they might have had of talking their way out of this was gone.

Petrel should have been afraid, but instead she was furious. Why did no one *listen* to her? Why couldn't they see what she could see?

Crab peered down at her as if she were something dug out of a fish's innards. "I have no idea why Orca tolerated you for as long as she did."

"Mam didn't *tolerate* her," snapped Dolph. Her dislike of Crab was obvious, but her dislike of Petrel and Fin was greater. "Orca just—just ignored her." She gestured back along the passage. "What are we waiting for? You want the two of 'em off the ship, don't you? Everything'll right itself once the stranger is gone."

"It will indeed," said Crab. He turned to the woman by his side and said, "Find a rope. A long one."

The woman hurried away. Crab nodded at the men who held Petrel and Fin captive and they began to move.

Now Petrel *was* afraid. She dug in her heels, and was dragged along the passage, her feet catching on the rivets. When they came to the ladders, her captor did not loosen his grip, but lifted her body and carried her upward.

Petrel tried to think. Who would help them? Squid, surely,

or Krill, if she could only get a message to them. Who else? No one. There was not a single other person on the ship who cared about her.

Except Mister Smoke and Missus Slink.

Was it one of the rats she had seen earlier? Perhaps they already knew what had happened. But even if they did, how could they save Petrel and Fin from being thrown overboard? How could they stop Crab? What could they do against a ship full of cruel men?

They're servants of the sleeping captain, thought Petrel. *That's what Mr. Smoke said when he made me an honorary rat. Maybe THEY can wake him!*

She had no idea if it was possible. But she must tell them about the ship, and about Crab, before it was too late.

And so, as she and Fin were carried up the Commons ladderway, she set to work on her gag. She could not use her hands—they were held firmly against her side. But the lanterns were far enough ahead that no one could see her face, so she grimaced and chewed at the gag, trying to loosen it. She screwed her face up, and rubbed the edge of the gag against her captor's arm, as if jolted by the climbing.

No one spoke to her. Even Dolph had fallen silent. They climbed past other crew members several times, and Crab announced, "We have caught the stranger, who is the cause of all our misfortune. Soon things will turn around."

And the folk they passed nodded and said, "The sooner the better."

At last Petrel felt the gag loosen. They were past

Dufftown by then, with no sign of Squid or Krill. *Only good thing about this is the pack ice,* thought Petrel. *At least Crab can't throw us to the Maw. At least we won't get chomped up by those great big teeth.*

It was a comfort, for someone who had always believed the Maw would get her in the end. But not much of one. Petrel worked her jaw frantically, trying to get the gag out of her mouth.

"I expect," said First Officer Crab from somewhere up ahead, "that Albie will have the lectrics fixed within the hour, once the stranger is gone. Once this *untidiness* is rectified."

The man who carried Petrel growled his agreement.

Not likely, thought Petrel. *If Albie says it's a couple of days, then it's a couple of days, and chucking us overboard ain't going to make a scrap of difference.*

But although her mouth was now free, she didn't waste her breath arguing with Crab. She'd only be able to get a few words out before she was gagged again, and she must make every one of them count.

She waited a few seconds more, trying not to tense up and give herself away. She licked her dry lips. Drew cold air into her lungs.

Then she shouted at the top of her voice. "Mister Smoke, there's a strange ship out there, wants to hurt the *Oyster*! And they're throwing me and Fin overboard! They think we murdered Orca but 'twas Crab—"

A hand clamped over her mouth, silencing her. Crab raced back down the ladderway, crying, "Shut her up! Why are you letting her talk such nonsense? Make sure her gag's tight this time."

Then he climbed back to the head of the procession, muttering, "We are tidying things that should never have been untidied in the first place."

The rest of the climb to the afterdeck was without incident. Petrel wondered desperately if Dolph believed her. She wondered if Mister Smoke or Missus Slink would come.

Probably not.

Her fear grew.

The afterdeck, when they stepped out onto it, was dark and cold. Fog crept over the ship like a gray blanket, and although there was a moon, its light came fitfully. High in the rigging, the wind fiddles played a mournful dirge.

Crab coughed and his breath froze on his beard. "The quicker this is done, the better." He turned to the woman who had brought the rope.

"Wait," said Dolph. "Why does she keep saying you killed Mam? Why would she say that?"

"She would accuse anyone to avoid punishment," said Crab. "A person would have to be mad to listen to her." He raised his voice. "However I am not a cruel man and will not send them to a lingering death. Remove their outdoor clothes so they will die quickly. Then lower them onto the ice."

Petrel trembled and tried not to think about what was coming. Beside her, Fin's eyes were white-rimmed with horror.

The woman with the rope unslung it from her shoulders. "Quickly now," said Crab, and Petrel's captor pulled Petrel's sealskin jacket and trousers off, leaving her in her ship clothes. Then he dragged her forward so that the end of the rope could be tied under her arms.

Petrel was shaking so much that she could hardly stand. She tried to loosen her gag again so she could cry out for mercy. She rolled her eyes at Dolph, and silently screamed, *'Twasn't us! Crab's the one who killed your mam, not us!*

Dolph looked uncertainly at Crab, but said nothing. The rope tightened around Petrel's chest and she found herself suddenly lifted off the deck and dropped over the rail.

She grunted with the shock of it, and grabbed hold of the rope. She had never in her entire life been off the *Oyster*, never felt anything under her feet but the reassuring safety of the deck or the ladders or the nets.

Now there was nothing. She swayed in midair for a sickening moment—and began to fall.

At first she thought they had decided to drop her. But then her descent slowed and she clung grimly to the rope, knowing that she was going to die soon, but not willing to have it happen just yet. The great bulk of the *Oyster* rose and rose above her, and she wished she could reach out and touch it, but the angle of the hull was too far away.

When her feet hit the ice, she stumbled and skidded. *It's just like the afterdeck,* she told herself. *You have to be careful.*

With fingers made clumsy by the cold, she undid the knot around her chest and watched the rope snake upward into the grayness. She took the gag out of her mouth and wrapped it around her right hand for what little warmth it could give her.

Then she walked gingerly across to where the *Oyster*'s battered hull disappeared into the ice, and stared at it, with tears turning to frost on her face.

It seemed like forever before the rope swung down again with Fin on the end of it. The bitter cold was galloping into Petrel's bones, and her ship clothes felt as if they gave her no more protection than paper. She began to wonder if perhaps Crab had changed his mind about the boy, and she was going to be left all alone down here.

"Wouldn't matter a-anyway," she whispered, shivering. "I'll b-be dead before I know it. Having a bit of company won't make any d-d-difference."

But it would. She knew it would. And when she saw Fin's legs dangling above her she cried out with relief, and was ashamed, because now he was going to die too, and she shouldn't be glad about it.

Still, she *was* glad. "Better than being alone," she said fiercely, as she undid the rope.

Fin swallowed and nodded. And as the rope slid upward, out of their reach, he wrapped his arms around Petrel and they clung to each other.

CHAPTER 22

AN ARMY OF MEN

The ice beneath Fin's feet groaned and his teeth chattered uncontrollably. *I am going to die,* he thought, *and it is probably just as well. Because when Brother Thrawn discovers that I have failed to carry out my mission, my life will not be worth living.*

He still found it hard to believe that things had gone so completely wrong. He had tried and tried, but the ship had defeated him. The ship—and Petrel.

It was not her fault, he knew that. All along, she had merely done what she thought was right, just as he had. She had fought for her ship, while he had fought against it.

He was glad she was here with him now. He was glad she would never know how close he had come to betraying her.

As his shivering grew worse, he wondered what would happen next. Would Brother Thrawn and the Devouts come storming across the ice, thinking that the demon was dead? Would they find Fin and Petrel before it was too late? He hoped—

Actually, he was no longer sure what he hoped.

He looked up at the hull of ship, rising so enormously above them. "Nothing c-can save us now, can it?"

"Not unless Crab changes his m-mind," said Petrel, "which ain't going to happen."

"Is the ice strong enough to hold us? Will it c-crack under our feet?"

"I r-reckon it's strong enough. It f-froze up quick and solid like it d-does sometimes. We'd have fallen through already if we were going to."

"Oh . . . We are f-friends, are we not?"

In answer, Petrel hugged him tighter. Then she said, in his ear, "T-tell me about your m-mam and da."

Fin pulled back a little way and stared at her. "W-what?"

"I d-don't want to think about what's coming. I'd think about m-*my* mam and da if I could, but I don't remember 'em. T-tell me about yours. What're they like?"

"M-my father died before I was b-born," said Fin. "My mother—" He broke off, as a far-too-thin face swam out of the recesses of his memory and placed itself firmly in front of him. His heart ached, but for the first time in years he did not try to push the face away.

"M-my mother—" he said, and stopped again.

"Better t-talk quick," said Petrel, "'cos the blood's f-freezing in my veins already."

"I h-have not thought about her for a l-long time."

"'Cept when you were feverish. Then you c-called her *Mama.*"

"I d-did?"

206

Petrel nodded.

"I—" said Fin. "I—"

"Was she k-kindhearted?"

"Yes."

"Did she l-love you?"

"Y-yes. But when I was three years old, she t-took me to the Citadel and g-gave me to the Brothers, so I w-would not starve." Fin's voice cracked. "I d-did not want to go."

He remembered how frantically he had cried and screamed and kicked. In the end, Brother Thrawn had locked him in the punishment hole, and left him there with the rats until he learned to be obedient.

"These B-Brothers," said Petrel. "They the ones on the other ship? The ones who w-want to kill us?"

"Yes," said Fin.

Petrel peered around uneasily. "We'll fight 'em if they c-come. Here, move around a b-bit." And she jumped up and down on the spot.

Fin jigged from foot to foot, though it made no difference to how cold he was.

"Why do the B-Brothers hate us so much?" asked Petrel.

Fin did not want to talk about the demon, so he merely said, "B-because of the machines. They are v-vile contraptions that make p-people lazy. They can s-steal a person's soul. They must be d-destroyed—"

He paused, hearing his own voice as if for the first time. What he had just said did not make sense. He had been on the ship, surrounded by machines, for days. And had they stolen his soul, even when he was sick and helpless? Had they done *anything* other than drive the ship and keep the crew warm?

He was not sure. Perhaps his soul *had* been stolen. Perhaps that was why he was so confused.

"What h-happened to your mam?" asked Petrel. "After she g-gave you to the Brothers."

"I-I do not know. I think she probably d-died."

"Maybe she d-d-didn't. Maybe she just went off to another—another d-deck or something. Maybe we could g-go and find her. When we g-get off the ice."

Fin nodded, though they both knew they would never get off the ice. Death was rushing towards them, and nothing could stop it. "We—"

Petrel raised her hand. "Shhh! I heard something."

"What?"

"I don't know— *Look! Up there!*"

A spark of hope flared in Fin's heart. A *third* person was being lowered on the rope. "Have they sent someone t-to rescue us?"

Petrel sighed as the figure kicked and struggled all the way down. "No such luck. It's D-Dolph. Look, she's all tied up."

The older girl's feet skidded on the ice, and Fin ran to untie her. As soon as he had freed her hands, Dolph tore out her gag, tipped her head back, and screamed at the ship, "You greasenosed fish carcass! I'm going to k-kill you, Crab! I'm going to cut out your l-liver and feed it to the Maw! Coward! T-traitor!"

The rope slid upwards. Fin could have warmed his fingers on Dolph's rage, it burned so hot.

"Murderer!" she shrieked. "I'll use you as t-toothy bait. I'll—I'll—"

"Save your b-breath. He's gone," said Petrel.

Dolph snarled at her. "This is all your fault, rat-girl. You're the one who k-kept saying it was him murdered M-Mam. He must've thought I believed you, 'c-cos he waited till everyone else had gone b-back inside, then he grabbed me." She glared upwards again and shouted, "Soup-brain! P-penguin-breath!"

The breeze had gone and the wind fiddles were silent. Fin rubbed his face. He was feeling dreadfully tired.

"I'm going to get you, C-Crab," shouted Dolph. "Either me—or my g-ghost, we're going to—"

There was a flurry in the air above her, and something fell onto the ice. Fin stared in disbelief, wondering if the cold was making him see things that were not there.

"It's our j-jackets!" cried Petrel. "And t-t-t-t-trousers!"

Dolph pounced on her own outdoor clothes and began to pull them on with frantic haste. Petrel and Fin had been longer on the ice, and were slower to move. But in the end, helping each other all the way, they managed to drag the trousers and jackets over their freezing limbs, and put their mittens on, and their hoods and ice masks as well.

It was only when they were fully dressed, and the cold no longer chewed quite so ferociously at their bones, that Petrel shouted, "Who's up there? Is that you, Squid?"

The only answer was a slither of noise. Fin leaped back, just as the end of a rope hissed down the side of the ship and hung quivering in the night air.

"It's Squid," cried Petrel. "Or K-Krill!"

"It's for m-me, not you," muttered Dolph, and she grabbed the rope and began to climb.

"Dolph, wait," said Petrel.

The older girl ignored her. But she could not ignore the weakness that the cold had already drilled into her limbs. She managed to climb to a point just above Fin's head—and there she stuck, grinding her teeth and snarling.

A small gray body slid down the rope towards her, one of its legs sticking out to the side.

An imp! thought Fin.

"It's Mister Smoke," cried Petrel. "Dolph, g-get off."

Dolph didn't move. She stared at the rope as if she could climb it by sheer force of will. The imp crawled over the top of her and dropped onto the ice.

Fin's heart was bumping against his ribs. But Petrel fell onto her knees beside the imp and whispered, "You heard me sing out!"

"I *saw* you, shipmate," said the imp in a rough voice. "Right back when they grabbed you. Me and Slink've been busy ever since. We're takin' you elsewhere as soon as reinforcements arrive."

"The rat talks," muttered Dolph, still clinging to the rope.

Petrel ignored her. "Where are you taking us, Mister Smoke? There's nowhere 'cept the ship."

"And the rat-girl talks back," muttered Dolph. "I should've guessed."

The imp looked up. "'Ere they come."

Fin followed his gaze and cried out in disgust. Dolph sprang away from the rope as if it were on fire. Down its length swarmed countless numbers of black rats, leaping and jumping over one another, running across each other's backs and dropping onto the ice in a squeaking, writhing mass.

Petrel stared at them in astonishment, and Dolph glowered. But Fin shrank back, feeling as if he were three years old again, and trapped in the punishment hole.

"Don't fret, shipmate," said the imp, and he let out a piercing whistle, far too loud for his small frame, that calmed the rats down a little and kept them away from Fin's feet.

"How can these"—Fin gulped, trying to control his loathing—"these creatures help us?"

"Don't know," said Petrel. "But I reckon we've got a chance now! Quick, jump around. Stamp your feet. We've got to warm up."

Fin jumped up and down. But Dolph watched the rope hungrily, and when it slithered up into the fog, like a broken promise, she turned on Petrel.

"That was our last hope, rat-girl. You should've kept it here."

"You wait," said Petrel, who obviously trusted the imp she called Mister Smoke. "You be patient."

Fin had to force himself to keep moving. He was afraid that if something didn't happen soon he would lie down on the ice and fall asleep, and nothing would wake him. Not even the rats. Not even Petrel.

But then Mister Smoke said, "'Ere we go." And down the side of the ship, dangling from the end of the rope, came a sled made of driftwood and whalebone, with more rats clinging to every part of it and tumbling down the rope behind it.

Whatever Petrel had been hoping for, it wasn't this. Fin could hear the disappointment in her voice. "What's the use of a hunting sled, Mister Smoke? Where can it take us? To more ice? Who'll pull it? Us? We're having enough trouble standing upright. Besides, we don't want to go anywhere 'cept the ship. We gotta wake the sleeping captain."

"Don't you go gettin' ahead of yourself, shipmate," said Mister Smoke.

He whistled again. The sled dropped onto the ice, its whalebone struts rattling, and Dolph pounced on the rugs that were strapped to it. She took three of them, and Petrel and Fin took the rest and wrapped themselves up until only their eyes were visible.

Meanwhile, the rats were swarming over the end of the sled, where the long traces joined the whalebone. These traces looked as if something had chewed at them with sharp teeth, leaving hundreds of holes, each one just big enough for a rat or two to poke their heads through and take the weight of the sled on their chests.

"On ya hop, shipmate," said Mister Smoke.

As Fin watched in confusion, Petrel mounted the sled, saying, "Where's Missus Slink?"

"She ain't comin'," replied the imp.

The rope spiraled upward again, and this time it did not reappear.

"Where are we going?" asked Fin, who had not moved. "Where are you taking us?"

Mister Smoke replied with another question. "'Oo's crew are you on, shipmate?"

Fin swallowed. His mission was a failure and his old life was gone. He was not yet sure how he felt about it. "Petrel's," he said.

"Then you'd better climb up next to 'er, or you'll be left on the ice, and we won't be comin' back for you."

Dolph had been listening to all this with a blank face. Now she too moved towards the sled. Immediately, a thousand rats swung around in their traces to bar her way.

"Rat-girl," said Dolph with an uncertain sneer. "Tell your *kin* to move."

"It's not Petrel who orders 'em," said Mister Smoke. "It's me." He turned to Petrel. "You want to take 'er with us, shipmate? You want to save 'er life?"

The breath hissed between Petrel's teeth. "No, I don't, Mister Smoke! She was gunna leave *me* on the ice, without thinking twice about it!"

Dolph looked away. "I wouldn't want to come with you and your stupid rats anyway," she muttered. "I'd rather die by Mam's ship."

It was clearly bravado. Petrel laughed. "Remember the tar buckets? This is payback, Dolph!"

The imp made a small sound. Petrel glanced at him, and her laugh faltered.

Mister Smoke's head was tipped to one side, and his eyes glittered. He was the only creature on the ice without a cloud of breath around his nose, but it struck Fin that there was something very real about him. Something very *human*.

"What?" said Petrel.

"Nothin'," said the imp.

"I'm not taking her!" said Petrel.

"I never said a word, shipmate."

Petrel scowled at him. "I got good reason to leave her here, Mister Smoke. It's payback. It's the way of the ship."

"So it is. And it's been goin' on for generations. Tribe against tribe, windin' down through the years. Your own mam and da are dead because of it."

That hit home. Petrel winced and said, "Stop it, Mister Smoke! Stop trying to make me do something I don't want to do!"

The imp said nothing. But his previous words still hung in the cold night air, and Fin could see that Petrel was moved by them, despite herself.

She glared at Dolph through ice-rimmed lashes. Then she said, "I spose—"

Dolph hunched her shoulders, expecting the worst.

Petrel sighed. "I *spose* she can come with us."

Mister Smoke nodded approval. Dolph flopped onto the sled, angrier than ever. "Shove over," she muttered.

Fin squashed closer to Petrel. Mister Smoke climbed up behind them, his leg dragging, and let out one of his piercing whistles.

The rats began to move.

Each rat was only small, but there were so many of them that the sled immediately jerked forward, sliding over the ice in fits and starts. Fin, Petrel and Dolph clung to the whalebone struts.

Mister Smoke whistled again, and the rats fell into a smooth gallop, their frosted backs bobbing up and down as they raced squeaking across the ice. Fin looked over his shoulder. The fog had lifted without him noticing, and the *Oyster* loomed up behind the sled like a vast fortress, dark and silent.

Nor'east of it, something moved. Fin stared. An army of men was tramping across the ice towards the *Oyster*! The moonlight glinted on axes and grappling hooks, and when the men saw the sled they shouted, and some of them broke away from their line and started after it.

The breath seemed to freeze in Fin's lungs. He knew that he should throw himself off the sled and warn Brother Thrawn that the demon still lived, but his body would not obey him.

Beside him, Petrel cried, "It's them! The men from the other ship! Mister Smoke, we have to go back. We have to warn the *Oyster*. We have to wake the sleeping captain!"

But Mister Smoke merely whistled, so that the rats picked up their pace and the men fell behind.

Dolph reached across Fin and grabbed Petrel's arm. "Make him turn back. *Make* him."

"Please, Mister Smoke," cried Petrel, "we can't just leave 'em!"

"Can't do anythin' useful back there, shipmate," said the rat.

He hopped onto Petrel's shoulder. "Go for'ard, that's what we 'ave to do."

"But *where*? There's nowhere to go."

"North," said Mister Smoke. "That's where we're goin'. North."

"Mad," muttered Dolph, in a voice that trembled with fear and fury. "The creature's mad." And she hunched down in her rugs and did not look back at the *Oyster* again.

Petrel gripped Fin's gloved hand. "North?" she whispered, her eyes enormous. "What's north? Nothing 'cept ice and sea, which is not a comforting thought! And what about the sleeping captain? We're sposed to *wake* him!"

Fin did not know what to say, so he said nothing. Mister Smoke crouched on Petrel's shoulder, his eyes fixed on the ice.

The rats galloped faster.

PETREL HAD ALWAYS TRUSTED MISTER SMOKE, AND SHE DID not want to stop now. *He knows what he's doing,* she told herself grimly. *It's just not clear to the rest of us yet.*

The sled hit a patch of rough ice and she jolted against Fin. The runners swished. The rats squeaked as they ran. The bitter wind gnawed at the rugs, trying to find a way through.

"Mister Smoke," said Petrel, peering into the darkness, "this ice is getting a bit thin. We'd best turn around."

The old rat didn't answer. He hopped off her shoulder and hauled himself onto the front of the sled, his tattered ears pricked.

"Ice is getting *very* thin," said Dolph. Like Petrel, she knew about ice. Everyone on the *Oyster* did, knew it in all its forms. And what they were traveling over now was too wet.

"Mister Smoke?" said Petrel, more urgently.

Mister Smoke whistled. But instead of turning, the rats surged forward, their paws sending up tiny spurts of melt water.

"What's the creature doing?" shouted Dolph.

"I don't know! Please, Mister Smoke!" cried Petrel.

Beside her, Fin gripped the seat of the sled. "Where is he taking us?"

"Wherever it is, we're not going to get there," shouted Dolph. "Listen!"

The sound that Petrel heard was such a dreadful one that her heart almost stopped. She crawled forward to where the gray rat clung to the front of the sled. "Mister Smoke," she cried. "The ice is cracking!"

Petrel's voice was cracking too, with fright. What did Mister Smoke think he was doing? He had promised to take them to the sleeping captain, at least she thought he had. She tried to remember what he had said, but the ominous sounds beneath her had driven everything else out of her mind.

She would have leaped off the sled, but it was going too fast. The rats squeaked to each other as they ran—*they* knew the danger. But Mister Smoke's whistles drove them on, and their steps did not falter. The sled hissed over the treacherous ice, and spray rose high on either side.

Petrel crawled back to Fin and Dolph, and the three of them clung to each other, all hatred forgotten. They heard a loud crack beneath them, and cried out. The sled jerked down, then up again. It slowed to one side and jolted back on track.

"Mister Smoke—" shouted Petrel.

But the desperate cry died in her throat. Ahead of them, the ice was splintering and cracking, as if the dreadful black waters of the southern icecap had grown sick of waiting and were rising up to meet them.

Rising . . . and rising . . . and the ice tumbling away on every side with a great roaring sound, like stars falling from the night sky . . .

And out of the midst of the roaring came teeth, each one bigger than a full-grown man, and jaws that opened . . . and opened . . . as the sled and its hapless passengers hurtled forward.

Petrel shook from head to toe. "The Maaaaaw!" she wailed.

Her cry echoed across the ice, in tandem with Mister Smoke's whistles. The rats plunged onward. The massive head rose higher.

Petrel screamed in fury and despair. Everything she had ever believed about Mister Smoke was suddenly wrong. He had betrayed her, had brought her and Fin and Dolph to their deaths.

Then there was no more time to think. With one last flurry of speed, the rats and the sled plunged between those terrible jaws.

And everything went dark.

CHAPTER 23

THE MAW

WHEN PETREL WOKE UP, SHE WAS SURE SHE WAS DEAD. She was pleased that she had missed the painful part, where she had been crunched between the Maw's great teeth, but she was annoyed too. She didn't *want* to be dead. She wanted to be back on the *Oyster*, helping to drive that army of cruel, shouting men away from her home. She wanted to wake the sleeping captain. She wanted to ask Mister Smoke why he had betrayed her.

But there was no chance of any of that now. She wondered if there were ships in the afterlife, and fried toothies. And friends.

There were certainly no fried toothies in this part of it. All she could smell was salt water, with maybe a bit of oil mixed in.

Beside her, something stirred. "Fin?" she whispered. "That you?"

"Where are we?" mumbled Fin.

"Dead, I reckon."

"What was that—that *monster*?"

"The Maw. It chewed us up and—" Petrel broke off. She was thinking a little more clearly now, and she didn't *feel* chewed up. She didn't feel dead either. She felt more or less the same as she always had, except for a few more bruises.

But if she wasn't dead, where was she? And where was Mister Smoke? And Dolph?

That last question was answered almost immediately. Petrel heard a groan from somewhere behind her, and twisted around. "Dolph?" she whispered.

Another groan. Then, "Blizzards! My ankle!"

Petrel crawled towards Dolph's voice. She had to feel her way past hundreds of rats, all of them sprawled on their stomachs in attitudes of exhaustion. *They* were certainly not dead. They squeaked at her as she passed, annoyed at being disturbed.

"Dolph, where are you?" whispered Petrel. Her hand bumped against something that was not a rat.

"Ow!" said Dolph. "Watch where you're going!"

"Is that your ankle?"

"It *was*," snarled Dolph, "before you clomped all over it."

"Sorry."

"Where are we? Where's that stupid rat of yours brought us to?"

"Don't know. Wish there was some light." Petrel held her hand up to her eyes, but the darkness was so absolute that her fingers were invisible.

"Hey, Fin," she said. "You cold?"

"Not as cold as death," said Fin, from just behind her.

"Me neither. Maybe the Maw spat us out again. Didn't like the taste."

"Then we'd be back on the ice," hissed Dolph, "or twenty fathoms under water, and too dead to make stupid comments. It can't have swallowed us after all."

"But it *did*, Dolph. You know it did. You saw it."

Fin cleared his throat uncertainly. "Could it be that we are—in the monster's belly? I cannot think of any other possibility."

Dolph gasped. Petrel stared in Fin's direction, and an awful chill ran down her spine.

He's right! That's where we are! Inside the Maw!

The darkness seemed to crowd around her. "D'you think it knows we're here?" she whispered, and immediately regretted the words. They made it more real, somehow. They gave the darkness an intelligence, an inward-turned eye.

A hunger.

Now even Dolph's voice wobbled. "P'raps it's—keeping us for later."

"Like—like putting a toothy on ice," agreed Petrel. "For the next day."

She fumbled for Fin's hand and was not surprised when she felt Dolph squeeze her other hand. She squeezed back, and the three of them huddled together, united in terror.

When something roared beneath them, they all flinched. "What's that?" hissed Fin.

The roaring grew louder, and the darkness began to tremble.

"It's swimming, I think," whispered Dolph. "Taking us deeper."

Petrel could feel the movement now, a powerful, rhythmical surge that jammed the three bratlings against each other, then pushed them apart. She braced herself against it, and wondered what the monster would do when it finally decided to eat them.

Will it spit us forward and crunch us between its teeth? Or will it just swallow, and we'll get squished up in its guts?

One would be just as painful as the other. She was glad her mam and da had been killed before they were thrown to the Maw. She wished desperately that it was the crew of the other ship stuck down here, and that she and Fin and Dolph were back on the *Oyster*. But at the same time she felt a sense of inevitability.

"Always knew the Maw'd get me," she whispered. And so she had. But she had never imagined, not for a moment, that it would be Mister Smoke who betrayed her. That hurt more than anything.

"Petrel." It was Fin, murmuring in her ear. "What will happen when the men from the *Retribution*—"

"That the other ship?"

"Yes. What will happen when they attack the *Oyster*?"

"They won't win," said Petrel quickly. "They *can't* win."

"Will the—the sleeping captain wake up?" asked Fin.

"Sleeping captain doesn't exist," said Dolph.

"Don't you be so sure of that, Dolph," said Petrel. "I know

where he is—least I think I do. I was going to wake him and tell him about Fin's ship . . ."

Petrel's voice trailed off, as she thought of the army of men tramping towards the *Oyster*. In her imagination, every one of those men was twice as big as Krill and three times as vicious as Albie. What if no one told the sleeping captain about them? What if he stayed asleep, when he should be defending the ship?

What if everyone on the *Oyster* died as a result?

She ground her teeth. "I don't *want* 'em to die," she said aloud. "I want to get out of the Maw's belly, and back to the ship to wake the sleeping captain. And he'll strike all those men dead, and—and—and you and me'll take the *Retribution*, Fin, and go and find your mam."

It was absurd, and Petrel knew it. But it made her feel better.

"We should stand up," she said.

"Why?" asked Dolph.

"So we can dodge when the Maw tries to chew us."

Dolph snorted. But she stood up all the same, balancing on her good leg, and Fin stood too, and the three of them put their backs together and waited. The Maw surged and twisted around them, taking them who-knows-where.

Petrel had no idea how much time passed. The intense darkness magnified every heartbeat, every movement. It might have been half a watch—or only a few grains of the hourglass—before she heard a dragging sound.

The three stiffened, and pressed against each other. It was impossible to tell which direction the dragging came from, or what it was. But it was coming closer—they could hear it quite clearly.

And then it stopped, and was replaced by a rough voice. "You there, shipmate?"

"Mister *Smoke*?" said Petrel, amazed.

"That's me, shipmate. You all right?"

In a flash, Petrel's astonishment gave way to anger. "What's it to you if I am, Mister Smoke? I trusted you, and you gave us to the Maw! You tried to kill us!"

"So are you dead, shipmate? You don't sound dead to me."

"Not yet, no thanks to you."

"Hang on," said the rat. "There's something missin' from this conversation."

There was a scraping sound and an oil lantern flickered to life. As the yellow light spread, Petrel stared around in stunned disbelief.

She was standing on a porous deck, with black rats flopped on every side of her. Metal arches glinted above her head, disappearing into darkness where the light did not penetrate. The arches supported something that looked a bit like the hull of the *Oyster*, except here it was made of overlapping plates that moved rhythmically against each other.

Petrel looked at Fin, and he gazed back at her, dumbfounded. "We are inside a machine," he whispered.

Petrel nodded slowly. *That* was undeniable. But what—

The truth struck her, and she glared at Mister Smoke, at the gleam in his eye. "It's a ship!" she said accusingly. "The Maw is an underwater ship!"

Mister Smoke looked mysterious and pleased at the same time. "Knew you'd work it out, shipmate. Backup, that's what the Maw is. You gotta have backup. Ain't I told you that over and over again?"

Petrel's anger flared higher. All that fear! All that terror, for nothing. "You should've told us," she said. "You should've—"

"Where's this thing taking us?" interrupted Dolph.

The rat's eyes shone with mystery. Petrel scowled at him. "You stop all these secrets, Mister Smoke! They scare me half to death, and I want to know the truth. Where are we going?"

"Back to the *Oyster*," said Mister Smoke. "Where else?"

Fin caught his breath. "Back to the *Oyster*?"

"How'll we get past those men?" asked Dolph. "They'll be right around the ship by now."

The rat said nothing. Petrel sighed. "More secrets, Mister Smoke?"

"Secrets within secrets, shipmate, and all of 'em kept for three 'undred years. But it looks like they're about to be dragged into the light." And he limped away.

For as long as she could remember, Petrel had been able to judge how fast the *Oyster* was going, and its direction, even when she was curled up in one of her nests, deep inside the ship. But now, in this strange vessel, she was lost. It swam, in that odd rhythmical way, and she balanced herself against the movement and tried to understand.

We're inside the Maw!

She had a thousand questions, and a thousand more that she hadn't thought of yet. She wished she knew how far they were from the *Oyster*, and how long it would take to get there. It was a terrible thing to be sitting helplessly while death and disaster marched on her ship.

She kicked the nearest arch. "Those men could be climbing the hull by now."

"Someone'll see 'em from the bridge," said Dolph, who was sitting down again, nursing her ankle.

"Who? Crab? He's probably too busy *tidying up*. He'll have the whole crew standing in a neat row, just in time for 'em to be slaughtered."

"If Mam was still alive—"

"But she's not, is she? She got herself killed, just when we needed her."

"It wasn't her fault," snapped Dolph. "Crab betrayed her—"

"She shouldn't've trusted him," said Petrel, with a sizeable snap in her own voice. "*I* didn't trust him."

"You don't trust anyone."

"I've got good reason for that," said Petrel, and she glared at Dolph until the older girl reddened and looked away.

The deck rumbled and swayed beneath their feet. "Go faster," whispered Petrel.

Despite the evidence, she couldn't quite bring herself to think of the Maw as a ship. It was the monster that had followed the *Oyster* for centuries, the monster that everyone feared. The monster that had chased Petrel through her dreams, year in, year out.

Now she wanted to skitch it onto the army of men. "Go as

fast as you can," she whispered to the metal arches. "Crash up through the ice and swallow 'em. Chew 'em to bits—"

She broke off, thinking of all the corpses that had been thrown over the side of the ship, year after year, century after century. Petrel had thought—*everyone* had thought—that the Maw *ate* them.

But it wasn't alive. It *couldn't* have eaten them. So what had it done with them?

She remembered how nothing on the *Oyster* was wasted. Everything was used for either food, clothing or fuel. Maybe the Maw was the same! Maybe there was a digester back there in the darkness, and an engine, just like the ones on the *Oyster*, and Mister Smoke overseeing their workings, the way he seemed to oversee everything else.

Her thoughts were interrupted by the old rat's voice from somewhere aft. "Hang on, shipmates!"

Petrel grabbed one of the metal struts just in time. She heard a muffled clang and the deck beneath her jolted violently. Dolph yelped. The black rats woke from their exhausted sleep with a great squeaking and protesting, and the shadows from the lantern cavorted like ice devils.

And then everything was still.

"Reckon we're there," said Petrel. "Reckon we're right up against the hull."

"Impossible," said Fin. "The ship is icebound."

Petrel's breath quickened. "Reckon we're *under* the ice!"

"Then how can we get on board?"

"Don't know."

Mister Smoke shouted again, "Time to move, shipmates."

"Don't you go without me," said Dolph, and she struggled to her feet, clinging to one of the metal struts.

Petrel picked up the lantern and put her shoulder under Dolph's arm. "Fin, you go on her other side. You can hop, can't you?" That was to Dolph.

The older girl nodded. "Can't dance though."

Which was, Petrel realized in astonishment, a joke.

Petrel and Fin made their way slowly aft, with Dolph between them. She leaned heavily on their shoulders and winced with every step, but made no complaint. Their feet rang on the metal deck.

Mister Smoke was waiting by a hatch in the wall. It had no clamp, but otherwise it looked more or less like the hatches in the *Oyster*. Petrel heard scratching sounds, and the rasp of metal against metal.

"Must be a double hatch," she whispered. "The Maw and the *Oyster* must be screwed up tight against each other so we can get through with no water coming in."

It was an amazing thought, but there was no time to dwell on it.

"Where will we come out?" asked Fin. "Somewhere near the—the sleeping captain?"

His voice was odd again, and his jaw set. When Petrel tried to see his eyes, he turned away from her. "I don't know," she said. "Mister Smoke?"

But the rat was watching the hatch, and waiting.

More rasping sounds. Petrel shifted from foot to foot,

thinking about the men they had seen raging across the ice. The dreadful fervor of them. The hatred in their cries and the axes in their hands.

If they thought they could just climb onto the *Oyster* and take over, she told herself, they were wrong. The *Oyster* was a ship of fighters. From birth to death, the crew fought the sea and the ice and the long winter nights. They fought rust and decaying machinery. They fought storms so terrible that stories were told about them for years afterward.

And they fought each other.

"Those men are gunna get a fright when they come up against Albie," she said, and Dolph nodded.

Neither of the girls mentioned the fire and its aftermath. But they were both thinking about it. About the lack of lookouts. About the rattle of pipe messages and the hammering, and how those sounds would drown out the clang of grappling hooks hitting the rails.

The crew of the *Oyster* might be fighters, but if they were taken completely by surprise . . .

"Mister Smoke, what are we waiting for?" said Petrel. "Can't we hurry?"

To her relief, there was a final rasp and the hatch creaked open . . . and there on the other side of it, her eyes reflecting the lantern light, was Missus Slink, pedaling lopsidedly at a tiny treadmill, which was geared to cogs and wheels and levers, all of them sliding over each other to unseal the hatch.

"Missus Slink!" said Petrel, and for just a second or two everything seemed almost normal.

But then Mister Smoke was urging the three of them through the hatch, muttering, "No time for greetings. In you go, in you go, mind the step, watch that lantern."

The black rats surged after them, making Fin grimace with disgust.

"Don't worry about *them*," said Petrel. "There's worse things coming than a few rats."

"Yes," said Fin, in that same strained voice. "I know."

Missus Slink was treadling the other way now, and the hatch was closing. Mister Smoke scrambled up beside her. "How's things above the waterline, Slink?"

"Not good. Those grappling hooks are taking hold, and no one up on deck to stop them. There'll be feet climbing the hull any minute, axes a-waving and skulls a-breaking. The past is catching up with us, Smoke."

"We have to warn the crew," said Dolph. "That's the first thing to do. Second thing is to kill Crab."

"We tried to warn 'em before, and they wouldn't listen," said Petrel.

"They'll listen to me," said Dolph.

"Who will? Albie? I doubt if you'd get near him, he'll be so busy. You could try Crab, I spose, before you kill him."

"Krill then. And Squid."

"They'll be busy too, trying to set things to rights. By the time you get through to 'em it'll be too late."

Dolph shook her head, knowing Petrel was right, and not liking it one bit.

"What we've gotta do," said Petrel firmly, "is wake the

sleeping captain. That's what I've been saying all along. Isn't it, Fin?"

Fin's lips moved, but he made no sound.

"There's no such thing as the sleeping captain," said Dolph.

"There is! That's why we're here!"

Behind them, the hatch clanged shut and the two rats slid down from the treadmill. "Come on, come on," said Mister Smoke, clambering up onto a narrow metal walkway. "Mind your feet, don't waste time. You still got that knife of yours, shipmate?"

"Aye," said Petrel.

For all the rats' urging, they could not hurry. Fin and Petrel had to edge sideways along the walkway, with Dolph hopping between them. Petrel could hear the ice grumbling against the hull and the rattle of pipes in the distance. She felt as if her heart were swelling in her chest, out of sheer excitement.

We're going to wake the sleeping captain!

But then she thought she heard the distant *clang* of a grappling hook, and the sound of feet climbing the side of the ship. She winced, and held the lantern higher so they could see where they were going.

This space had never been a hold or a storage area. The hull pressed in on one side and the bulkhead on the other, leaving no room for anything much except the walkway. It was a bit like one of the tunnels, only bigger, which was a relief. Petrel didn't feel like crawling, not with the cruel men so close, and her heart drumming so violently within her.

The walkway ended abruptly in a veil of old cobwebs. And

there in front of them was a table, bolted to the deck, and a metal box strapped to the top of it.

It had obviously been there a long time. The metal straps were rusty, and the box was half skewed out from under them.

Dolph's fingers gripped Petrel's shoulder so hard that it hurt. "What is it?" she hissed.

Petrel brushed the cobwebs away and stared at the box. She had thought it would be bigger. She had thought it would be as wide as Krill, at least, and taller than Albie, and decorated with grand designs.

She had thought it would look more . . . important.

Out of the corner of her eye she saw Fin slip his hand into his pocket. There was something about the look on his face that made her uneasy, but then Mister Smoke said, "Lift us up, quick," and Petrel forgot all about Fin.

She scooted out from under Dolph's shoulder and lifted the two rats onto the table. Mister Smoke's paws fussed at the straps until they fell away in a shower of rust. Then he limped up and down the lid of the box, inspecting it.

"No damage," he mumbled. "Should be fine. Won't know until we see the evidence though. Are you ready, Slink?"

"Ready long ago," said Missus Slink.

"'Ave we done our duty?"

"We have, and nearly wore ourselves out in the doing of it."

"Is the world safe?"

"It is not, and you know it. But times change, and a body's got to change with them. If we don't wake him now, he might never wake. Lift the lid."

It was a moment before Petrel realized that those last three words were addressed to her. "Oh," she said, and she stepped right up to the table and grasped one side of the lid with shaking hands.

Dolph propped herself against the bulkhead and said, "I don't believe it." But there was a growing uncertainty in her voice.

Clang, went another grappling hook. More boots climbed upward.

"Fin, come and help me," whispered Petrel.

Fin didn't move. Mister Smoke and Missus Slink went very still, their polished eyes fixed on the boy.

"Shipmate?" said Mister Smoke, and there was an edge to his voice that made Petrel shiver. "Hope I'm not wrong about you, shipmate. Hope you're on the right crew."

"Course he is!" said Petrel. "How could you doubt it, Mister Smoke?"

"Let the boy speak for 'imself," said Mister Smoke.

"I—" said Fin, and it seemed to Petrel that there was some sort of battle going on inside him. "I—" He jerked his shoulders, as if there were something wrapped around them. A net perhaps. Whatever it was, he gasped once, twice. Then he stepped forward, on the other side of the box from Petrel, and grabbed the lid.

It was not easy to open. The weight of three centuries had bound it in place, so that Petrel felt as if she were trying to lift the entire history of the *Oyster*, with its countless births and deaths, its icy winters and bountiful summers, its wars and fishing seasons and hunger and hopes and expectations.

It seemed impossible, but it must be done. Petrel and Fin braced themselves more firmly and hauled at the lid. They gritted their teeth and bent their knees. Dolph hopped forward to join them, and they all squeezed their eyes shut and heaved with every muscle in their bodies . . .

The only warning they received was a hiss of air, as sharp as an indrawn breath. Then the lid flew upwards, so suddenly that they staggered and cried out.

Petrel was the first to recover. She bent over the box, still panting. Her skin tingled. Her eyes filled with tears.

"It's the captain," she breathed. "It's the sleeping captain."

CHAPTER 24

THE SLEEPING CAPTAIN

FIN WAS EXPECTING SOMETHING MONSTROUS, SOMETHING THAT he could loathe and fear. Something so horrible that he would be able to ignore the light in Petrel's eyes, and do what he had come here to do.

But the boy in the box was anything but monstrous. He was no bigger than an eight-year-old child, and his silver face was beautiful. He lay so peacefully in his bed that it seemed a pity to wake him.

Fin swallowed, and gripped the spanner in his pocket.

"He's real," said Dolph in a choked voice. "I never thought he was, and neither did Mam. But he's real."

"He's going to save us," breathed Petrel, and she reached out her hand, then pulled it back again, as if she wanted to touch the boy but did not dare.

Missus Slink had no such concerns. With a great creaking of her joints, she clambered down into the box and stood on the boy's chest. A small screwdriver appeared in her paw.

"Now this," she said, "is the tricksy bit." She undid a panel in the boy's shoulder and put the screws carefully to one side. Beneath the panel were two holes. It looked as if something was missing, although Fin, who knew nothing about either machines or demons, could not imagine what it might be.

"Don't forget the screwdriver, Slink," said Mister Smoke, who was balanced precariously on the edge of the box.

"My circuits aren't that rusty," said Missus Slink crossly, and she carefully laid the screwdriver next to the screws. Then she climbed back up to the edge, and teetered next to Mister Smoke.

Clang. More boots climbed the side of the ship. And more. And more.

"Quick!" said Missus Slink to Petrel. "Get on with it!"

"But how do v wake him?" asked Petrel.

"Take out your knife," said Mister Smoke.

Petrel hesitated, then took her knife from her pocket.

Mister Smoke raised a paw and tapped first his own neck, then Missus Slink's, next to the green ribbon. "Now slit our throats."

"What?" Petrel dropped the knife with a clatter. Dolph put her hand to her mouth, her eyes wide with shock.

"You 'eard me," said Mister Smoke.

"No!" said Petrel, her voice shaking. "No, it'd kill you!"

Mister Smoke and Missus Slink exchanged glances. "Will it kill us, Smoke?"

"Mebbe. Mebbe not. There's no tellin' with these things. It has to be done, all the same."

"But *why*?" asked Petrel.

"You want to save the ship, girl?" said Missus Slink.

"Of course she does," said Dolph.

Fin said nothing. He wished they had never returned to the *Oyster*. He wished the Maw had kept going, kept sailing until they were far, far away from Brother Thrawn and the demon.

He wished he could persuade his fingers to let go of the spanner.

"I *do* want to save the ship," said Petrel. "But I—"

Missus Slink's voice overrode her. "You want to save Squid and Krill? And Albie?"

"I don't care about Albie! I'm not going to kill *you* to save *Albie!*"

"Save one, save 'em all, shipmate," said Mister Smoke. "All them folk workin' away to set the ship to rights, not seein' the danger that's upon 'em. All the old 'uns. All the bratlings. You gunna sacrifice all of 'em 'cos of a couple of rats?"

"You're not just a couple of rats! You're my friends!"

Mister Smoke was unmoved. "You want those men to win?"

"No, of course not! But—"

As Petrel hesitated, a pounding began, far above their heads. It echoed off the walls of the little cabin and boomed up and down, forcing its way into every corner of the ship, drowning out the creak of the ice and the pipe messages and the turbulent beating of Fin's heart.

"What's that?" cried Dolph.

"Reckon it's the invaders," said Mister Smoke, "bangin' on the deck with their axes." He looked at Fin. "Am I right, shipmate?"

Fin forced himself to nod. In a voice that sounded far too calm for the way he felt, he said, "Brother Thrawn will be leading them, or at least that was the plan. They will not enter the ship, not while the crew is still alive. They would be lost in its passages. They must draw the crew out, and this is how they do it."

"But if anyone goes out," cried Petrel, "those men'll be waiting for 'em! They'll cut 'em down as they step through the hatches. They'll slice 'em to pieces!"

"Yes," said Fin. He imagined Krill roaring up the Commons ladderway towards the afterdeck. He imagined Squid—

"You gotta wake the captain, shipmate," Mister Smoke said to Petrel.

"I *know* that!"

"And there's only one way to wake 'im."

Above their heads, the pounding ceased abruptly. "It's started," whispered Petrel. "There's folk up there fighting and dying."

Her breath sobbed in and out. Mister Smoke squinted up at her and said, "Right about 'ere, shipmate." And he touched his throat again.

Tears spilled from Petrel's eyes. "I can't," she whispered. "Don't ask it of me, Mister Smoke. I'll do anything else, but not that."

Something twisted inside Fin's chest, and he found himself saying, "I will do it."

He regretted it immediately, but Petrel was already handing him the knife. She kissed the top of Mister Smoke's head and cuddled Missus Slink so tightly that the rat protested, "Mind these old circuits, girl."

Petrel put Missus Slink down gently, in front of Fin. Then she turned her back, as if she was afraid she might try to stop him. "Don't hurt 'em," she whispered over her shoulder.

"It won't 'urt a bit, shipmate," said Mister Smoke, and there was a tenderness in his voice that Fin would never have expected from such a creature.

He did not expect Dolph's reaction, either. She touched the old rat's head with surprising gentleness and murmured, "Thank you for saving our lives, Mister Smoke. I will not forget you."

Fin licked his lips. The knife felt too eager in his grasp, as if Brother Thrawn were forcing his hand. But Petrel was there too, on the other side of him, so that he did not know which way to move.

I will do this part, he told himself. *And then make up my mind.*

Mister Smoke and Missus Slink lined up in front of him, their eyes unreadable.

"Once I have cut—" said Fin. "Ah— Once I have done it, what happens?"

The rats looked at each other. "Do you know what comes next, Slink?"

"Not me, Smoke. That's outside our circle of reference. They'll have to work it out for themselves."

"Right." Fin nodded. "Perhaps you should lie down. On your backs. I—"

They will not feel it, he reminded himself. *They are not really alive.*

He placed his hand on Missus Slink's furry chest. It felt warm, though that was impossible. He could have sworn that he felt her heart beating, though that was impossible too. Missus Slink gazed up at him with ancient silver eyes . . .

In the end, it was easier than Fin expected. The knife was sharp, and the spot Mister Smoke had indicated seemed to welcome the blade. The cutting edge sliced through fur and something else, and came out the other side.

Fin half expected to see blood, but there was none. With a grimace, he poked his fingers into the wound and touched a—a *thing*.

It came away in his hands, a tiny colorless box with wire knitted in intricate patterns across it. As it left her body, Missus Slink's eyes closed and she sprawled lifeless on the table.

Fin put the little box to one side and turned immediately to Mister Smoke. Across the way, Petrel's back was rigid.

There was another box inside Mister Smoke. Fin placed it next to the first one, and let the knife fall to the deck with a clatter, wondering why he felt so bereft.

The light of the lantern dipped. The sounds of the ship and the grating of the ice against its hull wound together in a plaintive lament. The two rats lay limp and silent.

Petrel looked over her shoulder, her face shiny with tears. "Is it done? Are they—Are they dead?"

"I think so," whispered Dolph.

Fin had never admired Petrel as much as he did then. For all her grief, she did not hesitate. "Then— Then we'd b-better get the captain awake, quick as we can," she said.

With trembling fingers, she picked up one of the tiny boxes and slid it into the silver boy's shoulder. It fitted perfectly.

Petrel picked up the second box. She was steadier now, though the tears still rolled down her cheeks.

"We're going to wake him," she said, and Fin couldn't tell whether she was talking to him and Dolph, or to the bodies of Mister Smoke and Missus Slink, or to Brother Thrawn, so far above their heads. "We're *all* going to do it." And she handed the box to Fin.

He took it, feeling as if he were dreaming. *It is not too late,* he thought. *I could drop this device onto the deck and crush it beneath my foot. Then the sleeping captain would never wake. And the world would be a better place . . .*

Or would it?

He had always accepted the notion without questioning. He had accepted everything Brother Thrawn had told him.

But now he must think for himself. He must choose.

What it came down to, he realized, was coldness versus warmth. Death versus life. The Devouts versus the crew of the *Oyster.*

Fin thought of his mother. He thought of Krill and Squid and Albie, and a hand on his shoulder, and a shield at his back, and a girl who fought for her people, even when they treated her badly.

And in that moment, he knew that Brother Thrawn must not be allowed to crush the *Oyster,* the way he crushed everything else he touched. Fin could not bear it. All that noise silenced. All that chaos. All that life.

He gripped the little box tighter and looked down at the beautiful silver face of the sleeping captain. One final doubt crept into his mind. What if it *was* a demon? What if this was the biggest mistake he had ever made?

"Quick!" said Petrel. "What are you waiting for?"

Fin looked up and met her worried gaze. He must tell her the truth; he owed it to her.

Before he could lose his nerve, he blurted it out in one long breath. "I told you that the Devouts forced me to come with them, but I lied, I *wanted* to come, I was supposed to kill the sleeping captain."

Petrel's eyes were enormous. "*What?*"

"But," said Fin firmly, "I will not do it!" And he pushed the box into the hole.

Later, when there was time to think, he wondered what he had expected. A whirring? A thudding, like the *Oyster*'s engines?

There was none of that. No sound. No ratcheting of joints or rattling of metal. The boy's eyes merely opened.

And he smiled.

At least, Fin thought he did. The silver face did not move, but there was a warmth in it, a sense of joy and wonder.

"Hello," said the boy, and his voice was as full of strangeness as the *Oyster* itself.

Fin gulped. "H-hello."

Petrel's face was still pale with shock from Fin's revelation. But once again she knew what must be done. "I'm Petrel," she said to the boy. "This here's Dolph and that's Fin. We need you, Cap'n! There's cruel men come to destroy the ship."

The boy sat up, as smooth as the silk of Brother Thrawn's robes.

"They're on the outside decks already," said Dolph. "We have to hurry."

"They are the Devouts," added Fin. "Led by Brother Thrawn. They have come from the other side of the earth, hunting a demon. They have come to kill everyone on the ship."

Petrel shot him one sharp glance, then looked back at the silver boy. "We need you to stop 'em, Cap'n."

The boy climbed out of the box, his limbs moving with such elegance that Fin longed to take him apart and see how he was made. Except—Except the boy was so alive. So real. Far too real to take apart.

Far too real to smash.

"I know two thousand years of history," said the silver boy. He hopped down from the table. "I know the rise and fall of civilizations, and how to rebuild myself if I am injured, and the position of every screw in this ship."

He paused. "But I do not know how to stop the Devouts."

"What?" said Dolph, as if she hadn't heard him properly.

But Petrel said fiercely, "You *must* know! Shipfolk are dying up there, and you're sposed to save 'em. That's what you're for!"

The boy shook his head. "I am for knowledge, not war."

The small cabin seemed to grow colder. Fin swallowed. "Can you not kill the Devouts with a glance? Can you not boil the blood in their veins? Destroy whole cities?"

"No," said the boy.

The children looked at each other in dismay. "Then what's

the use of you, Cap'n?" cried Petrel. "We killed Mister Smoke and Missus Slink to wake you, and now you can't do anything. We killed 'em, and we shouldn't've—"

"Killed them?" said the silver boy. His long fingers touched Missus Slink, slid into the wound Fin had made, twisted something, adjusted something else. Then he did the same to Mister Smoke.

On the table, the two rats raised their heads.

Petrel gasped. But when she scooped the rats up and hugged them, they said nothing. And when she asked anxiously, "Are you all right, Mister Smoke? Missus Slink?" they still said nothing, but sat silent in her grasp, as if they could no longer speak or think for themselves.

A single tear rolled down Petrel's face.

"Forget 'em," said Dolph. "We've wasted too much time already. Forget the captain too. If he can't fight, we can." She took a step, and yelped with pain.

"Your ankle," said Fin. "You can't walk—"

Dolph hissed at him. "Doesn't matter! I'll crawl all the way up to the afterdeck if I have to!"

"Wait," said Petrel. With a visible effort she dragged her eyes away from the rats and stared at the silver boy. "We've gotta think."

"There's no *time* to think," said the older girl. "We're crew, ain't we? We should be up there!"

But Petrel's eyes were darting from side to side, as if she were trying to calculate something. "Knowledge," she muttered. "Does that mean you know what time it is, Cap'n? I've lost track, 'cos of being inside the Maw."

Without hesitation, the boy said, "It is just past three bells of the morning watch."

Petrel closed her eyes, and for a moment she looked more uncertain than Fin had ever seen her. But then her eyes sprang open again and she said, "We have to go *now*."

"That's what I said!" cried Dolph.

"No, we're not going to fight. We're going to the bridge deck."

"What can we do there?"

"You'll see," said Petrel. She pulled a face. "Least I hope you will. Come on. You too, Cap'n." And she tucked the silent rats inside her jacket, and hurried towards the far end of the little cabin, where there was a door with a circular handle.

Dolph tried to hobble after her, and yelped again. The silver boy tapped her on the shoulder. "I am strong," he said. "I could carry you, if that would help."

They all stared at him. Dolph laughed uncertainly. "The sleeping captain, carry *me* . . . ?"

"Good," said Petrel, as if it were already settled. "Let's go."

The boy *was* strong, despite his smallness. He lifted Dolph in his arms as if she weighed no more than a loaf of bread.

Petrel picked up the lantern, saying, "Stay close. Don't fall behind."

Fin grasped the spanner, which was still in his pocket.

Then the four children—one of them silver-faced and

carrying the lost knowledge of generations inside his slender body—began to climb upward through the ship, knowing that above their heads a battle was raging, and that all the advantage was with the Devouts, and none at all with the crew of the *Oyster*.

CHAPTER 25

BROTHER THRAWN

PAST THE SILENT ENGINES THEY RAN. Past the digester and the batteries, up the first steep ladders with their iron rungs, up the next ladder until they were on the Commons, and up again. There was no time for caution, no time for ducking around corners to avoid folk. But neither, to Petrel's growing dismay, was there anyone to avoid. Apart from the babies and the youngest bratlings, who were presumably still huddled amidships with a few adults to care for them, everyone must be trying to fight their way out onto the open decks.

Trying and dying.

Petrel climbed faster, her mind spinning like a whirlpool. Fin's last-minute confession had shocked her, though it explained so much. The uncomplaining weight of the rats inside her jacket made her want to weep. The emptiness of the passages, the thought of what was happening above, the slim hope that she might be able to do something about it—

Fin's footsteps echoed hers. Dolph urged them on from the rear. "Quick, Petrel! Quick, Fin! Don't drop me, Cap'n!"

They passed Dufftown and kept climbing. Petrel thought she could hear shouts of fury and screams of pain from above, but it might have been the creaking of the ship or the grinding of the ice. The Commons ladderway seemed to go on forever, as if Brother Thrawn's malice had slithered down into the ship and changed its structure.

We've got to stop him. And with that thought, Petrel led the way up the last short ladder to the bridge deck.

There was no one there. Everyone who could work had been busy setting the lectrics to rights and mending the fire damage. And now they were trying to force their way out onto the fore- and afterdecks, determined to defend their ship.

Crab should've been on the bridge, thought Petrel, running along the last passage. *He should've seen the grappling hooks come over the rail. He should've stopped the cruel men before they got a foothold.*

But it was too late for recriminations. Petrel darted onto the bridge. The sun was a fingertip below the horizon, and the air outside the windows was pearly gray. It should have been beautiful. But below them, on the open decks, terrible things were happening.

Petrel put the lantern down, threw open the hatch that led outside, and ran aft, with the others close behind her. Out into the freezing air. Out into the screams and howls and clash of weapons rising from below.

She could hardly bear to look down. Every hatch on the

fore- and afterdecks was open, and the *Oyster*'s crew were trying to fight their way out. But they were at a terrible disadvantage. Only two men could climb through the hatch at a time, and however well-armed those men were, however fierce, a dozen or more Devouts waited for them, and struck them down as they emerged.

Petrel saw Crab fall, and five Officers, one after the other, behind him. At another hatch, Krill was fighting for his life. The deck in front of him was red with blood, and the cries of the Devouts, floating upward, were so full of savagery and hatred that Petrel shrank back. Her idea for stopping the attackers seemed pitiful now. She wished desperately that the silver boy could throw down lightning, or summon up an ice storm.

But he could not. It was up to her. The Nothing girl.

"What do you wish me to do?" asked the captain, putting Dolph down.

Petrel glanced at the horizon. "Stand next to the rail. Closer! *Closer!* Quick, now! Stand right here, and look down at the afterdeck."

Fin and Dolph stared at her, puzzled, but did not speak. The boy captain took a step forward and stood, looking down at the carnage . . .

And at that moment, as Petrel had calculated, the first rays of the sun rose above the horizon and struck his silver face. He shone as bright as a comet, and the light bent down to the deck and dazzled one of the attackers.

Just one.

The man looked up—and stopped in his tracks. His

quivering hand rose to point at the boy captain. His mouth gaped and no sound came from it.

The man next to him looked up. And the man next to *him*. And the man—

It was like a sickness, thought Petrel. A winter sickness that started with a single person and spread through the crew so quickly that one moment everyone was healthy and the next they were all coughing and sneezing.

The men below her were dumbstruck. Horrified. Afraid.

Can you not kill the Devouts with a glance? Can you not boil the blood in their veins?

As the invaders stared up at the silver boy, waiting for his terrible weapons to strike them, the men and women of the *Oyster* poured out of the hatches to defend their ship.

But then *they* looked up too. And *they* were dumbstruck. Petrel could see Albie, his cunning face blank with shock. And Krill and all his folk, staring up at the captain, their weapons limp in their hands.

Within seconds, the afterdeck went from a scene of death and destruction to total silence. Even the wind fiddles were still. Even the useless straining turbines.

It won't last, thought Petrel. *They'll be fighting again as soon as they get their wits back, which means more blood. And Albie and Krill still don't know what's going on. I've gotta tell 'em!*

Her breath was a cloud in the morning air. She could feel the doubt gathering inside her. What if no one listened? What if they looked straight past her, ignored her, treated her as nothing?

"No!" she told herself firmly. "I'm *not* nothing! Never was! Never will be again!" And she stepped straight past the doubt, stepped forward until she was standing beside the silver boy.

"This is the captain!" she shouted to the folk watching from below, and her words fell like an axe upon them. "He's the sleeping captain, only now he's awake!"

She saw the sudden understanding in Albie's face, and in Krill's.

"And those folk"—Petrel pointed to the Devouts, with their strange round hats pulled over their ears and their layers of scarves and jackets and ugly brown robes—"they've come to *kill* him!"

Her words woke the invaders from their stillness. They had thought the demon was safely dead, but now here he was, directly above them. Alive. Awake.

Most of them turned tail and ran. With their hands shielding their heads and their axes forgotten, they raced for the ship's rail and began to slide frantically down the ropes.

Behind them, the *Oyster*'s crew roared with fury. Albie raised his pipe wrench and bellowed, "After 'em, shipmates! Don't let 'em escape!"

But the boy captain, up on the bridge deck, bellowed louder. "Let them go, Albie."

The Chief Engineer stopped in his tracks. As far as Petrel knew, he had never taken an order in his life, not from anyone. But this was the sleeping captain—though he was no longer asleep. And what was more, he knew Albie's name.

Petrel looked at the silver boy, startled. *How did he know that?*

"Let them all go," cried the boy. "Krill, let them go."

He knows Krill too!

The captain's orders made no difference to the Devouts. In their panic, they crowded each other and pushed and shoved, so that some of them fell off the ropes onto the ice, and their companions left them there without a backward glance.

"Good riddance," shouted Skua, who had joined his da.

But not all the Devouts had run away. Petrel saw movement out of the corner of her eye, and spun around. A small group of men had climbed onto the aft crane, and now they stood there, glaring up at the boy captain with such loathing that Petrel could almost feel it.

Even before Fin spoke, she knew that the man at the front of the group was their leader. His thin face was set in disapproving lines, as if everything about the world disappointed him. He was as cold as midwinter—but at the same time, there was a feverish air about him, that Petrel could sense even from this distance. An air of hatred, and the determination to shape the world to his will, no matter what the cost.

"Brother Thrawn." Fin's whisper sounded as if it had been cut out of him with a knife.

"Do you fear that man?" asked the boy captain in a quiet voice.

"Yes. No. I—I don't know," answered Fin.

"Don't look at him," whispered Petrel. "He *wants* you to look at him, I know he does."

It was true. The eyes of Brother Thrawn's companions were fixed on the boy captain. But Brother Thrawn was watching Fin. And Fin was watching Brother Thrawn.

By this time, Albie had spotted the men on the crane too. He began to urge the crew after them—but then he stopped and shouted, "What about *them*, Cap'n? Shall we get 'em down?"

The silver boy looked at Petrel, who shook her head. "Wait," said the boy, holding up one hand.

Albie waited.

Brother Thrawn took five precise steps forward. "Initiate," he said, and his voice was like a shard of ice on the morning air.

Petrel felt Fin tremble. She thought of what it must have been like for a small boy to be at the mercy of such a man, and she stepped closer to her friend, so he would know she was there.

"Initiate," said Brother Thrawn again. "I am pleased to see you."

He didn't sound pleased. He sounded furious, in a secretive sort of way, and Petrel wasn't at all surprised when Fin didn't answer. She wondered if he *could* answer, or if all the breath had gone out of him, the way it had gone out of her when she saw the Maw rearing up through the ice.

The sun was rising higher now, and everyone else was blinking. Brother Thrawn did not blink. "Now you must act," he said to Fin. "This is what I trained you for. This is your moment. The fate of the world lies in your hands. Now you must act. Now—"

There was something horribly hypnotic about that flat,

cold voice. Petrel found herself nodding, as if Brother Thrawn were talking to *her*. She blinked.

"Fin," she hissed. "Don't listen."

She didn't think Fin heard her. All his attention was fixed on the awful figure of Brother Thrawn.

"Raise your weapon, Initiate," said the Brother.

It was only then that Petrel realized Fin was still carrying the spanner, his fingers clenching and unclenching around it.

The boy captain touched her arm. "Should we do something?"

Petrel looked at Fin. He had retreated behind the old blankness, and only his hand showed his distress. "Wait," she whispered to the captain, though she was not at all sure it was the right thing to do. "Just wait."

"Listen to me, Initiate," said Brother Thrawn. "Raise your weapon."

Slowly Fin raised the spanner. It seemed to weigh a ton, and despite the cold air, sweat sprang from his forehead, as if one part of him were fighting with another part.

"Do you see the demon beside you?" Brother Thrawn's voice was no louder, but it seemed to envelop the whole ship. "Do you see the vile creature?"

Fin nodded.

"No," whispered Petrel, but she did not move.

"You must crush it," cried Brother Thrawn. Some of the flatness had gone from his voice, and in its place was a thinly concealed triumph. "Crush it, and join the Inner Circle. Crush it and save the world. Crush it, boy, and win yourself a name!"

As the spanner rose, the sun seemed to pause in its journey. Down on the afterdeck every face was a mask of dismay. Petrel held her breath.

Fin's mouth opened and shut. His chest heaved. He lifted the spanner high above his head, so that the parts of it that were not rusty shone almost as bright as the boy captain.

Then he shouted at the top of his voice. "I *have* a name! It is *Fin!*" And he threw the spanner at the terrible figure of Brother Thrawn.

The spanner spun through the morning air, turning over and over, like a seal in the water. It spun like something joyous, thrown by a small bratling. It spun like life itself, homing in on the man who had denied that life.

Brother Thrawn did not duck or try to avoid his fate. Perhaps he was courageous, in his own cold way. Or perhaps he simply did not believe that one of his Initiates would turn against him.

The spanner hit him on the forehead. With a cry, he dropped to his knees. He tried to stand—once, twice—then sprawled facedown and did not move again.

CHAPTER 26

NORTH

THE MEN AROUND BROTHER THRAWN STOOD STUNNED, LOOK-
ing from Fin to their leader and back again. But then understanding gripped them and they set up a wailing so loud that it
hurt Petrel's ears. They lifted Brother Thrawn's body as carefully as an egg and lowered it from the crane, shuffling past the
Oyster's crew members as if they were not there.

"Is he dead?" whispered Petrel.

"I do not know," said Fin. "I do not care."

It took the Devouts several minutes to find a way of lower-
ing Brother Thrawn to the ice. Someone—Petrel thought it was
Skua again—shouted, "Just drop him. He won't feel it," and
laughed. But everyone else stood silent and threatening, until
the Devouts were gone, and their mournful cries fading in the
distance as they retreated to their ship.

Only then did they look up. And now their faces were as
bright as the morning.

"Cap'n!" cried Krill.

"Cap'n!" shouted a dozen other voices, and then two dozen, and then a hundred. And before Petrel knew it, she and Fin and Dolph and the silver boy were wrapped in a great rolling swell of sound that rose and fell with joy.

"Cap'n, Cap'n, Cap'n!"

It seemed to go on forever. And when it began to die away at last, Skua climbed onto the aft crane, and picked up the spanner that had clobbered Brother Thrawn. "Fin!" he shouted, waving the spanner above his head.

The sound rose again, as everyone forgave Fin for being a stranger, and bellowed his name at the tops of their voices. "Fin! Fin! Fin!"

Dolph waved from the bridge deck. "Dolph! Dolph!" cried the crew.

No one shouted for Petrel. They had heard her when it counted, but now they looked past her, as if the habit of ignoring her were too great to be broken.

She wasn't surprised.

Not really.

She told herself that it didn't matter.

Not really.

She was about to turn away when a single voice said, "Petrel."

It wasn't the cry of acclamation that the others had been. It was quieter. More thoughtful. More of a suggestion than anything else.

"Squid," whispered Petrel.

No one else said anything, not immediately. The folk near Squid looked at her, puzzled.

"Petrel," said Squid again, a little more definite this time.

Near the rail, Krill crossed his beefy arms, peered up at the bridge deck and boomed, "Yes, Petrel."

"Who?" said a woman nearby.

"Where?" said a man.

And within seconds the whole deck was whispering back and forth, back and forth. "Who's Petrel? What are they talking about? Did Krill get a bang on the head, do you think? There's no one else up there except the Nothing girl."

Petrel couldn't bear it. She felt a great heat inside her, a great noise that would not be silenced. Before she could lose her nerve, she strode back to the rail and said the words that she had said to herself earlier. Only now they rang out across the afterdeck, too loud to ignore.

"I'm *not* nothing! Never was, never will be! I'm Petrel! Quill's daughter. Seal's daughter too!"

And she stood there in the morning sunlight, not hiding, not ducking away. Just stood there, so that they *had* to see her.

For a long moment there was dead silence, broken only by the creaking of the ship and the distant cry of gulls.

Then someone said, "So *that's* her name."

And someone else said, "I didn't know she *had* a name!"

"I always thought she was a half-wit."

"Me too."

"But she can't be, can she? She's the one who shouted earlier. Told us what was happening. Showed us the sleeping captain."

"Quill's daughter, heh? Sounds just like her mam . . ."

The murmuring stopped abruptly. Feet shuffled. Eyes fell, as folk remembered things from twelve years ago. Things they had done. And not done.

It was then that Squid said, for the third time, "Petrel!"

A quiver swept through the gathered crowd, like wind on water. Gradually, folk began to whisper again, but this time their voices were so quiet that Petrel couldn't catch what they were saying. Not at first, anyway. But then she heard her name.

"Petrel," said a woman.

"Petrel," said the man next to her.

And suddenly the whole afterdeck was filled with voices, all of them shouting, "Petrel! Petrel!" and folk craning their necks to see her as she stood beside the captain, and beaming up at her and stamping their feet.

"Petrel!" they cried, "Petrel! Petrel! Petrel!" as if they were trying to make up for the last twelve years.

The girl they shouted for could hardly believe what was happening. She looked at Fin, who smiled at her.

"Wave!" mouthed Dolph.

Petrel waved, and the resulting roar of approval almost knocked her off her feet. Ice fell from the turbines, and folk dodged it, laughing. Gulls fled in all directions.

But the shouting could not go on forever. As it died away, folk rushed for the bridge and squeezed inside, as many as could fit.

When the boy captain walked in, with Fin and Petrel supporting Dolph between them, all the talking stopped and a shyness fell upon the crew. Those at the front of the crowd regarded the silver boy with awe. But when he began to question them about who had died in the fighting, and about the fire and what they had done so far to mend the damage, their shyness vanished, and before long they were asking his advice on myriad things, foremost of which was fixing the lectrics as quickly as possible so they would not all freeze to death.

The boy captain answered their questions with a knowledge of the ship and its crew that astonished everyone, including Petrel.

But then she realized. *He's got Mister Smoke's and Missus Slink's memories. That's what we did with the little boxes, we gave him their memories. It had to be done, but now he's got it all, and they've got nothing.*

Sadly, she hugged the placid bodies inside her jacket. With the excitement over, she was feeling slightly sick. She wanted to be somewhere quiet, to mourn for the rats who had been her only friends for so long.

She knew they weren't really gone. All their knowledge was there inside the boy captain, along with the memory of everything they had done over the centuries.

But it wasn't the same, not for Petrel.

Around her, voices rose and fell. Krill talked loudly of getting rid of the tribes and working together for the good of the ship, and a surprising number of folk agreed with him. Dolph told everyone about Crab's treachery, and about the rats and the Maw.

At one stage, Albie bullied his way to the front of the crowd, whacked Fin on the back and said, "I'm the one who rescued you in the first place, lad, don't you forget that! It turned out to be the right decision, despite what certain folk said at the time."

His words were no surprise to Petrel. Albie would always be where the power was. Where the decisions were being made.

But it *was* a surprise when he whacked *her* on the back and said, "This is a proud moment for our family. I always knew you had great things ahead of you." He grabbed Skua's shoulder in a punishing grip. "I said so many times, didn't I, son?"

"Reckon so, Da," mumbled Skua.

Petrel was still a little afraid of her uncle. But she had meant what she said on the bridge deck. There was to be no more hiding. No more scuttling round the edges of the crew. Apart from anything else, the captain was going to need her. After all, how could a boy of silver and wire, however cunningly made, know that Albie was lying? How could he know that Skua was afraid of his da, and that Squid had a warm heart, and that Dolph had loved her mam and was still grieving?

But Petrel knew those things, and a thousand more. Despite her sadness, she grinned at Albie, which surprised him so much that he dragged Skua away without another word.

Gradually folk set about the business of repairing the ship, and the crowd thinned out. When everyone but Fin, Petrel and Third Officer Hump had gone, the boy captain turned to the chart table, his delicate fingers tracing the course that the *Oyster* had followed for as long as anyone could remember, and for centuries before that.

"The man who made me," he said, "thought that the world would be righted within a hundred years, no more. He thought that by the time I woke, people would have given up their hatred of machines, and be crying out for the knowledge that I carry within me." He looked at Fin. "But I do not think that is the case."

A furrow appeared above Fin's blue eyes. "The Devouts still hate machines," he said slowly. "But the people in the villages— Their lives are so hard. They starve and die young. I believe they would welcome anything that made things easier."

"Then we must help them," said the captain, and his finger strayed from the old course and began to trace a new one.

Petrel's breath quickened. "You mean, go north?"

Behind her, Third Officer Hump gasped. "North? Are you *mad*? I mean, north, Cap'n? Is—um—is that wise?"

"I believe so," said the boy captain.

"The Devouts will try to stop us," said Fin. "They are everywhere. They are more powerful than you can imagine."

"So is knowledge," said the boy captain. "Our expedition will not be without resources."

Inside Petrel's jacket, something wriggled. Then a rough voice mumbled, "I 'ope you've got backup for this expedition, shipmate."

Everything around Petrel seemed to grind to a halt. She

opened her jacket. "Mister *Smoke?*" she whispered. "But I thought—"

Mister Smoke's silver eyes peered up at her, bright with mystery. "You gotta have backup, shipmate," he said. "And if no one gives you any, then you gotta build it yerself."

"Mind you," said Missus Slink, poking her nose out, "we didn't quite get the hind leg circuits right. You might have to carry us for a bit till we fix them."

"Um— All right," said Petrel, not knowing whether to laugh or cry, and wanting to do both at once, because there was more joy in the world than she could ever have imagined.

AND SO IT WAS THAT, EARLY NEXT MORNING, IN THE PEARLY light before dawn, when the whole crew had worked together to get the engines going again, and the *Oyster* had forced its way out of the pack ice into clear water, the silver boy gave the order to turn north.

"Are you sure, Cap'n?" asked Third Officer Hump, who was now First Officer.

The captain nodded. "We are going back to the world."

"We are going to change things," said Fin, who stood on one side of the captain.

Petrel, who stood proudly on the other side, said, "We're going to find Fin's mam!"

"North it is, then," said First Officer Hump.

From inside Petrel's jacket, Mister Smoke cried, "Full speed ahead, shipmate!"

"But watch out for those valves," said Missus Slink. "They're not as young as they could be."

Petrel laughed. First Officer Hump swung the wheel. Third Officer Dolph—newly appointed to the position—banged out a rattle to Albie in the engine room.

And as the sun rose above the horizon, the ship turned and sailed north, like a bright light heading into darkness.

SUNKER'S DEEP

The Hidden series—book 2

LIAN TANNER

PROLOGUE

THEY CAME TO THE MEETING SHORTLY AFTER MIDNIGHT, SEP-
arately and secretly. Professor Serran Coe was the first to arrive, and he greeted the other three with his finger to his lips.
Not a word was spoken until they were in the basement, and
even then, with the university abandoned above them and a
dozen locked doors between themselves and the outside world,
they were reluctant to name the things they were talking about.

"Has he gone?" whispered Professor Surgeon Lin Lin, a
small, sharp-eyed woman with night-black hair.

Serran Coe nodded and a flicker of regret crossed his face.
"Two weeks ago. The ship sailed under cover of darkness."

Ariel Fetch leaned forward, her long earrings tinkling.
"Did you give him the instruction? The one we agreed
upon?"

"I built a compulsion into his circuits," said Coe. "It will
come into play when he crosses the equator on the return voyage."

"If there *is* a return voyage," growled Admiral Cray, who was Lin Lin's husband.

The others began to protest, but the admiral spoke over the top of them. "Nothing is certain, and you cannot tell me otherwise. I have just learned that five of our best ships were sunk last night, and their officers murdered! By their own crews, mind you, who then deserted en masse to join the Anti-Machinists." The admiral's waxed moustache twitched in disgust. "This whole thing is spreading quicker than anyone thought possible. There are even rumors that the government is teetering! And what do we four do about it? We run, we hide, we send a mechanical child to the far southern ice, hoping that one day he will return and be compelled to seek out—"

"Hush!" said Lin Lin, and her husband broke off his rant. The building above them creaked ominously.

"It is only the wind," said Serran Coe in a tired voice. "It has been rising all week."

The admiral grumbled, "Look at us, jumping at shadows! Why are we not out there fighting the mobs?"

His question momentarily silenced the other three. Then Ariel Fetch sighed and said, "You may be a fighter, Admiral, but we are not. And even if we were, we could not turn back the Anti-Machinists. Their time has come. All we can do is try to preserve as much knowledge as we can, so it is there when people want it again."

"Pah!" said the Admiral. "They will never want it again! They are fools and criminals—"

His wife interrupted him, "Then you should be glad that we are leaving them behind."

Her words fell like a blow on the tiny gathering. Serran Coe loosened his stiff white collar and said, "You are going to do it? I thought you might change your minds. It is so—extreme."

"Extreme, it may be," said Lin Lin, sitting up very straight, "but I refuse to live under the rule of the Anti-Machinists, and I am not the only one who thinks that way. Besides, the medical papers we are taking with us must be preserved for the future. Even your mechanical child does not know everything."

"When will you go?"

Lin Lin's calm voice gave no hint of what lay ahead. "Another week, at least. It will take that long to gather family and friends." She smiled wryly at her husband. "Which means there is still time for a little fighting if you wish it, dearest."

The admiral took a deep breath through his nose and let it out again. "Nay," he said. "Nay, you are right. We must follow our plans to the very end. I just hope—" He scrubbed his fists against his knees until the blue cloth crumpled. "I just hope it is worth it."

Nine days after that meeting, Professor Surgeon Lin Lin and her people left. They told no one where they were going, and no one had time or inclination to ask; the government was on the brink of collapse and the city was in uproar.

Screaming mobs rampaged through the streets, determined to destroy the machines that they blamed for all the wrongs in the world. They smashed automobiles and typewriters, omnibuses and telephones. The police were helpless against them. The army, brought in by the collapsing government, destroyed its own gun carriages and joined the mobs. Everyone else, frightened and confused, barricaded their doors, telling each other that the madness *must* stop soon.

But they were wrong. The long harsh reign of the Anti-Machinists was only just beginning.

THREE HUNDRED YEARS LATER

SHARKEY SQUINTED ONE-EYED THROUGH THE THICK, GLASS porthole. He was searching for scraps of metal—metal that'd be covered in weeds by now and colonized by barnacles, so that it looked no different from the rocks around it. But it was here somewhere, seventy-five feet below the surface of the sea, and he was determined to find it.

"Two degrees down bubble," he murmured.

"Two degrees down. Aye, sir!" cried eleven-year-old Gilly, and she turned the brass wheels that tilted the little submersible's diving planes.

In the bow, eight-year-old Poddy's hands flew across the control panel, trimming the boat and keeping the direction steady as it sank. Further aft, Gilly's younger brother, Cuttle, braced his bare feet on the metal deck, waiting for orders to change speed. Pipes gurgled. Dials twitched. Above the children's heads, the ancestor shrine maintained a silent watch.

"Ease your bubble," said Sharkey.

"Ease bubble. Aye, sir!" Gilly turned the wheels the other way.

Outside the porthole, the green light that filtered down from above touched thick strands of kelp and a shoal of codlings. The throb of *Claw*'s propeller was like the beating of Sharkey's heart.

He straightened his eye patch and sang the last part of an old Sunker charm, under his breath.

"Below to find,
Below to bind—"

It must have worked, because almost straightaway, he saw something out of the corner of his undamaged eye. "Starboard twenty," he said.

"Starboard twenty. Aye, sir!" cried Poddy, and *Claw* began to turn.

When they were on the desired heading, Sharkey said, "Midships."

"Midships. Aye, sir!"

"All stop."

"All stop. Aye, sir!" And Cuttle threw himself at the motor switches.

Gilly came for'ard, ducking past the periscope housing and wriggling around the chart table. "Have you found something, sir?"

Sharkey wasn't sure, not really. But he always sounded confident, even when he had no idea what he was doing. "Aye. There, where the kelp's thickest," he said.

Young Poddy hooked her toe under the control panel and

leaned back on her stool. "Adm'ral Deeps *thought* you'd be able to find it, sir. And she was right!"

"'Course she was," said Sharkey, hoping that the strange-looking bit of rock really was scrap metal from the giant submersible *Resolute,* which had broken up somewhere near here ninety-three years ago.

"Has he found the boxes?" called Cuttle.

"Not yet," said Gilly. "But he will." She bobbed her head in the direction of the ancestor shrine. "Thank you, Great Granmer Lin Lin. Thank you, Great Granfer Cray."

For the rest of the morning, *Claw* cruised back and forth through the ropy kelp, while Sharkey stared out the porthole, half-dizzy with concentration.

At the end of the forenoon watch, Gilly struck the bell eight times. *Ting-ting ting-ting ting-ting ting-ting.* "It's midday, sir. We're due back on *Rampart* soon."

"Mmm," said Sharkey. "I want to find at least one of the boxes before we go."

From the helm, Poddy said, "You could ask Lin Lin and Adm'ral Cray where they are, sir."

Sharkey said nothing. His fellow Sunkers venerated their dead ancestors, but at the same time, they seemed to think that the spirits were like some sort of boat crew, and all he had to do was whistle and they'd come running.

Poddy glanced out the helm porthole. "Look, sir, there's a dolphin! Maybe it's the spirit of Lin Lin! Maybe she's going to show you the boxes!"

Sharkey sighed in a long-suffering sort of way. "Lin Lin talks to me when it suits her, Poddy. So does First Adm'ral Cray—"

The younger children bobbed their heads respectfully.

"—and *that* is just an ordinary dolphin."

"Oh," said Poddy, disappointed.

The dolphin swam idly away from them, and Sharkey watched it go. His eye flickered downwards. There was something—

"There!" he said. "Port full rudder."

"Port full rudder. Aye, sir!" Poddy's small hands brought *Claw* around, as smooth as sea silk.

"All stop."

"All stop. Aye, sir!" shouted Cuttle.

"Hold us right there," said Sharkey, and he gripped the lever that worked the retrieval device.

Like the underwater vessel that housed it, the device was called "the claw." Sharkey pulled the lever back and it ratcheted out from the side of the little submersible and spread wide its talons. It wasn't easy to use with only one eye; Sharkey had to compensate for the fact that he couldn't judge distances as well as he'd been able to before the accident. And he didn't want to wreck the box. Now that he'd found it, he was sure it'd be a good one, crammed full of surgeons' secrets with not a drop of water seeped in to spoil it.

Gilly eyed the chronometer. "We're due back on *Rampart* now, sir," she said.

Without looking up, Sharkey said, "Send a message turtle. Tell 'em we'll be late."

". . . Aye, sir."

There was no argument, of course. Discipline on the submersibles didn't allow for arguments. But as Gilly scratched out a note and took one of the mechanical turtles from its rack, Sharkey knew what the middies were thinking.

He won't get into trouble. But we will, even though we're just following his orders!

It was true. Because of who he was, Sharkey could get away with being late, whereas the middies couldn't.

Still, that was their problem, not his.

It took him another ten minutes to juggle the box into the side airlock. As soon as it was secure, he murmured, "Mark the position."

Gilly squeezed past the ladder to the chart table. "Position marked, sir!"

"Half-ahead. Take her up to periscope depth."

As *Claw* moved forward again, the planes tilting, the bow rising, Sharkey sat back on his stool, pleased with himself. He knew what the other Sunkers would say when they heard about the box.

Sharkey can do anything. Sharkey can find anything. Sharkey's a hero, a future adm'ral, born on a lucky tide and blessed by the ancestors. Thank you, Lin Lin!

The submersible leveled out, and he grinned. "Up periscope."

There was probably no danger from their enemies, not so far from terra. But caution was drilled into the Sunker children from the day they could crawl. Gilly crouched, her face pressed against the eyepieces, her feet swiveling in a circle.

Halfway round, she stopped and rubbed her eyes. "Sir, there's something strange in the Up Above. Like huge bubbles—"

Sharkey was already moving, snatching the periscope handles away from her.

"Sou'west," said Gilly.

The breath caught in Sharkey's throat. Gilly was right. There were three enormous, white bubbles floating through the sky with woven baskets hanging beneath them! And figures leaning over the edge of the baskets, pointing to something below the surface. And lines tethering the bubbles to—

To skimmers! To a dozen or more skimmers with billowing sails and their hulls low in the water, following those pointing fingers with a look of grim purpose.

"It's the Ghosts!" cried Sharkey, and his blood ran cold. For the last three hundred years, the Sunkers had dreaded this moment. "It's the Hungry Ghosts! And they've found *Rampart*!"

EARLIER THAT SAME DAY

As DAWN BROKE, TWELVE-YEAR-OLD PETREL LEANED AGAINST the rail of the ancient icebreaker *Oyster*, staring into the distance. Somewhere over there, beyond the horizon, was the country of West Norn.

"Will there be penguins, Missus Slink?" she murmured.

"Probably not," said the large, gray rat perched on her shoulder. A tattered green neck-ribbon tickled Petrel's ear. "But if my memory serves me correctly, there will be dogs and cats. And perhaps bears."

"Bears is further north," said Mister Smoke, from Petrel's other shoulder. "Don't you worry about bears, shipmate. There's worse things here than bears."

"You mean the Devouts?" asked Petrel.

"Don't frighten the girl, Smoke," said Missus Slink.

"I'm not frightened," said Petrel quickly. But she was.

For the last three hundred years, the *Oyster* had kept its course at the farthest end of the earth. Its decks were rusty, its hull was battered, and its crew had broken down into warring tribes and forgotten why they were there. All that had remained of their original mission was the myth of the Sleeping Captain, and the belief that the rest of the world was mad, and therefore best avoided.

But the Devouts, fanatical descendants of the original Anti-Machinists, had traced the *Oyster* to the southern ice, and sent an expedition to destroy the ship and everyone on board. Thanks to Petrel, they had failed, and the Sleeping Captain had woken up at last.

The Devouts thought the *Oyster*'s captain was a demon. But really, he was a mechanical boy with a silver face and a mind full of wonders. He knew sea charts, star maps, and thousands of years of human history. He could calculate times and distances while Petrel was still trying to figure out the question, and he could mend or make machines and lectrics of every kind. On his orders, the *Oyster* had left its icy hideaway and headed north.

"We are going to bring knowledge back to the world," he had said.

The voyage had taken more than twelve weeks, with several engine breakdowns that had tested even the captain, but now Petrel was about to set foot on land for only the second time in her life.

She heard a rattling in the pipes behind her and turned to listen. It was a message in general ship code.

SHORE PARTY PREPARE TO BOARD THE MAW. SIGNED, FIRST OFFICER HUMP.

With the rats clinging to her shoulders, Petrel slipped

through the nearest hatch and onto the Commons ladderway, which took her from Braid, all the way down to Grease Alley. She ran past the batteries, which were fed by the *Oyster*'s wind turbines, and past the digester that took all the ship's waste and turned it into fuel.

And there was the rest of the shore party, making their way towards the *Maw*.

"Here she is!" boomed Head Cook Krill, in a voice that was used to shouting over the constant rattle of pots and pans. "We thought you must've changed your mind, bratling."

"Not likely!" said Petrel, putting on a bold front. "Don't you try leaving *me* behind, Krill."

"We would not go without you," said the captain in his sweet, serious voice. "I *knew* you would come."

Fin just smiled, his fair hair falling over his eyes, and handed her a woven seaweed bag.

"Ta," said Petrel, and she smiled back at him, though her heart was beating too fast and her mouth was dry at the thought of what lay ahead.

The *Maw* was an enormous, fish-shaped vessel set to watch over the *Oyster* by its long-ago inventor. It traveled underwater, and the only way onto it was through the bottommost part of the ship. As the small party climbed through the double hatch, Chief Engineer Albie was giving last-minute instructions to his son, Skua.

"No mucking around, boy. This is a big responsibility, taking the cap'n and his friends ashore." In the dim light, Albie's eyes were unreadable, but Petrel thought she saw a flash of white teeth through his beard. "You set 'em down nice and gently."

It wasn't at all like Albie to be so thoughtful. By nature, he was a cunning, evil-tempered man who until recently had made Petrel's life a torment. But Petrel was so excited and nervous that she didn't think much of it. Not until later, and by then, the harm was already done.

"Aye, Da," said Skua.

"And come straight back when you've dropped 'em. You hear me?"

"Aye, Da. Watch your fingers, Da!"

There was a clang as the double hatch was clamped shut, and a moment later, the *Maw*'s engines roared to life and the interlocking plates of its hull began to move.

Thanks to Albie's instructions, their passage towards land was smooth and uneventful. Skua brought them right up close to the headland, where the drop-off was steep, and they jumped onto the rocks without getting wet past their knees.

"I'll be back at noon," said Skua, as he stood in the mouth of the *Maw*, tugging at his sparse red whiskers. "Watch out for trouble, Cap'n. And the rest of you!"

His expression was suitably serious, but it seemed to Petrel that as he stepped back into the shadows, it turned into something else. A smirk, maybe. Mind you, that was normal for Skua, who smirked at everything, and once again, she thought nothing of it. A moment later, the *Maw*'s huge mouth closed and the monstrous fish dived below the surface.

Petrel felt a tremor run right through her. *We're on land!*

She took a cautious step forward, and the ground seemed to sway under her feet.

"Mister Smoke," she hissed. "The ground's moving!"

"Nah," said the old rat. "It's because you've been on the *Oyster* for so long, shipmate. It'll stop soon."

Fin had been staring at the surrounding countryside with uncertain pride. Now he turned to Petrel and said, "This is West Norn. What do you think?"

The landscape stretched out in front of them, muddy and inhospitable. There were patches of snow on the ground and the air was cold, though not nearly as cold as Petrel was used to. A few straggly trees were scattered here and there, with a bird or two huddled on their branches, but there was no other sign of life.

Petrel would've liked it better if there'd been a good solid deck under her feet and the familiar rumble of an engine. But she didn't want to hurt Fin's feelings, so all she said was, "It's big, ain't it? Reckon you could fit the *Oyster* in its pocket, and it wouldn't even notice."

Behind her, Krill said, "What now, Cap'n? We head for the first village?"

The captain pushed back his sealskin hood and nodded. "Once we have introduced ourselves, we will explain the workings of water pumps and other simple machines that will make their lives easier. We will find out what they want most, and go back to the ship for supplies and equipment." He paused, his beautiful face gleaming in the early morning light. "Of course, I will ask them about the Song too."

Krill scratched his chin until the bones knotted into his beard rattled. "Now this is where you've lost me, Cap'n. I still don't understand this stuff about a song."

"There is nothing mysterious about it," said the captain. "Serran Coe, the man who made me, must have programmed it into my circuits. As soon as we crossed the equator, I became aware of its importance."

"But you don't know *why* it's important?"

"I know that it will help us bring knowledge back to the people. I know that I will recognize it when I hear it—the Song *and* the Singer. If I do not know more than that, it must be because my programming has been deliberately limited, in case I am captured."

He pointed due west. "Three hundred years ago, there was a prosperous village in that direction. We will start there."

EVERYTHING PETREL SAW THAT MORNING WAS STRANGE AND unsettling. She was glad of Mister Smoke and Missus Slink, riding on her shoulders, and of Fin, who walked beside her, naming the objects she pointed to.

"That is a fir tree," he said. "It does not lose its leaves in winter, like the other trees. That is an abandoned cottage."

Petrel clutched the seaweed bag, which contained dried fish in case they got hungry, and a telegraph device that the captain had built so they could talk to the ship. "Folk used to live in it?"

"Yes."

"What happened to 'em?"

"I do not know. They probably got sick and died."

The mud slowed them down, and the village they were heading for seemed to get no closer. But at last, Fin nudged Petrel and said, "*That* is a tabby cat."

Mister Smoke's whiskers brushed Petrel's cheek. "You sure it's a cat, shipmate? Looks more like a parcel o' bones to me. I can see its ribs from 'ere."

My ribs were like that not so long ago, thought Petrel, and she took a scrap of dried fish from her bag and tossed it to the cat.

"Captain! Krill!" called Fin. "If there is a cat, the village is probably close by. Beyond that row of bare trees, perhaps. But we should be careful. There might be Devouts."

The captain nodded, and waited for them to catch up. "That position accords with my knowledge. Mister Smoke, will you go ahead and see if there is danger?"

"Aye, Cap'n," said the rat, and he leaped down from Petrel's shoulder and scampered away.

"D'you really think there might be Devouts here, lad?" Krill asked Fin. "We're a good hundred miles or more from their Citadel."

"They have informers everywhere," said Fin. "And there are always rumors that someone has found an old book, or un-earthed a machine from the time before the Great Cleansing. The Devouts travel the countryside, trying to catch them."

Petrel listened to this exchange carefully. Fin knew all about the Devouts. He used to be one of their Initiates and had traveled to the southern ice with his fellows to destroy the

Oyster and her crew. But Petrel, not knowing who he was, had befriended him, and bit by bit, Fin had changed.

Now he's one of us, thought Petrel. *And we're going to find his mam.*

Her heart swelled at the thought. She knew that the main purpose of the *Oyster*'s voyage north was to bring knowledge back to a world that had sunk deep into ignorance and superstition. But as far as *she* was concerned, the search for Fin's mam, who had given him to the Devouts when he was three years old to save him from starvation, was just as important.

Mister Smoke returned with mud on his fur and his silver eyes shining. "No sign of Devouts, shipmates. Village is quiet as a biscuit."

Petrel looked towards the trees, feeling nervous all over again. "But what about the informers?"

"The Devouts who attacked us down south know we weren't beaten," said Krill. "I reckon they could guess we might come after 'em. And what with all that engine trouble we had on the way, I wouldn't be surprised if they passed us and got here first. So, we're not giving up too many secrets by showing ourselves to a few villagers, informers or not." He cracked his knuckles thoughtfully. "All the same, it won't hurt to take it slowly. How about I go in by myself, chat to a few folk, see what's—"

But the captain was already striding towards the village.

"Wait!" cried Krill. "Cap'n! Wait for us!"

In the end, they entered the village in a tight group, with the captain's silver face hidden under his hood. For her part,

Petrel was glad they were sticking together—and not just because of her fear of the Devouts.

For most of her life, she had survived by pretending to be witless. Shipfolk had called her Nothing Girl, and believed that she couldn't talk. Then the Devouts had attacked, and Petrel had spoken up at last, to save the *Oyster*.

Since then, she had grown used to speaking her mind, to proving over and over again (to herself as much as anyone else) that she was *not* Nothing. But that was on the ship where everything was as familiar and comforting as her own two hands.

This was different. This was *land*, and these villagers were strangers. She already felt out of place. *What if they take one look at me and decide I'm not worth talking to?*

To take her mind off such an ugly possibility, she whispered to Fin, "Wouldn't it be good if your mam was right here, in the first place we stopped?"

"She will not be," said Fin. "Look! There are the cottages!"

"They're small," said Petrel.

"And *dirty!*" Fin sounded shocked. "I knew people's lives were hard, but I had forgotten—"

He broke off, and they all stared in dismay at the little settlement. The cottages were made of earth and reeds, with more reeds for the roofs. Most of them leaned one way or the other, and the ones that didn't lean slumped in the middle as if they could no longer be bothered to stand upright. The snow between them had turned to sludge and, in some places, it was hard to tell where the houses ended and the muddy ground began.

"Is this the place you were thinking of, Cap'n?" murmured Krill. "It don't look prosperous to me!"

Petrel thought she saw movement, but when she jerked around, there was just a scrap of filthy curtain trembling over a glassless window. "Where's all the people?" she whispered.

"Watchin' us," said Mister Smoke, from her right shoulder.

"Scared," said Missus Slink, from her left.

They're not the only ones, thought Petrel. *Blizzards, I wish I was back on the ship!*

"Come," said the captain, and they waded through the mud to what seemed like the middle of the village. Krill looked relaxed, except for the muscles in his neck, which were as taut as staywires. Fin eyed the mean little cottages with a mixture of fascination and disgust.

They saw no one.

"Don't reckon they want to talk to us," whispered Petrel. "We might as well go—" Her whisper turned to a yelp as a rock flew out of nowhere and hit her on the leg.

Her instinct, honed by years of survival, told her to run for her life. But Fin grabbed her hand, and the captain stepped forward and cried, "We do not mean you any harm!"

A whisper came from one of the cottages. "Go away!" A man, from the sound of it, not wanting to be heard by his fellow villagers.

"We wish to help you," cried the captain. "We will teach you how to build a water pump so you do not have to carry—"

Another rock splashed into the mud by his foot. "Scat, the lot of yez!"

Somewhere, a baby started to wail, and was instantly silenced. The air was sour with fear.

Petrel swallowed. More than anything else, she wanted to be back on the ship. "Let's go," she whispered.

But the captain did not move. He raised his voice again. "We are also searching for a Song—"

"Scat!" hissed the man, a third time.

At which Fin suddenly lost his temper. "Is that all you can say?" he shouted. "You ignorant peasant!"

"Shhh!" said Krill.

But Fin wouldn't be silenced. "We came here to help you, and you will not even—"

A woman's voice interrupted him. "Our beloved leaders, the Devouts, are on their way." Unlike the man, she spoke loudly and carefully, as if she had tested each word beforehand to see how it would sound. "They will be here shortly after midday. They are always interested in travelers; you must wait and speak to them."

That stopped Fin in his tracks. "Let's go!" urged Petrel again. And this time, the captain listened to her.

"D'you reckon they'll tell the Devouts about us?" she asked when they reached the headland at last. She felt horribly exposed standing there in the open, with the hostile land at her back.

"Course they will," said Krill. "Didn't you hear what the woman said? She was warning us, which was right kind of her. Especially after the way a *certain person* spoke to 'em."

Fin reddened. "I—I did not mean to shout. But they *are* ignorant. That is the truth."

"They're scared," said Krill severely, "and with good reason, from the sound of it. And if they're ignorant as well, who made 'em that way, hmm? The Devouts, that's who. Seems to me you're in no position to go around shouting insults at folk, lad."

Fin was a proud boy, and Petrel knew that apologies did not come easily to him. But he swallowed and said, "You are right. I am—sorry."

Krill glared at him for a moment longer, then softened. "Ah, you're not doing too badly, considering where you came from."

"It is not long till noon," said the captain. "By the time the Devouts arrive, we will be gone." He looked over his shoulder in the direction of the village. "But I wish the people had liked us more. How are we to help them if they will not talk to us? How are we to find the Song?"

"Look at it this way, Cap'n," said Krill. "We mightn't have got any further with the song or the water pumps, but those poor folk told us more by their silence than they could've done with a thousand words. We've got a huge task ahead of us."

That stopped the conversation dead, and they waited for the *Maw* in silence, staring out over the water. Petrel kicked at a rock, wishing Skua would hurry up and take her back to the ship, where she belonged.

Noon came and went.

"D'you think he's forgotten us?" asked Petrel after a while. She shaded her eyes with her hand. "Can you see any sign of him, Mister Smoke? Look, over there, is the water moving?"

"That's the tide, shipmate," said the rat. "It's on the turn."

Petrel made herself wait another few minutes, then said, "He should be here by now. We'd best remind him." She took the telegraph device from her bag. "How does this thing work, Cap'n?"

"It is quite simple," said the captain, sounding pleased that she had asked. "I took a spark gap transmitter and changed the—"

"Sorry, Cap'n. I'm sure that's really interesting, but it's not what I meant. How do I *use* it?"

"Oh," said the captain. "It is like banging on the pipes. You tap the key, and it sends that same tapping to the device on the bridge."

"Dolph'll be on duty by now," said Krill. "Ask her what's happening."

But before Petrel could begin, the telegraph key began to move by itself, clicking out a message in general ship code.

At first, Petrel thought it must be a joke. She looked at Krill and he was obviously thinking the same thing. But then his smile died. Because Third Officer Dolph would never joke about something as serious as—

"Mutiny!" whispered Petrel. The word tasted so foul in her mouth that she could hardly continue. But Fin didn't understand general ship code, not when it was rattled out fast, so she had to translate the whole message, stumbling over the dreadful meaning of it.

"Albie's locked the First and Second Officers in their cabins and taken over the ship!"

"What?" said Fin.

"He told everyone that—that Skua came to fetch us—but we were dead—murdered on the rocks and—and the cap'n smashed to smithereens!"

"But that is not true!" said the captain. "I am not smashed. Why would he say it if it is not true?"

The tapping continued. Petrel felt sick. "Albie's saying we should never have left the ice in the first place, and—and he's demanding that the *Oyster* goes south again!"

Krill roared like a wounded sea lion. But the captain said, "Why would he *do* that? It is not logical."

Petrel thought of Albie's uncharacteristic helpfulness, and Skua's smirk. She thought of all she knew about the Chief Engineer, from a lifetime of hiding from him. "Reckon he prefers the way things *used* to be on the *Oyster*, Cap'n," she whispered. "With the payback and the treachery, and everyone being scared of him. Since you woke up, he's had to take orders, and he's not an order-taking sort of man." She stared blindly at the telegraph. "I *knew* he wasn't to be trusted. I did! I should've seen this coming!"

Small paws patted her shoulder. "So should we all," said Missus Slink. "But we didn't—"

"Hush, there is more!" said Fin, as the telegraph began to click again. "What is it saying?"

Petrel listened. The thought of the *Oyster* sailing south without them filled her with such horror that it was hard to concentrate. But the next bit of news was not quite so bad. "Dolph and Squid and a few others have—have barricaded themselves—on the bridge. They've got a bit of food and water—which means—which means Albie *can't* go south! Not yet anyway—cos they control the steering—"

The tapping stopped abruptly. Petrel shook the device, but there was no further sound from it. Quickly, she sent a return message, begging Dolph not to go south without them—*please* not to leave without them! But there was no reply.

"Cap'n," she said, thrusting the device into his hands, "it ain't working! I think your spark thing's broken!"

The captain inspected the device, then shook his head. "There is nothing wrong with it. The fault must lie at the other end, on the *Oyster*. A loose wire, that is all it would take."

"So, did Dolph get my message?" asked Petrel.

"Probably not," replied the captain.

Petrel stared at her companions, and they stared back. Krill looked as if he was going to explode. Fin's face was deathly white. Even the captain seemed dumbfounded.

"Then, we're stranded," whispered Petrel. And suddenly, the countryside around her looked more hostile than ever. "We're stranded, and the Devouts are coming."

ACKNOWLEDGMENTS

I HOPED TO GO TO ANTARCTICA WHILE I WAS WRITING *Icebreaker*, but never made it. As a result, I was more than usually dependent on asking endless questions. Many thanks to the following people.

Professor Gustaaf Hallegraeff of the University of Tasmania School of Plant Science, for helping me work out how the *Oyster* might be powered; Gwyneth Tanner, for a first-person account of dogsledding; Katherine Scholes, for the loan of her Antarctic photos; Captain Simon Estella, for arranging my tour of the icebreaker *Aurora Australis*; Murray Doyle, Ship's Master, for the guided tour of *Aurora Australis*, and for helping me work out some of Petrel's hidey-holes; Firefighter Andrew Mackey, for reminding me that water pumped into a ship must also be pumped out; Gosta Blichfeldt, for reading the manuscript and explaining how engines, digesters, and wind turbines might work together; and Professor Pat Quilty, ex-ANARE Chief Scientist, for information about seasonal events and weather.

For editorial advice and guidance, I owe thanks to Eva Mills and Susannah Chambers at Allen & Unwin, Jill Grinberg and Katelyn Detweiler at Jill Grinberg Literary Management, Liz Szabla at Feiwel and Friends and the redoubtable Peter Matheson.

My deep and sincere thanks to the fine people at Feiwel and Friends for giving *Icebreaker* a home in the U.S. My particular thanks to Editor in Chief Liz Szabla, who has proved a pleasure to work with, and to Senior Creative Director Rich Deas, for designing what has to be the best book cover ever.

And finally, thanks as always to my most excellent agents, Jill Grinberg in the U.S., and Margaret Connolly in Australia.